THE MAGIC CARPET

Jr

5 Walpole St
Weymouth

THE MAGIC CARPET

JESSICA NORRIE

To all the families I've ever shared stories with,
including my own.

AUTHOR NOTE

My story follows five families, but only one reflects my own heritage. I've written it because although there are – hooray! – increasing numbers of books exploring the experience of individuals from specific BAME communities, there are not yet enough stories that show many different heritages all mixed together, participating in and contributing to society. Yet such mixed communities have been the norm for decades in most UK cities. I taught in them for over thirty years.

When describing my characters, I have tried my best to add to the knowledge I gained in the classroom, and to inform their cultural and religious backgrounds both through formal research and talking with people I know. However, in stories often the most interesting characters are those who don't follow the crowd. So the characters in this book represent only their fictional individual selves. I don't intend them as objective spokespersons for any one religion, ethnicity, or cultural heritage; nor should they be admired or cause offence. Their family histories influence their personalities, but they do not define them. They are simply invented characters from a 21ˢᵗ century London suburb, crowding together on the page for the sake of telling one of many possible stories of how life was in the months that followed the 2016 referendum.

Friday 14th October
2016

The baby explores a range of squeaks and his tiny fingers uncurl and close again.

"No worries, Safiya, I'll take him out if he's noisy," my cousin Fawzia says.

We parents are proud, settling to watch our children perform. It's good of Fawzia, but maybe the baby will hear the words that mean nothing to him yet, and sleep a spellbound hour.

Through the drawn curtains falls a muted light. Pupils, cross-legged on the parquet floor, chatter behind their hands or drift in daydreams. The boys clash all angles and knees for space, and many older girls, woman-shaped already, hunch in discomfort. But all the chairs are taken, by staff posted around the edge of the squirming crowd or by parents with lap-bound toddlers struggling to slide away or merrily playing endless peek-a-boo. Latecomers squeeze themselves enough space to stand on tiptoe and crane for a view.

Clash! A boy swipes two cymbals together.

"Welcome!"

This head teacher has a deep, rich voice, a voice to take charge in an emergency, swell you or shrink you, invest your idea with worth or have you fret you'd disobeyed an unknown rule. It's a privilege to hear, low with wonder, threat, conviction, celebration. Even the whereabouts of toilets and fire exits sound grand when spoken by Mrs Dasgupta. How can the children follow that? Head teachers never take long to show you their egos, and this one deserves a gold medal.

Or perhaps not.

"Families and children, I'd like to remind you this is a big demand we're making on our younger pupils. Only just in the junior school, and here they are standing up in front of so many of you. Some of them only have little voices so please, turn off your phones and listen as carefully as you can. At least one of our special stories today will be told entirely in silence!" She lowers her voice to a dramatic whisper: "I think if we can be very quiet we shall see some magic today!"

We are hushed, as one. The wondering baby gazes from unfocussed eyes. Fawzia strokes his cheek with the back of her finger and fixes her eyes on the stage.

The curtains open.

EARLY SEPTEMBER 2016

ALKA MEHTA

Through the playground railings I see Mum's car on the yellow lines. That usually means we have to hurry but—

"Wow, Mum! You're sparkling!"

Mummy's in dazzling white jeans with a top that glitters like fireworks. Her eyes shine. She rests one hand on my head – "Hi, princess!" – and tosses back the thickness of her hair. My mum's the most beautiful of all the mums.

"Hey Priti, looking good! Is it today, then?"

The other mums gather round making screechy noises. Mummy's handing out the leaflets for *Priti Pretty,* with pictures of nails so shiny they have a white line down the middle and a star glinting like the teeth on the toothpaste box. Mummy's lips are like strawberries and her skin's even smoother than real life. Her eyes have stiff black lashes long enough to touch her eyebrows and they're soft like when she looks at Dad.

"Three for two treatments? I'll have six!"

"I'll have eight, no, nine – shit I never was no good at times tables!"

Screech, screech.

"You got mates' rates? For my cousin's wedding?"

Mum's friend Avni shakes her head firmly. "No, this is luxury! Priti's high maintenance, none of your market stall knock-offs!"

High maintenance? What does that mean?

Tall Avni grabs a bunch of leaflets – Mum told me they're called flyers. She makes them like a fan high above her head and twirls. We did spirals in Maths: the flyers fly a graceful spiral into waiting hands.

"Go us!" shouts Avni. "You lot just better come and spend your money! You know what Priti's bloke's like when he goes off on one, and as for me, I don't even want to show my name as business partner till we've made a profit. So get spending…!"

Something changes in the air. Avni's laughing so loud it hurts my ears.

I know how to stop Mummy frowning.

"Can I show my teacher?" I drag on her hand, pulling her back to where Miss Patel still waits in the sun at the classroom door, guarding the children who haven't been collected.

Mum's lips make their shiny wide smile. "It's my new beauty business – would you mind putting some flyers in the staff room, please? I could offer a special deal for a block booking."

"My mum can make anyone beautiful, Miss Patel. You should try her…"

Some other mums throw back their heads and laugh. I don't understand, but Mummy says "Bless you, princess," and Miss Patel's smiling and Avni's moved away…

Now Mandeep's grandma from our road gives Mummy a nod like a queen and takes a leaflet. What long wrinkly fingers she has! Perhaps she'll make the first appointment – but she hobbles off to catch up with cheeky Mandeep who always zooms away in circles round the playground the moment school ends.

"May I?"

Sky's mum's hand has cracked skin and ridged nails, like the pictures when Mummy was learning to do beauty. Perhaps even Mummy couldn't sort out that pudgy, freckly skin she has.

"I warn you it's not cheap," says Mummy. Her red nails are holding tight to the flyer.

"I might treat myself."

Then Mum has to give her the flyer and Sky's mum smiles like she thinks she's got a question right. Behind her Sky sticks out her tongue. I wish someone else lived next door. I wish Nathan did… Nathan often asks me about hair and clothes, and he takes a flyer, screwing up his eyes carefully at the picture of my beautiful mum.

"How very kind."

Nathan's dad is so polite he bows. It's funny to do that like a handsome storybook prince when he's so dull, all shiny glasses with his office bag slung sideways across his chest. But I do like Nathan. Now he's leaving already, talking with his dad about his day, threading through the families to the big metal gates.

The new girl's come so close she's brushing against Mum's leg. She's got huge eyes like her mum who's pulling her away. My mum stares.

"Wow! *She* doesn't need my help. She could be on the catwalk, even in those boring clothes. Who's her little girl?"

"She's new. Doesn't speak English. She's called Zo … Zo something."

"Ah. Probably not worth giving them one then."

I can see Mum worrying about her own clothes as she watches them walk away. But *I* think the glittery top and jeans are miles better.

"Nursery's out, Mum."

Mummy swings through the playground like a model herself, people still watching. At Sunil's class door it's the usual muddle, criers and spilt lunch boxes and flappy wet paintings. Mummy's minding her jeans and doesn't see Sunil. He snatches the bright flyers and throws them.

"Naughty Sunil! Bad boy! Pick them up, please!"

He bangs his arms tight round her leg, his kissy mouth whining "No" against her hips. I do my best to collect the crumpled flyers and the hard ground scratches my fingers. Mummy peels Sunil off and takes his hand hard. The playground's nearly empty.

"My days – is that a traffic warden? Dad'll kill me if I get a ticket! Run, both of you!"

MONDAY 12TH SEPTEMBER 2016

TERESA PERRY

One high point of my day – sad, aren't I? – is looking in Sky's school bag for letters home. It reassures me I'm a good parent if I read them. Often the letters are just demands for money, or the dreaded nit letter doing the rounds. But this request's right up my street and I stay in our dark hall reading.

Dear families,

We're asking you to participate in an exciting project… This term Year Three are working with fairy stories… blah … something about why children should know where fairy stories come from … *a project the whole family can participate in, grandparents, siblings, family members living abroad—*

"I'm hungry, Mum."

"I'll be there in one sec." – *We're giving each child a different story to bring home … we'd like you, your family and your child to work together to make it your own—*

"I'm *really* hungry! What's that word you say – ravenous? I could eat a house!"

"Horse."

"What? A horse then. And its mane and tail."

In the kitchen I cut fresh white bread in thick hunks and squidge on blackberry jam and start to tell her what the letter says.

"They want families to adapt a story together, then tell it at school when it's done. There's all sorts of ideas – it's exciting!"

"They're always getting us to do stories."

"Not at home, though. Look, they say *you could put your family in it.*"

Sky's cheeks bulge. She can't point out the obvious: that only means me.

"*Or tell it in another language…*"

"We don't speak another language."

The words muddle out though the bread and purple dribble runs down her chin. She scoops it back in, seeing how long she can make her tongue.

"Well, OK, but what about this: *change the setting…*"

"What's that?"

"The background, where the story happens: maybe change from winter to summer, or from a forest to a city."

Sky goes to the fridge for orange juice.

"Or it says you could … let's see, *bring it up to date by adding modern features* – or look, this is good – *Add more spells, wishes, monsters, palaces etc.*"

"Like a spell to find my cup. Why do you always take it when I'm at school?"

I reach for the cup from the top cupboard and watch as she spills juice – like me, she's often clumsy. But I'm determined to stay upbeat.

"The letter says we could each *write a different version. Or act it or even sing it and record it, then upload it to the school website.* Oh look, this is great: *We hope your family will join us in a performance of all the stories next month.*"

Sky bangs down the cup. Sticky juice sloshes on the counter. She waves her arms above her head, rotating an imaginary hula hoop.

"Ooh … ooh … and they lived ha-aaapily eeeever aaaafter!" Now she's crooning into a wooden spoon, and I hurt laughing.

She grabs the letter and reads out: "*You could make it happy… er or funny… er or even make it sad. You could ill… ust… rate it with drawings, painting, ph… otogr… photos. It's up to you! The only limit is your im… ag… ination!* We'd need painting stuff…" She's calming down. With calm comes doubt.

I look over her shoulder. "No, they say they'll help with art materials. Oh, come on Sky, we could do something brilliant together here. To surprise everyone!"

Perhaps Sky could be a chart-topping celeb in our story – with magic powers! Or why not both of us? I'm racing ahead already. So much better than the usual sums and spellings; creative, like someone somewhere's remembered what childhood should be.

"Which story are you getting, sweetheart?"

She shrugs. Well, let's switch off for a bit, she'll be tired after school. When her enthusiasm does grow, she'll probably sustain it better than me, with my fly by night bursts of excitement when my tummy fizzes and I can't keep my mind still. I tuck my knees under me on the squashy cushions to be comfy and my fat flesh spreads out wide. Sky's own legs stick out strong and straight as she concentrates ferociously on her iPad game.

How could I help her make more of herself?

She's sturdy, like me. She likes girly, gauzy clothes but her solid frame's better in plainer things or even school uniform, so I don't make her change when she gets home. What glossy Pritika next door with her diets and her skinny daughter must think of us! I just know she didn't want to waste a beauty leaflet on me. But we could show her, if we put our minds to it! First we'll get fitter: I'll find exercise we'd enjoy together.

Sky stabs the iPad screen, with an exasperated *tsk!* or *Yes!* She can go on like this for hours, but today she reaches her target fast and slithers off the sofa.

"I'm going to say hallo to Ten Pence."

Outside, the hutch smells musty. Ten Pence (my own childhood rabbit was Ten Pence) is fastidious about only pooing in one corner but if you don't clean the hutch every day the dirty straw does take over. Just as well we didn't get the long haired Chinchilla Sky wanted! Ten Pence jumps up on hind legs when Sky appears, grasping her front paws on the chicken wire, underbelly still white despite the squalor. Child and rabbit dodge their heads at each other for a few seconds' delighted greeting. Then Sky wrinkles her nose much like Ten Pence.

She pulls out the food and water dishes as quickly as possible.

"Aren't you going to wash them out?"

"No. Are you? They're disgusting."

"They wouldn't be if you ..."

Sky's already refilled the bowls and slammed them back in the hutch, holding her elbow firmly across the space left by the open door so Ten Pence can't escape.

"I'm fed up saying the same thing to you over and over. Ten Pence'll get ill if you don't take better care of her."

I follow Sky inside, pleased at least the kitchen – juice spill apart – is shining and the living room tidy. I pulled myself together today and cleaned. It would be nice if Sky commented, but if she notices she doesn't say. I love my daughter but I don't always like her. The thought strikes me she probably feels the same way about me.

We repeat the supper time ritual: "Eat your tomatoes."

"I don't like them."

"They're good for you ..." Tonight she wins. It's probably my fault, all that bread and jam.

Sky's playing behaviour ping-pong tonight – uninterested in homework, naughty with the rabbit, rejecting tomatoes – but her shower makes her a different child. We snuggle on the sofa now we don't fit on her bunk bed together, her soft, clean pyjamas soothing on the crook of my arm. Her thumb sucking, almost outgrown, returns, as I read a bedtime chapter of my own favourite childhood book.

"Who would you be, in this story?"

The thumb twists round, reflecting. As a child I always saw myself as the feisty heroine, but Sky surprises me.

"I'd be the quiet, thin one."

The character she means is frightened and undernourished. I hope she's not brooding on her own weight.

She slides off the sofa and pads away to the private world of the top bunk next door. In minutes her rounded back is turned, hunched shoulders and snuffles telling me she's asleep.

The long evening begins, and away from Sky's world of stories I go into the shadows. The counsellor said I'd benefit from outside interests, but the reality is, as a single parent, I stay in every night with myself for company. Sometimes I may as well go to bed when Sky does: here in Ditchfield Close no one's going to turn up and invite me to a ball. The samey night chugs on behind the pzazz of the telly. The spark from the school letter's burnt out. I drag my resentment, heavy like a suitcase with no wheels, through the French doors into the garden where the night air makes me feel better, at least for the time it takes to smoke one of the cigs I've promised myself I'll give up very soon.

Mr Chan

Last Friday we started Nathan's homework on the train.

"I have to read my book, Dad."

"Not too loud, we mustn't disturb people working."

His piping voice set off. It pierced the important silence; enquiring faces looked up from laptops. I sensed involuntary grins: businessmen perhaps remembering their own small loved ones still sticky in their cots when they'd left that morning. I was aware too of frowns from those who had simply had enough of children, parents themselves or not.

" 'Once upon a time in Greece' – where's Greece, Dad?"

"Greece is a Mediterranean country with a history of being very wise. Other countries learned from Greece, but now the Greeks are foolish and their country has lost the power it had."

I heard a snigger from the seat behind. But Nathan said nothing, used to me packing history and philosophy lessons into what his mother would no doubt have answered more simply.

" '… there was a king called Midas. Midas was not a bad king but he had one fault: he co…vet…ed beautiful things and never felt he pos…sessed as many gold vases as he wanted, to show off to other kings who came from all over the world to visit his palace.' "

My thoughts drifted. There are many men who these days *have* managed to turn all they touch into gold. They visit agents like me, to buy cheap buildings in a rat-ridden hole. Suddenly the area's sought after and they're rich men. Or women, of course. They juice fruit, give it a fresh name – "Eden" or "Nature" perhaps – and it becomes a household brand. They start a website, and suddenly the world's connected on social media, friends multiplied, acquaintances linked. But the original inventor never logs on because he prefers spending his time with real people. If I were Midas I wouldn't wish for gold, I'd wish for time. There's never enough.

Behind me in the draughty train somebody gave a hacking cough. I'd lost Nathan's thread.

"Miss Patel says we could make a film of it," he was saying. "But you'd have to be Midas. You could grow a beard and you look old. I'd have to be all the servants and people who sort things out for him when he can't do anything because it's all turned to gold."

I wouldn't – couldn't – grow a beard so I answered: "Actually you can do a lot with gold."

Again that snigger – someone judging how I bring up my son. My feet jiggled against the floor.

It's no-one's business if I teach Nathan the value of wealth! These stories are all very well but we must each make our way in this world and it's pleasanter when you can live in comfort, with jet showers and towels soft from the drier, when you can update to each new gadget and – most importantly – buy the latest safety devices so that there will never, never be another accident of the sort—

"Please listen, Daddy! How can we sort this out when you're always inside your head?"

Nathan pulled my sleeve and I admired the perfect dome of his glossy black hair. I tried to give him full attention.

"What do we have to sort out now?"

"How we're going to make everything turn gold when we film the story."

"We're filming it?"

He sighed. I shifted in the scratchy seat and stretched my legs as I stalled for time:

"Gold foil? Paint?"

"No, paint would make a mess. You'd tell me off."

It's true, I don't like the idea of paint in our pristine flat. I grasped an idea: "How about filming through a coloured filter?"

"Cool!" Nathan's enthusiasm was so sweet I forgave him the slang. The technical aspect caught my fancy. If you can change the saturation or the tone on a photo it must be possible on a video too. But this is clearly a major homework demand, less easy to assimilate into our day than the usual spellings and sums.

We rattled through darkening fields. Nathan wanted the tablet, to jot down his ideas. "Like you always say, before I forget." I can never get over his quick typing, and now I was alarmed to see him construct a table, with columns for characters, costumes, and settings. He explained what they've learned about storytelling.

"Settings – different to computer settings, Dad. I'll need one for the castle inside and out, one for the riverside where Midas bathes off the gold, maybe the servants' hall …"

Then his long list of characters … we were both dismayed.

"I can't act all these myself," he said, despondent. He'd listed vizier, valet, groom, butler, banker, gardener, princess, nurse.

"You certainly may not dress up as a princess or a nurse. That would be quite wrong. You'll have to put the action offstage."

"Offstage?"

"Where they can't be seen. So you can do without them."

"But that'd be boring, it'd be just boys talking," complained Nathan. "Can't I get Alka – she's in my class – to come after school one day to work on it?"

I wish Nathan would interest himself in football, in science … This acting, this dressing up is so girlish. I'm also apprehensive. As a single man I may be accused of – oh, I can't bear to think what, while somebody's daughter is in my home. But how can I explain this to Nathan? I must protect him, as long as possible, from the wickeder ways of the world.

He's always asking these days, to have children home to play. Is it so essential? We could work on this project together. He could learn from me ... practical, technical things, what to put in and leave out, working to a deadline.

"Alka doesn't talk much. She'd do what I say. Please, Dad, let me ask Alka to work with me and then – I don't know what story she's got – maybe I could help with hers too?"

"We'll see ... you'd be better doing it at school. You must just accept that's how it is."

I refused to let him reply, but I knew he was resentful. His schoolmates have their friends to play and it's no big deal; indeed I remember myself running wild with my friends around the Hong Kong streets. "Running wild" is a cliché; we were sensible children, we ran races only where space and people permitted, delving down alleyways and clambering terraces, the vertical explorations of Hong Kong as tempting as those at street level. If we were stopped by a fence or a closed door we went inside to study or debate, our attention on our clunky computers, on chess, on space ... Nathan is equally sensible but our situation in London is different. My mother was there, in Hong Kong, to provide snacks and wipe grazed knees ... various aunties too, and benevolent grandparents, guiding us into thoughtful pastimes. I don't remember being tempted by the girlish activities Nathan craves, but if I was, so many adults would have encouraged other interests to help me grow up healthy.

However, he *is* a good boy, Nathan, careful to do his homework exactly according to instructions. Always trying, always succeeding in reaching a higher standard. The blessed day he was born I said to my dear wife we would bring him up to aim higher with every action. She was medicated, confused by her ordeal. On her exhausted face, I thought I glimpsed a flicker of sadness, maybe disagreement, but I dismissed it. It wasn't like her to disagree.

Those minutes were fleeting. First he was a minute old, then ten, twenty and I stopped counting. Now every year he adds is another since his mother passed away.

Six years since Maxine died. Six years repressing my grief, working when our son sleeps, learning to cook and clean so he wants for nothing his mother could have provided. But the older he gets, the harder it is to provide everything alone. As the train swishes on towards our family weekend with his cousins, I begin to accept it may be time to seek an answer.

MRS KAUR

My grandson Mandeep lies on his tummy on the rug, legs swinging in the air, crossing his ankles, uncrossing…He is propped on his elbows with a book. The golden photograph of Sri Harmandir Sahib watches him from the wall. It is so lovely to look at them both.

"If I finish reading this can I do something else? Is it long till Mum and Dad get here?"

"Daddy-ji will be home later. As every day. And Mummy-ji too."

Aman is making money at his place of work. He buys and sells, buys and sells, what exactly he buys and sells I do not understand. His BMW will arrive home long after my grandson has gone to bed. I hope Suki is making money too, at her fashion shop of clothes, for if not, she will return in a bad mood. And there is really no need. We can easily give away more than the one tenth daan the Guru Gobind Singh required, and still have the radiators hot hot hot so Mandeep can swing his bare feet and I can become warm again after collecting him from school.

I have a list of jobs. I must pick beans from the garden, make filling for pakoras, marinate the chicken and wash the rice. I must massage my husband's swelling feet. But Mandeep is not a keen reader, and his parents want him to practise more.

"Please read me your story."

"You won't understand the English."

"I shall do my best. And when we have both had enough, you can put this in the page to mark where we are up to."

I pass him the leaflet I was given in the playground, all shiny nails and lips, too daring for me. I think even Suki would not like these bold designs. Mandeep hardly glances at the glossy colours. Why should a boy show interest in such mysteries?

My grandson reading does not pause for breath, and I think he should go more slowly or speak in different voices for I can decipher very little. There seems to be no beginning, no good or bad or special happenings, and soon, comfy on the velvet sofa in the warmth, I have closed my eyes and only hear one phrase: "*Fee fi fo fum*". It comes again and back again.

"*Fee fi fo fum*," I copy. It's a pleasure to feel the shape of the words in my mouth and push my lips wide, high, tight. Behind my closed eyelids I sense the lazy orange sun shining through the front window, as my mouth forms the sounds like a chant and forces them into the dry air.

Mandeep looks up. "That's not right, Bibi." His voice is sharp. "It's fe-*e-e-e fi fo fum,* then it goes on *I smell the blood of an English MUN.*"

"Oh, these do not sound nice words to me, Mandeep-ji. It means they are killing English people, in your story?"

Mandeep snorts. "It doesn't matter what it means, they just said I have to read it."

With my poor English, I can do so little to help Mandeep become more interested in his school work. His father and brother did not resist learning in this way he has, they would lap it up and ask for more, but this youngest child, to be truthful we can only call him lazy.

"Mandeep, I am sure it does matter. The person who is telling his story put everything there for a reason, you know. Even the blood, no, I think especially the blood."

My grandson's feet on the rug go thump!

"Why don't you stick to *Fee fi fo fum*? Don't worry about the blood bit."

My husband would tell him it is rude, to speak to me so. But I have to confess, until I can puzzle the book out for myself, he is right to imply I am no use to him.

And so I take his advice. Through the late afternoon and evening, I keep the words in my silent mouth; I roll them, bulge them and whisper them as in the shining kitchen, I marinate the chicken and stuff the pakoras, and even while I massage my husband's swollen feet. But I do not know what they mean.

Fe-*e-e-e*, fi, fo fum …

ALKA MEHTA

I can't find anyone who wants to read my book with me. Dad's not back, Mum's watching old *Hotel Inspectors* on TV, enjoying the dust and dirty habits people have even when they're running a hotel people pay to stay in. *Would you believe it?* she tuts.

When I read to Sunil he butts in with fuss and questions. I don't want to be clever older sister all the time. So after supper I go into the tepee in the garden. I read to the butterflies on the purple flowers Mummy said are called buddleia and the friendly blackbirds. I can just see them past the tent flap; the man smart in his black coat and his wife getting the food, worms and seeds, to make her husband sing sweetly. They're a happy family so I like them listening. I try to make it fun for them, with a high chirpy voice for the princess and booming for the men, but quiet so they aren't frightened away. I make Kalpita come for a while but she's worse than Sunil so I make her go away.

The sun begins going down. There's no pretty pink glow in the sky tonight. I mark the page with one of Mummy's bright flyers. The tired bees journey from one flower to another. They nudge right inside till I can't see them at all, then wriggle out backwards.

There's a shadow where the tent opens and Dad's standing there in his shirtsleeves, face turned up for the scent of the white flowers called jasmine. Does he know I'm here? His phone rings. He sighs and digs inside his pocket. When he sees the caller ID he makes a snorting noise and his voice sounds in a temper. It's fast, mixing Indian and business words. I'm trapped in the tent because I know he wouldn't want me to overhear. Oh! Those words are bad! He never swore in front of us like that.

The phone call lasts ages, long enough for the light to leave the garden. If only I was inside … Dad's pacing round the grass shouting and the neighbour bangs her window closed like she's shocked too. That stops him; with the phone pressed against his ear he runs in banging the French doors behind him. Quick like a photo I can't stop someone taking I see him lifting the inside handles, wrenching them against each other to lock them tight.

I'm left outside. Wind makes the tepee walls shiver and I'm shivering too, and my crossed legs shake so *Rapunzel*'s surprised in my lap. Outside the tent the sky's dark grey. Dad's gone through to the front. He didn't turn on the back-room lights. The birds are silent and there are no more busy bees. Now I want Kalpita but she won't come.

In the tepee it's chilly and damp with strange shadows on the cloth walls. I know the shapes are only the wind blowing Mum's fluffy pampas grass but from inside they look massive, like frowning trees looming. Or terrifying birds with enormous wings … they'll swoop down any minute! Their huge beaks will slash the tent, three swipes enough to gobble up a little girl who foolishly stayed in the garden at night, when shapes change and kind animals go cruel and insects bite and sting hard enough to kill, if you can't get quickly to a pill or find your asthma pump.

What time is it? The bathroom light doesn't go on for Sunil's bath. The tepee's a trap – be brave, break free! Leave the flaps tied shut so nothing goes there in the night. We don't want another trembling hedgehog covered in white blobs, like the one the animal welfare people took away when I was six.

I hammer on the thick glass of the French doors. Nobody comes. The kitchen door's locked too, with the side gate padlocked because it's not bin day. Someone must miss me! They're all inside; soon Mum will be bathing Sunil, then calling for me to have my hair brushed. Huddled on the steps I press my face against the glass but it's so cold … I breathe and the smudge of my breath on the window warms me up a bit and I can draw pictures with my finger. I'm not allowed. But it serves the adults right, leaving me out here so cold and alone … Shouts, THUD! from the front hall or the front room! I'm ten times more scared now! Something bad's happening in there and I can't reach anyone to make them stop.

Shut my eyes…put my fingers in my ears. My brain's crashing against my skull thinking what to do. Miss Patel says I'm sensible. She gave me a sticker for finding the answer to problems in books. The book I have today is inside the tepee. Only a few steps away, but in the blackness where it's too scary to move to find anything. Still, I remember: the story was also about a girl on her own; a girl shut in, not shut out. How did she escape? She was in a tower: I expect it was tall and round with only one small window high up. No electricity in the old days, just candles if someone gave her some. She too had a friendly bird that visited. She could just reach to lean out the window and someone might see her from the waist up. (She was very thin, like Mummy is now, and maybe like Mummy she wore silver bangles that'd clink against the glass.) The bird came in daylight but Miss Patel said we could change our stories: perhaps if she needed it badly enough the bird would come at night? It would tell the pampas birds to hush, and make sure no one pecked or gulped and it would keep me friendly company like Kalpita on a good day? Until someone comes?

In the story the princess was bored, not frightened. She was so bored the only thing to do was brush her hair and plait it, brush and plait, undo, plait again. I can use my fingers for a brush and do my own hair…then at least when they find me I'll have saved them one before bed task and they might be less cross. I pull my fingers through my thick black tresses. "Tresses" is a new word from my story.

The pictures show golden hair, but mine is much thicker and shinier than any white girl's. I think "tresses" was invented for Indian hair. Already I can make a plait so thick you have to make a fist to get your hand round it.

The bird in the story told the princess (called Rapunzel but that's ugly so I'll give her my own name, Alka, which means the girl with lovely hair – I wonder if Miss Patel knew that when she gave out the stories?) – the bird told Alka to make a rope of her hair and let it down from the window. Then when the prince rode by on his white horse he could climb up and save her and they could ride away with her behind and live happy ever after.

My thin fingers are five sticks, not a brush, and the ones on the hand I don't write with are useless. I need hundreds of bristles like on Mummy's brush from India. Even if I can make a rope plait, there's no prince riding by. How would he get in through the locked side gate? A prince would be taller than me. He could look over the garden fence to next door to see if there's a light or someone to call, but I can only reach the tiny holes Dad said are called knotholes. No one will see me through them.

So quiet out here now. It's gone quiet inside too, but if I press my ear against the cold glass and really strain I may hear something. There are two grownups and Sunil in there, I know, Sunil probably asleep by now with his round nappy sticking out like the bee bums in the blossoms and his thumb in his mouth making snuggly sounds. Mum says he should be out of nappies by now but at night it saves her changing the sheets every few hours, and it can wait... my father says *that's disgusting my son should be trained* and Mum says *I don't see you trying.* In the daytime even baby Sunil seems quite grown up, now he's in uniform for nursery school, sitting on a proper chair to eat. I like him being in nappies at night. It shows how different we are, me grown up and sensible and him just a cuddly baby.

But if I wasn't grown up and sensible, I'd have been tucked safely up inside like Sunil. I wouldn't know anything was wrong. I wouldn't be out here thinking I must try and do something to put it right.

Two clicks, the latch of the front door a long way away, and the remote click for the car door. When my dad got this new car he said what he liked best was the quiet engine. Now I almost don't hear it glide away from the house before the sound is gone.

Have they all gone? It's hard to think, with this frightened feeling big like choking. One long howl forces past the huge lump in my throat. I'm screaming my fear. I'm shaking with cold.

Nothing. We're used to sounds at night, foxes and cats and car alarms. No one ever looks. But making noise has unfrozen me. I can move now. I know what to do. I'll make more and more noise until someone, somewhere, does something.

I'm more used to seeing in the dark now. I find a stick. I start tapping gently on the French windows, but you have to hit the glass hard for a sound to go through. So I find a stone. I don't dare throw it – even though I'm angry! How could my parents leave me like this? I'm a child, they should be looking after me! I crouch and tap louder, nearly banging, then REALLY banging, staring through to try and see something. Inside the house is strange, darker than the garden now, nothing moving, no shapes even of the furniture that must be there, the long sofa and the old wooden chair we have to keep for Nana's bad back although it spoils the look of the room.

Tap, tap, TAP.

Bang, bang, BANG!

Between taps and bangs I press my nose against the glass. Aaah! A shape shows up close to mine, separated only by the thickness of the glass, I know what it is but at the same time I don't know; it's a face, my mother's face, torn, bleeding, she's screaming too and I hear Sunil wailing and Mummy's face comes close to mine, her teeth look like the horrible dog across the road and her eyes are white and her skin's glowing pale in the blank dark and then she lies down still and it looks all wrong the way she's lying…

It can't be my mum. It doesn't look like Mummy. I jerk away from the window. I'm stumbling back to hide from her terrible face. I rip the tepee cloth open and crouch inside, grabbing my book to protect my head from the thing that's hurt my mother. The thing may hurt me next.

My heart thumps so hard it feels bigger than I am. The thing'll hear it…

Somebody crashes against the gate on the other side – once – again and the wood rips off the posts – Dad will be even crosser! The somebody grabs me and holds me against slippery shiny material with a cold sharp strip of zip against my face and says "Don't worry, it's going to be all right!"

Sky's mum from next door. It's her voice, from inside a cigarette-smell hug. She's never done that before. I'm trapped inside the strongest, longest, hug I've ever known. I won't get out till she decides. Is she the thing that did that to Mum?

TUESDAY 13TH SEPTEMBER

SAFIYA AHMED

"**M**ummy, you're not making food, are you?" Xoriyo puffs out her tummy, gazing down with worry on her face. Each family visit for Eid-ul-Adha yesterday offered more goodies we couldn't refuse. By the time we got home my stomach felt like a bag hung round my neck on weights and Xoriyo, who normally scampers everywhere, could only just drag herself along.

"No, my love, don't fret. Let's look at your beautiful book from school instead."

We settle to the story of a flying carpet, its jewelled weave thick and heavy. Our old sofa becomes a nest of luxurious cushions blotting out the landlord's dingy room.

"Wow, look at all these colours ...!"

Tufts of orange and ruby weave through the carpet, turquoise shading into sapphire and jade green into pine and colours running away from my eyes. Below the carpet scenes stretch to the horizon at the edge of the page, hills, valleys, isolated farms and crowded towns, minarets and domes. Xoriyo traces a winding river to the sea, then jabs her finger back on the carpet.

"Pretend we're there too!"

"Yes! Imagine you're swooping up and down, gliding, falling, rising…"

"Ooof." She makes a face and holds her stomach.

"Oh, don't worry. Look, if the gusts become too hard the carpet calms the wind. 'Wind,' the carpet says, 'Go and play with the trees or flirt with the waves'."

On the page Xoriyo prods the tassels. The carpet is flat in the smooth air, flying calmly to the best destination. Xoriyo wonders at the landscapes spread across the double pages. She's enchanted by shadowed pink clouds that ride between the carpet and the ground. The pictures and the lulling words draw me on board with her. We're passengers, peeping over the edge, bathing our faces with pure droplets of iced water and, because it is a story, we feel no pain from the sharp cold.

Xoriyo's enchanted, but the altitude sums up my darker memories of a journey when I was younger than she is now, a journey she must never make. Nobody told my school, or even me, I was going away, but suddenly one day we were on a plane, all hard edges and pale grey plastic, cold metal hurtling through the sky until I was a day older, with films I might not watch. It was dull on the outward flight and painful like serpents inside me on the return, and I have only hazy notions of what happened in between, while we were away.

I remember turbulence: stewardesses whipping things away, passengers tensed and braced, even the fat businessmen no longer nonchalant, everyone lurching and gasping in the air.

On Xoriyo's magic carpet there are no such problems. No seatbelts, no metal trolleys, no pain inside, no weary ladies in lipstick and high heels with fake smiles like that mum with the leaflets in the playground.

"Let's invite guests on the carpet, Mummy. We'll offer them food and drink, like yesterday."

"Some of your new friends from the new school, would you like that?"

"No...o,...just people we make up."

Her talking voice, different from her reading voice, reinforces her imagined world. I snap my fingers and a genie appears, balancing a tray on one finger like the Cat in the Hat, with decorated glasses streaked with gold and magic bubbles.

"There's sherbert," Xoriyo suggests, "or hot chocolate..."

The genie has ruby juices and golden drinks like honey, sorbets and cocktails and warming winter syrups that glow through your body.

On the magic carpet with Xoriyo I'm a child again, whooping with joy and laughter, swooshing, swirling, fearless of the height. We're children together, but also wise: we know the languages of the places we see, our homeland and those of others. We can communicate with any of our fellow travellers...Xoriyo sees curving blue rivers far below and she knows they are called meanders; she sees oxbow lakes, murrains and wadis and she knows what all these are too. On the magic carpet we understand all people we meet: the goatherd, the engineer, and his toddling twins. We may choose to wear whatever we like from abayas to swimsuits. We are confident in our choices and violence and ignorance can do us no harm.

Really there is no reason my daughter should not make friends at this school, new friends, who can take this journey with us through fresh places and new joys. We can have every passport and none, here; we can belong and invite others to belong with us.

On the magic carpet we are free.

TERESA

Coming in through the garden last night, Alka glanced at the dark shape of the hutch and hesitated. Did she think my home no safer than hers, even for a few minutes while we waited for the police? The musty straw smelt stronger in the warm night and the rabbit might have been dead for all she knew. I fussed her inside quick.

The tidy lounge may have reassured her, with children's books, board games and coloured cushions like in magazines. That fresh coat of paint in the summer's made such a difference! I'm almost ready to take on new children and getting things ready is a tonic in itself. I need the money and Sky needs the company. She's getting selfish, I love her to bits but even I can see that.

Last night Alka climbed into my new IKEA armchair, lost and small. She's in Sky's class. They're not friends, particularly – she seems too quiet and serious. Her mum's very glam, not like me with my cracked hands and leggings and big jumpers. She's not looking as good as her flyer now. That's one new business off to a bad start.

"Call me Teresa," I had to tell Alka. Fancy being next door neighbours and her not even knowing my name! Of course you'd expect any child to be subdued last night, that or hysterical.

"Come on, let's have a big hug to warm you up!"

But she was tense, and trembled away from me. I tucked her under the pashmina I picked up in Oxfam, and she sat there all thin legs and huge dark eyes and masses of hair, pretending to drink the hot Ribena I'd made, until the social worker arrived with her little brother to drive them to temporary fostering.

"Thank you for having me," she said as she was led away. So old fashioned! It's what I was taught to say after I'd been to play in another child's house.

After they'd gone I felt excited and alive. I was the strong one for once!

To think I wouldn't even know it happened if I hadn't gone in the garden for a ciggie ... Those last three in the evening are the hardest to cut out. At least Sky's stopped complaining the house smells of smoke, or my clothes. As soon as I come in after the last one I take everything off and put it in the washing machine. By the time it's cold enough for a coat, I aim not to be smoking at all.

So I'd nipped out for the last one before bed and Alka banging on their French doors did give me a fright! I squeezed myself against the tree so I could peep over the fence without being seen, when that wailing started from inside ... Alka shot back into that little tent she's got.

"Police, please. There's a child locked outside and someone inside's been hurt."

"Wait for them to arrive. Don't interfere yourself," the operator said.

But it was only fencing, and the child was alone and terrified. I rammed the gate with my shoulder, broke through and grabbed her. Later the policewoman shrugged: "Probably just as well..."

There's satisfaction in having done the right thing. It was a bad business but it could have been even worse if I hadn't been there. Almost justifies smoking...no, that has to stop. I'm so relieved the social worker last night can't have seen any signs of it when she collected Alka, now I'm so careful. I showed I was a good person to look after children.

"All down to your quick thinking and common sense, Teresa, girl!"

Pat on the back time. A drink would've calmed my nerves, but why spoil a sensible day? I made herbal tea, and my goodness I slept well.

So this morning I'm getting the hutch cleaning stuff together when the social worker rings the doorbell. She's obviously checked out my child minding registration. She looks round like she approves. Good thing she didn't see the back way last night!

"We wondered if you'd pick Alka up from school with Sky – the little boy's going with a friend from nursery and the emergency foster carer who had them last night isn't available. The mother's injuries looked worse than they were but she won't be doing the school run. The grandparents are coming, from Leicester, but they won't be here until evening. If you could hold the fort till then, seeing as you're registered, it would help."

"I'd be only too pleased."

What a vote of confidence! I'll make sure I do a good job.

Half an hour later a policewoman calls. I go through what I saw, and she makes notes, but she tells me it's not a witness statement as such. Because after all, what did I witness? A women lying injured, through a window. I don't know how it happened. But I expect they'll investigate a frightened child being locked out.

Alka will need distractions, and since they're not natural friends Sky may need prompting to start off a nice game. I plump up cushions for a nest, and put Sky's dolls with her miniature china for a tea party. I'll get iced gems – they look pretty on the tiny plates. And cupcakes for us. Not the choccie biccies I buy for Sky's birthday teas, as we're not exactly celebrating anything (that would be tactless, in the circumstances). But I do want it to look cosy and fun and safe.

Outside it's even hotter than yesterday – a forty-year record, the radio said. The sky's that dense warm blue and the park's full of people lying on the hard dry grass in shorts with flip flops fallen off beside them. There's an empty bench, for soaking up the sun. There are purposeful joggers and cyclists in Lycra, and there's a group walking with ski poles. They look ridiculous but they don't half keep up a good pace. Others are chatting or daydreaming, checking out the late roses, wondering when the leaves will turn. It's all very civilised, no shouting, no aggression. When winter comes cold and lonely I must remember this afternoon ... I could be friends with any of these people. If one of them comes to sit next to me I'll ...

They don't. I go for a browse in the library, though there's less and less to choose every time. Outside there's a bramble hedge ... Blackberries are supposed to be an autumn thing, but they always seem to be finished once the school year has started. Thinking of school reminds me I've lost track of time. I must be punctual today of all days! (I'd never be intentionally late, though I know a lot of parents are, to avoid paying another half an hour to the child minder.)

Miss Patel steers me into the shade for a quiet word.

"She's very reserved." The teacher indicates Alka. "She's worked hard today, as always. She hasn't said anything."

Alka stands there on the warm tarmac, looking down. Waiting to see what will happen to her next, I expect. Sky chatters and I see Alka nod from time to time. Some girls hold hands, but not these two. Yes, she is very quiet.

Indoors, Sky's eyes widen at the cupcakes. She grabs the pink one, but Alka takes a neat bite and leaves the rest. She glances dutifully at the dolls, like she recognises my effort to entertain her but can't summon up enthusiasm. But she brightens at the sight of the cushion nest. Softly she asks, "Do you mind if I just read? This book is *Rapunzel* and I really like it."

This child is so polite it's unnatural. However she's reminded me of the school project. I ruffle through Sky's bag, and find *The Town Mouse and the Country Mouse.*

"Why didn't you tell me you had this, babe?" I say. Guilt! Alka's mum isn't there to call *her* "babe". Or whatever their pet name is.

Sky's tone is surly. "It's not fair I've got that story. There's no people, it's boring. I'm going to ask for something else."

I'm disappointed too, but I suppose we should persevere. It can't have been easy finding a different story for everyone. If all the children wanted to change their books it'd be a headache for the teachers. Alka looks up.

"You've got a rabbit, haven't you?" she says. "You could use it to tell the story instead of a mouse. Can I see it? We can't see it from our garden but Mum said that's what the smell is."

Children are extraordinary. Last time she saw her mum the poor woman was lying half dead on the floor, and now she mentions her in that matter of fact way…she seems to have forgotten she smelt the rabbit herself, last night.

But her idea cheers Sky up.

"The rabbit's Ten Pence," she tells Alka. "Poor old Ten Pence does stink, at the moment. She couldn't go visiting other rabbits. Unless Mum's cleaned her out today?"

I shake my head, ready to apologise. I'm so ashamed. Am I fit to look after children, if I can't even take care of a pet rabbit?

"So it's good you haven't cleaned her." Sky's motoring now. "We can do Dirty Rabbit and Clean Rabbit, or Poor Rabbit and Rich Rabbit. Poor people *are* sometimes dirty, because it costs money to be clean. You're always saying that."

Surely Alka's too young to look smug? But cleaning out the hutch would be something constructive to do together.

"You're not allergic to animal fur, are you?"

Alka shakes her head. She helps carry the cleaning gear and Sky skips ahead.

"Hey Ten Pence, you're going to be a star in my story!"

Is it my imagination or is Ten Pence's greeting a bit less enthusiastic today? Sky got my phone for photos of her usual hind-legged welcome at the chicken wire, but it doesn't last long and you can see she's breathing heavily, flanks heaving in, pushing out, in, out. Sky takes more pictures of her against the filthy straw and dark spreading dampness.

Despite the awful smell, when I lift Ten Pence out of the hutch Alka is fascinated. The rabbit herself is clean and I explain how fastidiously she keeps away from her own business (I don't mention she eats some of it) and show how even in these conditions her fur is still glossy and smooth.

Sky kneels in front of me.

"Give her to me first!"

I've taught Sky how to hold an animal. One hand firmly under the rabbit's bottom, not allowing any struggle, while you stroke with a regular, firm movement. She'll have to be persuaded to give Alka a go, but she'll get bored soon enough, she always does. If neither of them wants to hold the rabbit all the time it takes to do the cleaning, there's a box she can go in. It's cramped ... now she's bigger she should have a proper run, but that would need carpentry skills and materials and I keep shoving the idea to the back of my mind. Our rabbits always had runs when I was a child. I should have remembered that before I got Ten Pence for Sky. All I considered then was how good it is for an only child to have a pet. I didn't think enough about the feelings of the pet.

I rake out the soggy straw with an old brush onto some newspaper. The girls are partly preoccupied with Ten Pence, partly fascinated by what I'm doing. "She's a Dutch rabbit," Sky tells Alka. "Mum said a short-haired one was best ... they're smaller and they stay healthy easier."

Then in her most disgusted voice: "Ugh! Yuck!" When Alka begins copying her, a second behind and more tentative, I snap.

"Ten Pence is your rabbit, Sky. It's your responsibility to look after her as much as mine."

"I'm not old enough. You're the mum. It's your job to look after your children and their pets. No: *child*, and *pet*. Good thing there's only one of each or we'd really be suffering."

"That's enough."

Angry words well up inside me. Alka looks alarmed. I just manage to swallow them.

I bundle up the horrible newspaper in a ball.

"Push over the bowl of clean water."

I throw it straight in the hutch and begin swabbing out. I don't like Sky showing me up in front of other people, and it was tactless to mention mums looking after children when the only reason Alka's here is because her mum can't. Sky's getting very arrogant. I'll speak to her about it later when there's just the two of us.

"But it is your job," she persists. "And you're here all day; you could have done it ages ago."

Such a frightening feeling, when you sense control of your temper swishing away from you. I spin round, ready to let rip at Sky about everything that's wrong with life that stops me doing the best I can for her and the sodding rabbit – and she goes tense with that mulish look on her face she gets when she's preparing to give as good as she gets. She thrusts Ten Pence at Alka, who's not expecting her and fluffs the catch. The scared rabbit twitches, makes a sudden strong leap, and bounds across our grass and under the fence into the garden the other side. Sky freezes and it's Alka who jumps up. She runs across to the fence, lower than on her side, with posts and spaces between them. I'm surprised when she laughs.

"Look!" She's pointing. "She hasn't gone far, you'll catch her easily. She looks like a proper rabbit now."

I go over, my heart in my mouth: I hate having rows with Sky, and don't relish the job of trying to get Ten Pence back. But if we can't retrieve her I'll probably have to explain death – she'll be run over or mauled by a fox. At the same time I'm relieved Alka doesn't seem bothered by the rise in emotional temperature. And what she shows me *is* very funny: Ten Pence certainly won't go far while she has the neighbour's lettuces to detain her. She munches away, choosing the freshest lime-green leaves. Occasionally she eyes us as if to say, "You kept me in that hutch and all the time this feast was close by?" It's lovely to see her hopping free, in fresh sweet air. Sky comes over and mutely puts her hand in mine, before it occurs to her to grab more photos of Ten Pence behaving, yes, like a proper little rabbit.

"Do you have a carrot?" asks Alka. "Could we tempt her back with that? Your neighbour'll be cross about his lettuces. You stay here in case there's a chance to get her, and just tell me where to find a carrot."

What an extremely sensible child she is.

"No, I'll get something," says Sky, who knows to trim the carrot first, and Alka and I stay watching.

Ten Pence is just not interested, or not enough to come near the fence. She's pretty well stuffed with lettuce, and settles into a round slumbering ball in the middle of what's left. I dread facing the neighbours, who'll be back from work in an hour or so. If we can catch the rabbit, and if it rains tonight so they don't go out to water, perhaps they'll think it's slug damage? It's a bad example for the girls not to own up, but we need to get on with the neighbours and it may be discretion is the better part of valour. It wouldn't be the first time I've explained that proverb to Sky.

I'm too plump to get through the fence. Thin little Alka certainly could, but I can't send Alka into someone else's garden – what if her grandparents turn up when she's there, or worse still, the social worker? So we watch as Sky wriggles onto next door's land.

"Ow!" she mutters, managing to keep the exclamation under her breath as her cardigan catches on the rough slats.

Alka holds her breath beside me. Sky moves closer, crouching; the rabbit's nose twitches in her apparent sleep; she opens one eye a crack and shuts it again … we're not sure she knows Sky is there. We're all concentrating so hard the world has shrunk to the three of us and the rabbit in the patch of earth: hunters and hunted together in one moment of time.

My phone shatters the silence.

Ten Pence bounds with surprising speed given all that lettuce into the prickly shrubs on the far side of the garden and sits looking at us from an unreachable shelter.

At the same time we hear the doorbell, more faintly. Alka's grandparents! We can't leave Sky in the neighbour's garden, and we mustn't keep them waiting on the doorstep. They must be upset, and tired, with all that's happened in their family.

Alka's already turned to go back through the house, and Sky looks at me as though she can't believe it.

"Get back through that fence now, Sky. I mean it. We'll have to come back for Ten Pence."

At least she does as she's told. The grandparents on my doorstep can't possibly miss the slammed back door when Sky refuses to come back in the house, but I do hope they're too caught up in their fussy welcome for Alka to register the shouts of "I hate you!" and the wild sobbing from outside. Of course, by the time we've handed over bags and exchanged thanks and enquiries after Alka's mum and I've returned to face my daughter in the back garden, the rabbit is nowhere to be seen.

Mr Chan

Stand ready to jump off the train first, jog along the pavement from the station, briefcase swinging … What would the school do if I didn't arrive on time? I can't bear to find out. So I'm always there by six on the dot. But today I had to wind up a meeting most abruptly. I must urgently investigate other possibilities for Nathan so I can work a more standard day. He is growing up, after all. He shouldn't be disturbed by longer hours away from me.

The red man on the pedestrian light mocks my impatience and the beeps have barely begun before I'm on the school side, with just time to get my breath back.

Something's wrong. The play leader stands with a protective hand on Nathan's shoulder, my boy looking so morose he barely greets me. As we start towards home, a tear rolls slowly down Nathan's right cheek – it was always the right eye first, with baby Nathan and toddler Nathan, and so it still is with my boy nearly eight years old. A twin teardrop wells over his left eye. With the force of a storm suddenly Nathan is shaking with violent sobs.

There's no question of walking on. Nathan's beside himself.

"Calm down, now. Can't we deal with this at home? What on earth is the matter?"

"I … want … help … you must HELP me …" He can barely force out the words.

"Come, come …. Don't I help you with everything? I am your father, after all. It's my job to help you."

"You're not helping with this. You think I can do it myself – I can't!"

When Nathan is unhappy, I respond as the tides to the moon; pity surges inside me and I want to take his burdens on my back and relieve him of all his distress. Despite this instinct, I know he must learn to resolve difficulties for himself.

I do what I haven't done in a public place in recent years. I crouch down to his height, put both hands round his shoulders. I look into his eyes, and hold him still until the sobbing subsides. Other families collecting their children slow in curiosity, then discreetly speed away.

"We cannot have this spectacle in the street, Nathan." I modify my tone to be firm but fair. "You know I will help you, but you must calm down enough to explain what it is you want."

Bit by bit he controls himself; his sobs reduce to hiccups and gasps. A lorry thundering past gives him extra time to hide in the noise before he must speak. He can't keep still enough to look straight at me but he peeps shyly and I catch a watery smile that vanishes as soon as it came, like the sun behind clouds on a February day.

"I want," he mutters, as though if he says whatever it is quickly and quietly enough it will sound too reasonable to refuse, "a girl but I want it to be Alka – in my Midas story. I want you to *really* help us. Not just listen and nod like you did on the train. At after school club I was trying to work it out but I couldn't but if *you* help me *and* let me have Alka I can. I want it to be our story, that we've done together, you and me, Dad. But we need a girl in our story too."

A girl in our story...

MRS KAUR

*F*ee-e-e, fi, fo fum... It helps with the ironing. One
sleeve on the board, press down firm and draw
along a strong stroke fee-*e-e-e*; turn it over, *fi – eye –
eye*, front right side and between the buttons *fo – oh –
oh*, one *oh* for each button, front left side *fummmmm*.
Turn it over and do the back, four swift strokes, *Fee
Fi Fo Fum!* I finish all the grammar school shirts for
Gurdeep, plus six of my son's in record time. Like the
Cossack dancers I saw on TV I raise and stamp down
my feet! Swooping down I press on the last shirt.

"Humph!"

I'm satisfied; I flourish my elbows. Humphs and
flourishes – unnecessary but fun. Getting old you
can allow yourself the freedom of noises and gestures at home; in public you must be more discreet.

Oh dear. Mandeep is standing in the doorway.
He is fascinated.

"Well done, Bibi!"

He claps his hands and comes to me to do that
thing people do when they put their palms together
high in the air. I back against the ironing board.

"Take care – the iron is hot!"

54

He's a sudden statue, stock still. The statue speaks:

"Did you know your eyes glitter when you say *fee fi...*?"

I catch my breath to answer. It wears me out, this ironing.

"Well you see Mandeep, when I say *Fe-e-e-e, fi, fo fum* it helps me make progress fast! Now I can have chai and put my feet up. So maybe my eyes glitter because I am pleased."

"Would it help me?"

"To do your work quick, yes it would help you, but first you have to know *how* to do your work. What is your task, Mandeep?"

"I have to tell the story, my own way. I can't copy the words in the book. But I can't explain to you what they want. There's a letter from the school, I'll have to wait till Mum or Dad gets home."

So many times this happens when there is a letter from school. I have tried hard, but I find the letters so difficult to read. If I had my husband's command of English, we could have been doing what the letter says while they are at work. We could have it all finished ready to show them. Then they would be proud of Mandeep, and proud of me too for helping. But I do not know what the school wants. Aman always tells me *don't worry Bibi, you do so much for us anyway, and why would you need to read English when your Punjabi is so perfect?* He is so good to me, my son Aman. And every time he adds, "After all, Mandeep cannot read Punjabi, so you are equal!"

But we are not equal, for we live in this country and things are done in English.

Suki is kind also; she is a good daughter-in-law when she is not tired from her fashion shop. She says a different thing: "Why does the school always write such long letters with such hard words? Why don't they make it easy? There are so many parents who do not read English, it is not just you and the other grandmothers. If it was easier the children could read you the letter and you could get on with it. It's too late for homework by the time we come from work, and they are not helping us!"

It's kind of her to blame the school, not me. But after all, it cannot be so difficult, this work for a seven-year-old boy. I was at school and college in India, I was educated until I was eighteen years old and married. Today is my *Fe-e-e-e, fi, fo fum* day – maybe today I'll find I can read this letter!

"Fetch the letter, Mandeep. You will read this letter to your Bibi and together we will know what they ask us to do, *together*! You and Bibi will do this work! It will be a triumph, you will see!"

He still looks unsure. I insist.

"*Your* eyes will glitter too! Everybody's eyes will glitter!"

I am feeling very happy. I fetch barfi from the fridge, and we sit on the tall bar stools to eat the sticky white cubes and read the letter. They are so big you must cut them before you can fit them in your mouth and very very sweet to give energy to my old lady brain.

When I went to English classes, somebody had a good idea. They said sometimes you do not need to waste your brain to understand the first part of a letter, it's just polite things to see if you are listening. The important bit is in the middle. I run my eyes over the blocks of print on the paper and I point to the second one.

"Start reading there."

I hear the words "fairy stories" many times. What is this fairy stories, I ask, and Mandeep says he doesn't know. No fairies in his story, only a giant man, a giant wife and some magic beans.

We want this to be a pro...jec...a thing the w...whole family can take part in, grandparents, younger s...sib...lings, even family mem...bers who live a...broad...

"You see, Mandeep, I am *grandparents*, it is *my* homework too. *I* have to do it. *You* will perhaps be in trouble if *I* do not do my homework, so you must help me."

He laughs. My fingers push more sticky barfi in his mouth so it's too full to speak. I look at the letter myself.

There are big black spots on the left. I think of my friend at the English class and I tell Mandeep, "Only read this. The other part is not important!" When his mouth has just some crumbs spitting out a little bit, he starts to read me the big black spots.

- *Change the end to make it happier or funny or even sad.*

- *Add more spells, wishes, monsters, journeys and palaces etc.*
- *You could tell the story in another language or in your mother tongue.*

"What's mother tong … mother ton-goo?"

"It must be the language your mother speaks. For you it is most of the time English, but for me it was Punjabi."

- *You could act it or sing it and record it. Then upload your performance to our website.*

Mandeep giggles. "We'll have you with the ironing board, Bibi-ji! That will make them all laugh!"

I look at him. I try to keep a serious look but my lips break apart and make a rude noise. For a minute we cannot go on because we think it is so funny.

"We can do all the housework this way! Washing floor, peeling potato …"

"Cleaning the toilet!" shouts Mandeep. He laughs so hard I cannot understand straight away.

"No Mandeep! You cannot have your old Bibi cleaning toilet on video for whole school to see!"

"Washing the old socks … washing Mum's bras … *fee fi fo fum,* I wash the bras of Mandeep's mum!"

I have to take my glasses off and wipe my eyes with the hem of my sleeve. This is not like my own school days! He's rocking off the stool with chuckles. I save him with a big squashy hug and he is so happy he lets me do this. He doesn't run away like his older brother.

There is the sound of a key in the lock.

"Mandeep you must calm down little bit. There is your mummy-ji coming home..."

"*Fee fi fo fum*, I wash the bras of Mandeep's mum!" he whispers, loud as you can when you want it still to be a whisper. He gives me a naughty look and puts his finger on his mouth: "shush".

So I have a silly secret with my grandson. It is so lovely!

After supper Suki has a bath and Mandeep is supposed to be in bed. He calls me in as I pass his room. Usually I do not go in there on nights when Suki is home to do bedtime, and it is so sweet to see him lying in bed with his plaits free from his patka – his plaits are getting so long now! – all clean and relaxed. He wants to show me something on his tablet thing.

What is this mad thing? Men carrying ironing boards across rivers and on bridges. Mandeep pauses the film for me to see. They are on speedboats and climbing mountains, with their ironing boards. Somebody is underwater and he opens his board and starts ironing! Now here is someone ironing in Times Square – I recognise it because I went on a big trip with his Baba two years ago. Now a man is ironing on the back of a cow! Oh no. Not a cow, no, that will not do. But Mandeep giggles.

"We will make you do this!" he hisses. "You will be the first lady extreme ironing champion. You will be singing your *fee fi fo fum* song and you will be quicker than them! The star of the stage at school for all my friends and teachers to see!"

He pulls me down into a big hug and whispers the rude song about his mum's bra. And I have to squeeze him because I am laughing so hard I will fall if I do not hold on tight. Suddenly the English of his rude song is so easy to remember – maybe the other English words, ones I need more, will become more easy for me if we do this work together?

WEDNESDAY 14TH SEPTEMBER 2016

SAFIYA

"I couldn't wait for the end of school today, Mum."

Nor I for the end of work, so that after prayers and eating we could ride again on Xoriyo's magic carpet. But ride is a word the English use for horses and cars and trains. This is not a ride. It is a glide and a swoop and sometimes you have a strange dizzy feeling in your tummy, but not a sick feeling. The sensation is safe, but exhilarating.

I have been watching the news too much recently. My dreams are filled with violence and incurable pain. Xoriyo switches on the TV and there are the images again; soldiers, guns, turmoil, and people fleeing with their pans and blankets, their grandparents and the more fortunate of them in dusty cars piled high with parcels and scrawny children. I watch Xoriyo: her face is expressionless, she utters no horror or wonder or disbelief. She cannot become inured to this so young, yet neither can I bear to explain and destroy the disappearing fragments of her innocence.

"Let's look at your book, my love, we have better stories to tell."

With Eid al-Adha over, we need another special thing to occupy our minds.

The pictures in the book are so beautiful: they inspire us to invent our own stories leaving behind the words of the one they were painted for. In *our* stories we travel over lands of pink and gold, brownish rose for the earth, the streets and the sandy fields, gold and silver for the towers, the turrets and shining minarets. Dragons wait to be slain or pacified, laws to be passed or annulled, babies to be born and potions to be discovered. We may tell of a just battle, but there will be no long and messy war and the wounded will recover quickly and completely, retaining no scars.

Sometimes Xoriyo tells the story and sometimes I do. Our sentences fit together neatly. Each of us knows when to stop and when to take over. Xoriyo talks of colours and precious stones; I speak of feelings and ways of behaving. Doing this I think we are in a dream where nothing can go wrong for us. We know without thinking which tongue will suit best, now we have this story to tell. Sometimes our story blends with other words, from Somali poems and songs we have known all our lives. All Somalis carry poems inside, and these poems are now flowing into our story here.

The small lamps mute the shabby room. In the lower light even the landlord's clumsy furniture begins to match and the dreary décor blurs to something bearable. Sitting together on our big bed, with Xoriyo in soft pyjamas, the magic carpet is a refuge for my daughter and myself, the edges of the bed a drop into reality. I fear if we give our interpretation of this magic carpet story to the school as they have asked, we may lose something of ourselves. Yet the inspiration has been their gift to us and we must cherish it. Perhaps it would be good to share, to invite her classmates for the ride – but it would have to be Xoriyo who speaks the invitation.

I'm propped against the headboard and Xoriyo begins by sitting in my lap – she has grown so much it is some time since we did this. When she was a baby she would fall asleep as I sang her poems and told her stories, music and words my mother sang to me and her mother told her. Now she is too big, and soon she slides off my lap and snuggles against my shoulder instead. But those few minutes are so precious, arising from nothing more than a soft bed and a pretty picture book ...

"Look!"

She's excited by something she sees over the edge. Her voice dips low in awe. It surges louder and she sits forward, eyes gleaming, and points! She is so convincing I need barely pretend, I can see it too. Xoriyo's teetering dangerously, craning forward to reach her vision, likely to fall ... I take over. I must introduce something to calm her down again, for it is nearly time for sleep. I tell of our gentle flight over snow-topped mountains and green valleys with purple and pink flowers and chubby ponies grazing.

It seems to me we hear sweet music, not a definite tune but a series of lovely sounds, low, then higher but never piercing, and Xoriyo's eyes gradually close. I nudge her gently to her side of the big bed, safely cushioned from the darkness underneath, and cover her with woven shawls against the chill of the night.

From our magic carpet we saw no refugees, for nobody had lost their home. There were no banks, money being safe in these lands without thieves. Knives were only for cutting food, and guns had fallen into misuse. We saw no boats of desperate migrants, heard no screams of horror, and if we can stay on our carpet Xoriyo will never hear of rape or mutilation.

I stay on the bed watching over my sleeping daughter for a moment before turning out all but one low light. Before I move into the living room, where I shall watch neither fictional violence or real-life news this evening, I pick some threads from the carpet for myself and weave them into an imaginary shawl to protect my own shoulders from the threatening air.

ALKA

"Come and say hallo, Alka. Look, I'm home, it's all better now."

It's only *quite* better. When Sky's mum brought us home Nana opened the front door very slow, peeping round the edge like he was scared. His shadow was big on the other side of the glass. Nani was hiding behind him.

"Ah, safe home."

Nana stroked my hair. He put his hand under my chin to make me look up at him. At first it blocked my view through the lacy pattern of the glass doors to Mummy but then I saw her, lying on the sofa watching telly just like last time I saw her before the thing happened. It's even the same programme. Sunil ran past Nana but Nana had to wait because Sky's mum was still on the doorstep. I don't think they knew what to say to each other. She went away, quick.

Sunil hurled himself at Mum. I didn't want to see her white face with the blood and all the normal shapes looking wrong. But actually from here she doesn't look as bad as I remember. Her face has grey patches, darker under her eyes and her nose. *That* looks different. Bigger, maybe. Outside the grey bits her skin is pale. I don't remember the colours her face should be. Normally she always has make up on by the time she wakes me in the morning.

She's wearing old trackie bottoms she keeps for comfy days and only one bangle. Her hair's down loose, not plaited, which is not something she lets us see often. She looks like in the picture before she was married, when she was in school uniform and one day her friends didn't plait their hair because there was a competition to see who had the longest hair and plaits make it wavy so you can't measure them.

I had to go through the glass doors and now it's now, in the living room.

Nani is wanting kisses and hugs, then Nani and Nana sit down with the "ouf" sounds they make and Sunil goes running between them and Mummy and he can't make his mind up which pattern to make dashing from chair to chair. Nani stops him by getting up to go to the kitchen and then Sunil crouches by Mummy. He's trying to stop me getting as close to Mummy as he is. I start to push him out the way but before he can start wailing I realise I don't want to stay close to her. One of her eyes is red inside. Where it should be white. She smells a bit like the medical room at school, and her red eye isn't nice.

She puts her head down like the horse I saw at the riding school and brings all her hair over her face at once, like when you shake it over the bath to wash at Nani and Nana's house where there's no shower. She combs it back with her fingers but loose so it covers the red eye. Now she looks a bit silly, one-eyed, and also she's frowning. Perhaps it hurt her to move her head fast like that.

No, I don't want to be near her.

I back away until Nana puts his hard hands on my shoulders to stop me coming up against his sharp toenails and his sandals and bony knees.

Nani comes back with a tray of juice and biscuits.

"Oh, you're spoiling them, Mum."

Nani answers something in Indian language and Mummy says something back, a bit cross I think. We take the biscuits quick before anyone changes their mind, but I stay near Nana, until Nani brings him hot tea.

"Move in case I spill it, Alka."

Nowhere feels very safe.

Nana slurps his tea. "Tell me about your day at school, children."

Sunil puts two biscuits in his mouth together. His cheeks bulge. He shakes his head hard side to side to show he can't answer and crumbs drop out on the carpet. Everyone laughs except me. Why do they think he's so clever?

"Alka? What about you?"

"It was okay."

"What did you do?"

"Nothing. Stuff."

School wasn't nice today. I suppose it may get better tomorrow if other things get normal. *Quite* normal.

"Alka," says Mummy in a sharp voice. "Tell your Nani and Nana what you did at school today."

"Did you work hard, *dikri?*"

Nani is always gentle. I love telling her how good I was because she says "Ah!" and "Wonderful girl!" and "Of course Nani's granddaughter is a good girl who works hardest in the class." But today I didn't work hard, and another strange thing was Miss Patel didn't tell me off. We were writing our news, two days late because lots of the Muslim children were away on Monday and Tuesday for their Eid festival. I wrote the title and the date. Then I didn't want to write any more, and she looked over once but she didn't say anything. Janki next to me kept asking if I was ok because she's my friend, but she still got on with her own work. When she took it up to be checked I heard her tell Miss Patel "Alka hasn't written anything".

Bilal, who sits on our table went on about it for the rest of the day: "Why didn't she tell you off? Anyone else would get kept in to finish at playtime!" It felt like he was talking far away, about someone else. He doesn't usually talk to me at all, that was another thing that was different. Everything the last two days is so strange like the world has changed for me but not for the other children.

When we went for PE I followed them round the apparatus, not fast, not slow. Like always. There's nothing to tell about that and Nani doesn't understand PE anyway. She worries because we do it with the boys, not separate like when she was little. "Not

70

nice, you should talk to school," she always says to Mummy, so Mummy doesn't bring her to see our sports days anymore because the school will never change it just for her.

Back in class I found if I put my head close to the table top like I'm concentrating hard, and loosened my hair so it hides me, people didn't bother me so much. I didn't dare take the plait out completely because I wouldn't be able to get it back tight again, but I can make it loose enough to cover a lot.

All day I stayed close to a teacher. I didn't want Sky to come near me. Lucky she's not in my PE group, or she might have pushed me off the apparatus. She's furious. "It's your fault we lost Ten Pence!" she keeps hissing at me. To the others she says: "We had her home to tea after school yesterday, NOT because I like her but she lives next door and something happened so my mum said she'd help out. And when we were cleaning my rabbit's hutch she ran away and then just when we were catching her *her* grandparents rang for her and now we'll never see her again."

The other children look at me like I've been doing cruelty to animals. It's funny how fast they change. Yesterday everyone knew I was good and Sky could be the unkind one. Now they think it's me. The only one who didn't act like he believed her was Nathan. Nobody notices what he says and you never know what he's thinking, but it felt nice when the others were getting their work marked and he put his smiley chin on the table just like mine and whispered, "Don't worry, Alka. The rabbit'll probably come back. Do you want one of my stickers to make you happy again?"

I don't care about the rabbit – it was happier running wild in the lettuces anyway. That rabbit hutch was the second yuckiest thing I've ever seen (two yucky things I've seen in two days). But I can't say the truth about the hutch or they'll all think I'm just trying to be horrible back to Sky. She kept doing big sobs and everyone was putting their arms round her to make her feel better.

It got to the end of the day. "Sky's mum will be picking you up again," Miss Patel told me. This time Sunil was there holding one of her hands so I took his other one. "Not *her* again," grumbled Sky, but her mum gave me one of her smoky hugs.

"The rabbit running away wasn't your fault, Alka," she said, and that was all until we got here. She rang the doorbell to drop us off, telling Nana she'd call for me in the morning.

I don't want to go with Sky in the morning.

At school they say if someone is unkind to you, you should tell a teacher. It's the only thing you can do, whether it works or not. People aren't usually horrible to me, because I do good work and I'm kind. I wear nice clean clothes and invite them to my parties. So that was another new feeling, unkindness being done to me. Some children get unkindness all the time, like Xoriyo, but she never looks like she knows that's what it's meant to be. She's always smiling with the teachers like she doesn't need children to be her friends. And she can run very fast and tell her stories to herself or whatever it is she's saying in her own language, so she can shut them out as well as them shutting *her* out. Also she draws beautiful pictures. Perhaps she doesn't mind unkindness because she's used to it and I just have to get used to it too. But I don't really want to be like her. Anyway I can't speak much of anything except English.

Today I was alone like Rapunzel, with nobody knowing how bad I felt or explaining anything to me. I was alone but there was never a space without other children when I could tell Miss Patel.

"Sometimes school day good, sometimes it bad, heh, *mari dikri?*"

Nana slurps the last of his tea and reaches his arms to pull me close to his cheek. I'm lying across the arm of the deep chair, half on his chest. His skin is scratchy. I push my forehead against it to rub out my thoughts. His firm voice makes what he said not a question. Mummy sighs and closes her eyes and Nani tells us to come in the kitchen with her.

All I want is to snuggle somewhere soft and read my Rapunzel book. But Nani says: "Keeps an eye on Sunil for me, Alka." The book is all bent now, but I never got to finish it and I want to see what happens. Soon it will be time for Daddy to come home and maybe I can read Rapunzel to him if he isn't in a bad mood like two days ago.

If everything is all right for Rapunzel in the end then maybe everything will be all right for me, because I started reading her story the night the yucky things happened and in the story that was when everything went wrong for her too and she was shut up in the tower like me being shut out in the tepee.

Friday 16th September 2016

Mr Chan

Nathan's previous teachers have been maternal, cosy and warm, but this new Miss Patel is thin and seems efficient. She dresses smartly like a City worker, no flowery skirts and spongy sandals. Even her classroom seems uncluttered, formally planned for serious learning. I am impressed. I wonder how old she is.

"Please sit…" She points to the miniature table. My knees bang against the edge as I lean forward to inspect the exercise books she's laid out. There are satisfying columns of matching ticks and rubber stamped smiley faces, and long comments about what Nathan's next target should be. But his work isn't what I've come to talk about.

Miss Patel's colleagues all used to tell me how wonderful Nathan is, which got us nowhere, but she waits for me to speak with her head on one side. Her crisp white collar stays smart and perfect when she moves.

I don't know how to raise the subject of Nathan's feelings.

I flick through one more book to be polite, and clear my throat. "May I ask you…can you tell me who Nathan's friends are?"

She frowns. I'm surprised. Teachers never frown about Nathan.

"He…he's quite a loner, I think. I don't know them *very* well yet – we're only two weeks into term. He seems to get on with everyone, boys and girls, but I haven't noticed a special friend. He's very quiet…Of course, I'm new to the staff – his last year's teacher may be able to tell you more."

Last year I found his teacher overwhelming, gushing and smiley and difficult to pin down. I don't want to talk with her again.

"There's a girl called Alka." Does she tense when I say that name? Surely that's ridiculous. I must be projecting my own feelings.

"Yes, Alka sits here, on the same table."

That's better. I understand it's the table for the most intelligent children. On the wall behind Miss Patel are profile portraits the children have painted of each other. One is labelled 'Alka by Nathan'. It seems to be mainly hair, a pale skin and one brown eye like a capital A turned through 90 degrees. She wears a round yellow earring, greyed by the running black paint of her hair and too large. Perhaps he will see his classmates more accurately after we pick up his new glasses. Next to her somebody called Xoriyo – I wonder where that name comes from and if it's a boy or a girl? – has portrayed Nathan surprisingly well, even in profile showing the snooker ball roundness of his head. Every picture has the same sideways A. I imagine Miss Patel, in front of the impressed children, showing them the technique.

"You asked about Alka, Mr Chan?"

I look away from the painted children, down at my knees. "Nathan would like Alka to come to us. To play, well, I mean to work, on these stories you have given them. I'm not sure it's necessary myself, but he seems very keen. For her to be in the story."

"We've left it to the children to decide how they present their stories. If they involve each other that's lovely. I'll have a chat with Alka's mum..." She hesitates. "... or whoever picks her up on Monday."

"*Whoever* picks her up?"

"Mr Chan, people have different child minding arrangements. Alka goes straight home at the end of the school day when Nathan stays at after school club. It isn't always her mum who picks her up. I will pass your message on, but was there anyone else your son mentioned?"

Again, that flicker of tension. Would she prefer someone else? She doesn't say there's any reason why Alka should not be my son's friend. But I suppose she can't – I myself wouldn't want teachers talking about me to other parents in terms of my "suitability".

Tall red letters on the display declare: "We are all friends in Class 3P". Most of the names on the portraits are unfamiliar to me. Does Miss Patel think I should know more about these children, my son's companions for the past two years?

"Are there any boys he's close friends with?" There, I've asked what I really want to know. Cool Miss Patel sidesteps like a politician:

"Mr Chan, children this age are sometimes only beginning to form close friendships. It's quite normal, especially for boys, just to be part of the general group. I haven't had to sort out any arguments involving Nathan, which is always an advantage. But I get the impression he doesn't very often have other children to play with at home," – *impression* is polite: it's clear she *knows* that *often* is actually *never* – "and if you're concerned about encouraging his social development, a practical step you could take would be to let him share his things at home and play with others in an informal way."

"Did you, Dad?"

"Did I what?"

"Did you ask Miss Patel to ask Alka's mum if she can come here to do our stories together?"

He's pulling my hand, twisting his upper body round and stepping sideways like a crab so he can check my expression as we walk along. It reminds me we must collect the glasses he has been prescribed.

Now when I'd like loud traffic to make conversation difficult, the wide road is unusually quiet. There's no wind to carry my words away, not even birds or planes to distract us.

"She said … she would ask for us."

"What if you write an invitation, you know like a party invitation, and I give it to Alka?" Nathan, still looking at my face, trips on a crack in the pavement and rights himself fast before I can tell him off.

"Nathan, you must stop asking me about this. I've spoken to Miss Patel and she will speak to this little girl's family. Something will happen or it will not. I cannot make it happen faster."

"Oh, I do hope it does! Soon!" He's jiggling with excitement.

"In any case we will need to invite her mother or some other lady to come with her, she cannot come on her own to our house."

"Why?"

"Please stop asking questions. When we get home we'll work on your story together."

"But we need Alka straight away…"

Goodness, he is stubborn! I had never heard of this child before the story project began. Or, to be fair, perhaps he had talked about her and it didn't register.

"We'll get as far as we can without your friend and then we'll think what to do next. That's the best I can say for now. Look, there's a new BMW, this year's model. Do you see?"

Nathan doesn't care about the BMW. He trudges along with the school rucksack banging on his back. The lights ahead have changed and heavy lorries grinding past do now make it too noisy to talk. His head is on a level with their wheel arches and he puts his head down against the exhaust fumes in his eyes, good boy, as I have taught him.

He doesn't appreciate the step I took, seeing the teacher other than for school work. My father never had to do this, or even my mother. I can see them now: my father ferrying stock between producers and the shop or bantering with customers; my mother jointing poultry or coaxing cramped lettuces from her window boxes. I played in and out of the balconies and flats or got on with my school work. There was never anything like this project Nathan has. But he has fewer places to play than I did, and there aren't other children – if he had a sister there'd be no problem *her* being in his film. For although Miss Patel didn't seem to think there was any reason why I shouldn't invite children, including girls, to play with my son, she did point out it's complicated if you want to film them.

"I can check in our records if her family have given permission for her to be filmed at school. But you'd still have to ask them if they were happy for *you* to film her, in your house."

"In our flat," I say.

"Yes, your flat, wherever."

The traffic still thunders, as we walk through the petrol fumes and haze of the last block of the main road. It's just as well Nathan's downcast eyes can't see my wet cheeks. I just avoid tripping on the pavement myself, as I realise Miss Patel's wise advice regarding Nathan having playmates applies equally well to me.

SATURDAY 17TH SEPTEMBER 2016

SAFIYA

I would like to lie in, but Xoriyo is out of bed early as usual and her empty space reproaches me. I pull the shawl round my shoulders and make us tea, sweet and milky. In the living room the television is on but the sound is low and she has drawn back the curtains. The unpitying sun shows the room's every dent and stain but, oblivious, Xoriyo's crouched on the floor, swinging back and forward on her heels and mouthing the words of another picture book, a new one.

I once spent a day in the classroom at her old school. The well-meaning teacher wanted help with settling in a new Somali child, but the child was fine and I could sit back and observe. I was curious to see if Xoriyo's infant school experience matched my own memories. Afterwards I said to her:

"So many of your friends read aloud the words of a book, even when the pictures are beautiful and fascinating, and flick the page straight over without looking at them."

Xoriyo agreed. "Sometimes they haven't even read the right words, but they still turn over. Silly!"

The words make no sense and the poor children don't even realise. I thought, if only they would compare them with the pictures, they would understand what they've read is meaningless – and in fact, can we call it reading, if the words make no sense?

My mother taught me to treasure the contents of books, one of the most precious gifts she gave me and not diminished by other wounds. So I too have taught my daughter, beginning with the pictures in the free ones from the health visitor before Xoriyo could walk, pointing out the decorations around the page, the lettering and then the easier words. Soon she took over and began to show me. She may be indifferent to the contrast between our shabby garden and the neat drives with their gleaming cars around us, between our landlord's dreary choices and the smart bright rooms we see through other windows, but in books she notices colours, shapes and shadows; she spots details and she recognises images that recur from page to page. She used to share her pleasure in illustrations with my mother, peace be upon her. My mother would comment in dialect and Xoriyo would try to teach her the English and my mother would say, *too late, too late.*

"What are you reading now, my sweet?"

She looks up. "It's just a library book. But look..." and she points to a wonderful picture of a baby lying inside an enormous pink and yellow peach, cradled in the hollow where the stone should be. "I'm going to ask if I can use it for the project, then we could keep the magic carpet story all to ourselves."

The peach lies on a willow pattern plate, with the sharpest of knives beside it. It's been sliced in half, fortuitously without touching the baby, who even has a tiny towelling nappy. A man with black hair is waving his hands in the air in astonishment. His hair is like the baby's: straight, fringed, a gleaming circle of light around the crown. They both have round pink cheeks and dark eyes and the baby is smiling at the man. Behind him his wife's mouth is open in a round gasp of astonishment.

Xoriyo loves babies. She knows she will never have a brother or sister. I had to tell her, because a year or so ago she kept asking – one of her classmates had a newborn baby brother and she saw him in his pram in the playground at home time. I chose my words with care, for I realised if I told her I'd been ill when I had her, she might feel it was her fault. I didn't want to frighten her. I know only too well what nightmares a child may have alone in the dark, and although I share her bed I cannot always comfort her. I told her, you need a man to have a baby – I have not gone into details – and since there's no man, there will be no baby. Aren't we happy, together, just the two of us?

So I know why she likes this tale. A Japanese man and his wife long for children, but none come, and they grow old together and they regret it but they still love and care for each other. Then one day the man brings a peach home for his wife, and she marvels: it's the biggest, most glowing peach she's ever seen. She brings a plate and a knife and when the man cuts – there is Momotaro the peach boy!

"Isn't he beautiful? Just like I'd have, if we had one." Xoriyo traces her finger over the baby's chubby form and around the peach that cradled him.

I cannot let Xoriyo see that I am hurt. Nothing is her fault. In a sense this child can be a baby brother for her, just as the magic carpet is a safe place for us. My phone rings as we're turning the peach story pages again to think how we could use it, and the news I hear from my cousin Fawzia makes everything fit together perfectly.

I decide to buy peaches, although it's September, and never mind the price or how many shops we must visit to find them.

Mrs Kaur

"Today I'm going to write my story again to get it clear in my head."

Mandeep's mother will be pleased. He doesn't often want to write and the tutor she pays says if he doesn't practise more he won't go to the grammar school with his brother.

"I've made changes like they said – I'm calling the boy Mandeep – same as me!"

He puffs out his chest and jabs it with his finger, head on one side and an important expression. But already he's put the pencil down.

"Come and see what I'm going to use for the beanstalk!"

He pulls me out in the garden and poses next to the sunflowers we planted together. The stems are hairy and tough, the tall flowers casting shadows on Mandeep's patka. Aman was going to cut them down this weekend but I asked him to leave them. They look ugly he complained, the flowers are rotting and the leaves are curly brown. But secretly I think my son's happy watching football on TV instead. In the lounge his body is a diagonal line, his clasped hands behind his head against the sofa back. He crosses his ankles and his toes point halfway across the rug towards the screen. Aman's been an adult a long time but still I thrill to see my tall grown up son take all the space in the room. When something good happens his toes go up and when he's disappointed they stay still. His toes are discussing the match like the men on the TV. Ouf! What a lot those men have to say! Up, down go his toes! Aman is too old now for me to tell him sit up straight to be healthy. Anyway, if he is comfy he'll let us get on, no butting in, no cutting down our beanstalk.

Today there is blue sky and bright colours. The plant shapes have edges on such a sharp day. You do not get this in India where things blur in sunshine and soft rain.

"Brrr…" I pull my cardigan close. Straight away Mandeep is by me for a hug and our joke: "I'll keep your cardigan warm, Bibi." We pretend my cardigan is the old wrinkled thing that shivers, not my thin cold body underneath in the English chill. So we give my cardigan a big shaking hug together *brrr brrr brr*…"You're still cold!" His voice is impatient. He hugs me again, a hard bang against my body and I say:

"Maybe we go inside now, eh, Mandeep. And I see your story?"

"But Bibi you won't be able to read it."

Actually I am hoping he will help me read it and the letters will come together to make sense like the English teacher promised they would. In the class we had targets to reach. On the very first day, they talked about the end! *"At the end of the course, you will…"* then there were round black dots like on Mandeep's letter from school. One of the black dots said *"…be able to read and understand simple English sentences."* (I know because the teacher read it out for us and I was pleased. That is what I wanted to do so much!) But after four, maybe five classes I was not able to do this thing any better. Other people understood but I was in a muddle, stopping the teacher again and again with my questions. The teacher always smiling, saying "Well DONE!" It got on my nerves because it was not true, my work was not well DONE, and the other students were all waiting for me. There was ironing to do, and cooking, and the langar, and my husband grumbled: "Why do you go? If it doesn't make you happy?" So I stopped going. I was unhappy I hadn't succeeded. But I was very happy I didn't have to go!

Now I shall learn from my lovely Mandeep instead and we must have a sweet biscuit together to start us off.

But his writing looks different today. There are many more straight lines and all the letters are the same size.

"What have you done here, Mandeeep? Poor Bibi can't find any sense in this writing."

"There's this boy Tanveer at school and he's had a cool idea. He says, if we only write using capital letters, the teachers won't tell us off for *not* using them. I think they'll probably find something else we aren't doing right, that's what their job is. But I'm trying his idea here …"

Capital letters. Yes, I know these, at the front of my name and the football team and Sainsbury's. But Mandeep is frowning.

"… only if Tanveer's right I'm not sure why we bothered learning small letters in the first place."

No, I don't understand that either. I'm disappointed. I will have to ask him to write the story again, or ask Aman to put it into Punjabi for me.

"Don't worry, Bibi. Lots of people aren't very bright."

It hurts when he says that, but I give a silly grin like a clown to show I don't mind.

"Miss Patel says it's more important to be kind, and *you* are the kindest person I know. Can I have another biscuit?"

He's munching away, jabbing his damp fingertip on my clean worktop to pick up stray crumbs one at a time. To push away the humiliation I have another go reading his story. Gradually I can piece together the letters, comparing the shapes with the ones in the newspaper and sounding them out, part of a word first, another part next and reading out the phrases as we were taught in the class. Sitting in the warm clean kitchen with faint football sounds coming from the lounge, eventually I do understand his story. For the beanstalk he *has* used our sunflowers that we planted together. It was his own idea before I said anything. I am so pleased! At the top of the sunflower there is a massive kitchen like our kitchen but with even more islands and units and gadgets and machines. Machines for this and machines for that… There is a lady ironing and it is me! As I work I am singing *FEE FI FO FUM*. Mandeep has written it in lots of different colours to show all the different ways I sing it, and I can recognise the words and read them easy – easy peezy like he says. *Easy peezy* – more good words to roll in my mouth – *fee fi fo fum easy peezy, fee ee… easy, fo peezy, fi… yeezy, fumpeezy, fumpee…*

"YESSS!"

"Did they score?" Mandeep runs to the other room to see what is making his dad so happy.

I look back at the story. The lady ironing in Mandeep's story (me!) is doing a *fee fi fo fum* song… I recognise those words, but then the shape changes and I can't see the bit about her smelling blood and English people. Mandeep comes back. He likes to play football but he cannot concentrate on watching the long matches.

"I knew you didn't like that blood bit so I left it out."

"So we must think what she can say instead."

He skids across the polished floor on an imaginary skate board, aiming for the biscuit tin but I pick it up quickly and put it back in the cupboard.

"Mandeep, you cannot stop in the middle of the story like that. She must do another thing, something different."

"Oh yes you CAN! And oh no she WON'T!" He takes crayons and writes different colours for each letter:

"Look, I've done it in little letters so you can read it yourself, Bibi!"

the end

I can read the words but how can it be the end? I do not want to be stuck ironing at the top of a sunflower for rest of my story just because Mandeep is too lazy to write what happens next. Oh dear, he is so lazy!

It makes me shiver even though the oven has been on and the room is warm, to think of myself as an old lady left with all the tasks of the household while the men watch their football and the boys dance about at nothing. If I work on my English, my reading and writing, they will take my ideas seriously and **the end** will be a happier one for me.

MONDAY 19TH SEPTEMBER 2016

TERESA

Reminder **for** *all children in* <u>*Year 3*</u> (*Classes 3S and 3P*). *If you need help with materials or ideas for retelling your "fairy story" with your family, just ask your teacher! The closing date for entries for our festival is* <u>*Tuesday 11th October.*</u>

"Could we just start again, Sky?"

On Wednesday she wasn't too bad because they'd made a fuss of her at school after she told them about Ten Pence. We made a poster with a photo to stick up on the trees and Sky thought we could ask at doors if anyone had seen her. People do that for cats, so it might work for a rabbit… but actually I hope she'll forget the idea.

When we took Alka to school Sky walked ahead next to me with her face pointing the other way. Alka just trotted along quietly, poor child. I thought, an opportunity for me to show myself in my best light, and what do I do? I lose my child's pet! Fortunately Alka's grandparents started taking her, which gives me a chance to talk with Sky. Sometimes it's easier to resolve things when you're walking along.

But she sulked on, and then it was Saturday.

"I still want to go knocking on doors."

At first I wanted to curl up with embarrassment, but most people were kind. They knew, when I told them which day we'd lost Ten Pence, she'd be dead by now, but they smiled at Sky, promised they'd keep an eye open, looked carefully at the photo and said how sweet she was. Obviously there was no point calling on Alka's family, and there was no way I was going to have the neighbour the other side put two and two together about what happened to his lettuce patch. For the same reason I changed my mind about putting up posters, so by the time we got home from our first trip round the close Sky wasn't speaking to me again.

"I'm going to my room!"

She flung herself on her bed with theatrical sobs. She's a fantastic actress, I'll give her that. Hitting the mattress that hard must have nearly winded her, but she kept up the heartbroken pose.

"I'm sorry love, but these things happen..." And worse, but I won't go into that.

We keep the blinds shut so we don't see the empty hutch. At least now it's clean, so I can get rid of it on eBay. I'd better leave it a bit, or she'll think I've given up.

What a miserable week. First the "incident" next door – Alka's mother still hasn't shown her face. I can hardly ask the grandparents what actually happened. They look so miserable and the only time I saw the dad he was getting out of his car with an expression that said "Keep Out". You'd think he'd have thanked me for sheltering his child, and the fact he hasn't makes me think Alka's mum getting hurt *was* something to do with him. All clean and smart he is, with his shiny BMW and carrying his laptop…. But still waters run deep. It's often the clean and tidy ones who are the worst when it comes to domestic violence – if that's what it was – and now the thought has entered my head it makes me shiver just to see him turn into the drive and I'm relieved I'm not spending time with his children after all. Even if him swanning around with his designer suits and his special number plate does suggest they could easily pay me instead of putting on those poor tired looking grandparents.

That said, I've found out some good things about this road. I didn't realise how many of Sky's classmates lived here, some her friends, or could be (some – well, I can't see it). New local playmates could take her mind off Ten Pence, get her sharing nicely again. When we moved here last year she did have children in to play occasionally, but her best friend left and there were other problems. Not only with Sky, with the class as a whole: lots of difficult behaviour and bullying and not only children but also parents falling out…. It happens sometimes, said the head teacher after a series of stroppy meetings. The solution was to mix the children up into new classes when they returned in September. I was one of the parents who thought it a good idea, but some went on moaning – I think they'd moan whatever the school did, to be honest.

I hope the groups in the new class will settle down. Her friends don't have to be people like us, after all. It's not as if there *are* many, round here.

On Sunday morning we knocked on the doors in the close that hadn't answered before. It's amazing how different the houses here look when you start going up the paths: some really smart with plantation blinds and new reg cars, and others sad somehow, like they got left behind, like the one with the chipped old gnomes or the few like mine that still have wooden window frames. You can tell which are rented and where the old people live.

Intriguing spicy smells wafted from one of the bigger houses even before the door was opened. This owner was slim and elegant, with a crisply ironed shirt and designer jeans and his long thin feet bare. Men in turbans look so graceful – something to do with the upside-down V shape on the foreheads, seems to streamline them. An incredibly happy looking boy came running up behind, and pushed past his legs.

"Hello Sky! She's in my class, Dad!"

Sky went all shy. She hid behind me and peeped out with a coy look.

"Come on Sky, don't be silly…" She's not shy at all really, and now she's so big for her age it looks daft when she pretends.

"Please, come in." The man gestured courteously – would not hear of us standing on the doorstep to tell him why we'd come – and in no time we were sitting on shiny white bar stools in a kitchen like something from a magazine – units to die for – and there was an old lady in a sari and a big thick cardigan serving us with different kinds of Indian snack.

"Hot! I warn you! Not for children, innit!"

She pointed at one bowl, laughed and produced an alternative for Sky and the boy; a tupperware of those huge Indian sweets. Massive orange and pink chunks of syrup and sugar, and the boy broke one in half and gave it to Sky. I was embarrassed when she screwed up her face and refused to try it, but the grandmother gave the widest grin I've ever seen.

"Sensible girl! Don't take sweets from strangers, innit?"

The old lady offered her a chocolate biscuit instead. Which she did take, and then another.

There was a child's exercise book lying on the island unit and the boy said it was his story for the school project. For some reason he and the grandmother couldn't stop laughing when he spoke about it. That made her cough and wheeze for ages until her handsome son banged her on the back and made them all calm down. They said they'd check their shed for Ten Pence .... What a beautiful house though, and through the French windows the garden looked so well kept. I shouldn't think a stray pet could hide for long in a garden as tidy as that. Even the tall sunflowers didn't look as clumsy as I think they normally do.

Not everyone answered their door of course. There was an elderly couple who seemed suspicious, and one man who was deaf. We didn't get anywhere with him. Some teenagers looked completely bored and dazed at the same time, as though we'd arrived from another planet and they didn't even know what a rabbit was. Sky was pulling my hand to get away from them almost before I'd finished saying why we'd knocked. Then we were at the corner where the close meets the main road. There's a modern block of flats – expensive, I bet – on one side and on the other a house divided into two maisonettes, with two front doors like ours. Nothing designer about this: yellow flouncy net curtains upstairs that I've noticed before, a leftover from last century that no one's dared call vintage yet. Neither doorbell answered, perhaps because Sky was kicking at the slimy cracked tiles with a look of contempt on her face. I was just pulling her away when a corner of the yellow curtain twitched and a small brown face looked out and then vanished again.

"It's Xoriyo, from school," said Sky. "She's new, she's really odd…"

It was too late to leave. The left hand door was opened by a tall slim woman wearing a long straight skirt and loose top. She was pulling her headscarf forward to cover her hair. She had the most amazing bone structure. The only way people would ever not admire her face would be if she got one of those veils that cover your whole face. Niqab, I think they're called. She stood at the foot of the dark stairs enquiringly, her daughter turned in against her side with her arms round her hips. The child smiled timidly at Sky, a more genuine shyness than my daughter's performance earlier. I started to explain, and then the child interrupted, speaking rapidly to her mother in their own language, whatever it is. But the mother shushed her.

"Speak English, Xoriyo, these people will not understand."

Suddenly the child, Xoriyo, was positively gabbling about our rabbit, telling her mother how upset Sky had been in school that week, and how Alka was there when the rabbit got lost, and everyone'd had a go at Alka so now Alka was sad too, but Alka seemed sad anyway because something'd happened—

Her mother and I interrupted her both at the same time. Looking at the woman I realised although we were streets apart culturally and in our lives, we both recognised instinctively whatever had happened in Alka's house was not something the children should be discussing on the doorstep. Then Sky burst out: "You speak really good English! Why don't you do that at school?" At the same time her mother was saying "Don't you speak English at school? Why not?" and the child, Xoriyo, was half grinning and half looking worried and explaining, "Oh, I just understand it but I don't speak it. Then nobody bothers me ..."

Her mother was clearly disturbed.

"Well, don't worry," I said. "Just let us know if you see the rabbit..." and we turned back down their broken path to where the front gate would be if there was one. Sky had forgotten all about sulking and was saying "… but Mum, it's weird, she *never* speaks English at school, I didn't even know she could…", and I was thinking how interesting people are when you take your eyes off your own life and get a glimpse of theirs. All of a sudden someone was waving from the other pavement and it was that small, round-faced Chinese boy I've also seen around the school. I didn't remember him wearing glasses, though.

"Don't tell me he's in your class too!" I said.

"Hi Nathan!" called Sky, and she'd have run straight across the road to him if I hadn't stopped her to make her look properly. She didn't do any shy/not shy act with this one, I noticed, just stared at him. Nathan. I like that name.

"Good morning," said the man with him, his father I assumed, a very clean, smart-looking Chinese gentleman with a polite smile and shiny glasses like an older version of Nathan. Where have all the clean, polite smiling men been all my life, I wondered, or is it only Asian men that have manners round here? For the second time that morning I felt scruffy and clumsy. This one looked like if he'd had a hat, he'd have tipped it to me. Of course he didn't have a hat.

"Did you find your rabbit?" Nathan was asking.

"You lost a rabbit?"

"Yes, Dad, I told you all about it." He grinned at Sky with a hint of a shrug. "My dad never listens," he said.

"Please, Nathan—"

"Oh, don't worry, my daughter's always criticising me too."

I was trying to put him at ease. He looked hurt and anxious, standing there with his back to the privet hedge that skirts the car park of the flats. Why don't children realise their parents have feelings too?

"I have a lot to think about," he said, spreading his hands in a hopeless sort of way. "But I am sure your daughter is good to you. We should not criticise our children either."

I felt reproved. I'd only been trying to show a bit of solidarity. But he was going on:

"Nathan, is this little girl in your class? Perhaps you would like to invite her to be in your story if she lives nearby and her mother can come too?"

Nathan looked at Sky, grinned vaguely and shook his head. "No, I've chosen Alka," he said, and honestly you'd have thought the handsome prince had rejected Cinderella in favour of her ugly sister, the way Sky's pleased expression suddenly changed.

"I mean," added Nathan, who seemed a nice boy underneath but I suppose he just knew what he wanted, "Sky could help but I want Alka to be the princess."

Now his father shrugged. "Honestly, this homework with the fairy stories," he sighed. "It seems to be more trouble than it's worth. Your name is Sky? It's a beautiful name and now my son has made your face cloud over."

I often wish I hadn't called her Sky. When she was born, she had such blue eyes and I did think Sky was a lovely name. I didn't foresee the piss-takes that began almost straight away. But I don't think this man was joking; he was just proud of his clever turn of speech. You could see Sky was trying hard not to cry, and I felt a sudden rush of love. Unlike her storms earlier, these were true tears. Her feelings were genuinely hurt.

"You must apologise, Nathan."

"Don't worry—" I'd spent half the morning telling people not to worry.

"I'm sorry, Sky," said Nathan. He didn't seem to be just repeating it, like most children when they're told to apologise. He was simply keen to explain exactly what he meant. "I hope you find your rabbit. And you *can* help with my story. When I've got the main parts done with Alka, I'll let you know."

It wasn't the best way to leave it, but it would have to do. They turned into the flats and I'm not sure why we didn't walk away ourselves straight away. We watched the father jab a code on the entry phone and then they disappeared. I've often wondered what those flats are like inside – the smart, white building with its flat windows and wide balconies is so unlike anything else in our close. Sky wasn't the only one to regret we hadn't been invited in but she put a brave face on it.

"I don't want to play with him anyway. Not now he's got those stupid glasses."

I should have reproved her for that – presumably he only wears them because he needs to – and in fact I should get *her* eyes checked. But their initial greeting had been so enthusiastic, and then ended with such disillusion. Children are always funny when they meet outside school, so amazed there's an existence elsewhere they forget they aren't particularly close in their normal daily world. It kind of summed up the weekend: a disappointing muddle. People had been brilliantly friendly and even if we never find Ten Pence we've met some lovely neighbours. Or begun to meet them. But Sky couldn't see that.

Now it's Monday evening and the story project reminder in the school letter just makes me feel inadequate. But at least I'm down to two cigs and no way will I go out for a third now.

TUESDAY 20TH SEPTEMBER 2016

MR CHAN

"She's not my friend," Nathan insisted. "She's ok but she's ever so bossy."

It would be much easier, now we have met, to have this Sky – her name is so beautiful – in our flat because we could have her mother too. True, her appearance was not appealing – why do moles attract more attention when there has been an attempt at concealment? But she seemed polite. I caught something there, between us … Nathan tells me the little girl is an only child and I saw no wedding ring. Perhaps they are one adult one child in their home too. There was such sympathy on her face when I expressed my frustration with this storytelling project. Maybe she too thinks the children would be better with spellings and sums. Maybe she too is anxious about whether she is doing everything the correct way for her child, or maybe such anxiety affects fathers more, and she has the instinctive mothering skills that Maxine showed for the short time she could.

We hung up our jackets. Nathan filled the water jug and slotted it into the Nespresso machine. I must order new pods, there are none of my usual ones left. But who knows, perhaps I'll prefer the stronger ones. I have become set in my ways; some changes will do no harm.

"…although she's very good at acting." Nathan's tone was thoughtful.

"Who is good at acting?"

"Sky. She makes up plays. They practise them in the playground, her and her friends, and then at story time they show them to us. Sometimes. Well, she asks Miss Patel nearly every day, but Miss Patel doesn't always say yes."

"Are the plays good?"

"They never have a proper story. They're more about Sky and her friends, so they can dress up and sing songs and dance and…show off. But she *is* good, you can always hear what she says and she can do loads of different faces and voices."

"So why not ask her for your King Midas story?"

"Because I want Alka."

We were back where we'd started. The green light on the coffee machine stopped blinking.

"Drop in the pod for me, and press start." Nathan usually loves to do this, but he was preoccupied. He shook his glossy head violently as he does when trying to get a decision to settle in his mind. Then he removed his new glasses and looked up at me so trustingly. He said simply: "Alka's beautiful. I want a beautiful girl in my story. Do you see, Dad?"

A tidal pull of love for Nathan took me unawares. I do see. He cannot begin to know how well I see. We both want a beautiful girl in our story.

SAFIYA

"**D**id you speak English at school today?"

Xoriyo is mute, cross-legged on the sofa, rucking up the shawl underneath. It looks uncomfortable but she doesn't shift. Her books are still in her bag. She's shown no interest in proceeding with either of our stories. She puts the television on and stares as though she's watching. I tug hard at the remote to get her to relinquish it.

"Xoriyo! I'm not going to make supper until you tell me why you won't speak English at school!"

She has put on a headscarf as tight as she can and now she pulls the ends crosswise over her mouth and holds them trapped against her cheeks.

As for school, if she doesn't speak English there, when does she ever open her mouth? There are as far as I know no other Somalis in her class for her to talk with. That's one reason I was pleased to get this maisonette, to give us a break from Somali London claustrophobia. Her Muslim classmates may have Arabic lessons at the mosque, but that is not language for playing. We've established the other child, Sky, was not lying. Despite myself I'm impressed if my daughter has maintained silence for nearly three weeks.

"No one is an island" – I agree wholeheartedly with this English saying. Why would my own daughter want to make herself one?

Crossness won't yield results – it certainly didn't yesterday. I go to where she sits stiff and defiant on the sofa and put my arms around her. I will not pull the headscarf like I did the remote control. Instead I stroke gently from the crown of her head over her neck and down her shoulders, back to the top and start again. Gradually she relaxes.

"The children don't like me."

"I'm sorry to hear that…but what makes you think—?"

"So if they think I don't speak English I don't have to play with them. I don't want to play with people who don't like me. Also then the teachers don't give me hard work, that if I can't do it they'd say I'm stupid."

She fiddles with the end of her headscarf, not looking at me.

"Is the work easier at this school, then?"

"It is if you don't speak English. I get to sit on a table with a boy who doesn't talk in any language and another boy who shouts, and there's a special teacher who sits with us and does everything for us."

"But why should you want that?"

"Because then I won't make mistakes and the others won't laugh at me. Or if they do, Mrs Carmel – that's the special teacher – protects me."

"But it sounds as though you're not trying to make friends any more than they are! Why would you not want to make friends?"

I am bewildered. I know my daughter is independent, self-sufficient... I'm proud of her for this. She can play by herself for hours, tell herself stories, do without many toys or much company to entertain her. I do think she should know about her heritage, so we speak Somali here at home whenever she wants to and I'm teaching her to read it. Her bilingualism and her independence are useful gifts. And she's sporty, so other children want her to score their goals and win their prizes, even if they often leave her out of their team celebrations. But there's more to life than sport, and she needs also to be able to take her place in society, whichever part of society she ends up in, to integrate and melt into the background if need be, to hide and adapt and grow...

"I might leave this school like I left the other school. Then I'd leave my friends like I did before and miss them like I do now. It's better if I just get on with things by myself."

My heart aches. Although I see her point of view, her way of reacting is not the answer. But for now I place that part of the problem on one side and make an agreeing sound. I reach my arm around her and she snuggles a touch more against me, letting go of the headscarf at last.

"You are not learning things if you are doing only easy work. Don't you find it boring?"

"Yes, it *is* boring, but what's good is I'm the best on my table. That's better than being the worst in another group."

My poor little daughter!

"Why didn't you tell me this is how you're feeling?"

She shrugs. The scarf falls away and her grin reveals more of her usual self but she's still looking away from me to where the television would light the now dim room, if I'd let her have it on. It's a challenging grin, not a happy one. She speaks quickly, spitting out the words:

"You have your secrets. Why can't I have some too?"

WEDNESDAY 21ST SEPTEMBER 2016

ALKA

"Alka, would you take these clean clothes up to Nani's room please?"

Nani doesn't like the narrow stairs to the loft. There's a turn she's frightened of. She says she can't fit her foot all on the step at once. Nani's feet are not big, for a grown up, but she wears huge slippers that make them bigger. Nana too dislikes the stairs. So once they come down in the morning, they stay down.

After school I like to help Nani and Nana, because they are helping us, Mummy says. They're going to stay a long time. It feels safer that way, because grandparents are always the same whatever happens. So many other things are different, like, when she came home from hospital, Mummy wanted to sleep in my room. I have to sleep on the top bunk in Sunil's, with the Incredible Hulk wallpaper that gives me nightmares and all Sunil's stupid toys that are so big with hard bits I trip over. In the daytime he puts his cold metal cars and trains in my bunk even, and when I come in I have to throw them all out, but quietly not to wake him. I climb up, make sure I have them all, climb down, and put them gently on the carpet where we won't tread on them in the morning. Sometimes I have to go up and down two or three times. Sunil isn't having anyone in to play at the moment which is good because there would be even more mess, but bad because he follows me around wanting me to play instead.

It's quiet in the loft, and sunny. Nani and Nana's bed is so tidy, the bedspread flat with no wrinkles, the cushions exactly next to each other. I give myself a hug in Nani's warm dressing gown hanging on the door. I can't reach high enough to get my arms in the sleeves, but I can wrap the two sides across me and the soft fleece reaches to my knees. If I step very slowly I can pull the door with me so it feels like Nani's moving towards me to bring me into a cuddle. I go forwards and back inside her dressing gown. I get the smell of her to enjoy without her waving me away because she's busy. She's busy more than when they used to come to stay. Mummy used to do most things then, and Nani used to sit in an armchair and laugh she was learning to be lazy in her old age.

I stay inside her dressing gown for a little while to make it feel like she wants me to be safe in the room. Then I take a look round. Nobody will hear me. I know because last year, after the room was finished and they'd laid the carpet, I came up and nobody could find me, and Mummy said my footsteps must be light like a fairy. The builders' footsteps weren't light, they went bang creak bang creak

SMASH when they dropped their hammers. It felt so quiet when they went away.

Nani (it must be Nani, because she does the most puja) has moved one of the bedside tables into a corner to hold the mandir she always brings with her so she can pray. It's soothing to trace the patterns in the wood with my finger. Last time Nani was here I helped her clean the mandir, because she said my tiny hands were better at picking sticky dust out of the delicate holes and corners where the wood's carved to look like lace. This time she hasn't asked me yet – perhaps she's been too busy downstairs. Ganesh sits watching me, and I get a dizzy feeling until I've found all four of his arms. Nani used to tell me about him often because he's her favourite god, but it's not easy to remember all the stories so really she needs to tell me them again. There's a garland of flowers round his neck, and Nani has left him an apple after her morning puja, but I think he'd prefer sweets. One of his tusks is broken which is something to do with using it to write a story. He holds a lotus flower, which I guess is just to look pretty, a bowl of sweets (but not real ones, poor Ganesh) and a thing a bit like an axe. I don't know why one hand is empty or what the thing is he's holding with his trunk but I do remember why his trunk is always curved. It's to show when there's a problem, he can always find a way round it.

Maybe Ganesh could help Mummy get back to normal?

On her dressing table Nani has a big old hairbrush from India. It's so heavy it hurts to hold it up against the top of my head, but the brush part is too soft. It won't go through the thickness of my hair which is tangled because nobody plaited it this morning. I drop my hand down, holding on to the handle like the builder held the end of the hammer. In the big centre glass my face looks serious. I try to surprise the seriousness away by doing a wide smile but the seriousness knows it's not real. Then I try plaiting my hair myself but in the mirror everything goes the wrong way so I stop. I lift the hairbrush to make it look as if I'm banging myself on the head and I make a scary face. That doesn't look real either. I wish I could act like Sky, and make people believe who I was being. Or even notice when I'm just being me.

I want to see what I look like from the side – my profile. Miss Patel said it was called that when we drew each other at school. But although I twist lots of different ways I can't get that exactly right either.

So. Now I'm going to look at the view of outside from up here. I've tried not to think about our garden since that horrible night or about Sky's since we lost the rabbit. We can't see out from downstairs as Mummy has the curtains closed a lot. It's for her headache she says, and also in the front I don't think she likes people seeing in. In Sunil's room when the curtains aren't closed for his baby bedtime I just stay away from the window. But up here I can see everything if I'm brave enough to look. When things aren't right people need to be brave, and up here I have Ganesh to protect me.

The back window first, to get it over with. I can stand right inside it with a triangle of wall both sides and the window across my chest. A dormer, the builders called it. But I can't see the tepee or the empty hutch unless I drag the heavy dressing table stool over to stand on. Grownups would come and see what the noise was. So I don't need to be so brave after all.

At least I tried. I can be proud of that. Now for the front. Here the window is flat on the roof, called Velux. It works on a swivel which the builders showed me when the room was new. Nani has opened it to air the room, and I can just poke my head out over the ledge and watch what's happening in the street from high up like a bird.

I'm Rapunzel. She had a mirror, and a hair-brush, and a window high up. Below her was a for-est, a garden and a river. One day her prince rode past on horseback. He rode past and rode back, and rode past again and each time he wondered, "What is that strange tower with only one window so high, here in the forest with the river flowing by?" Then one beautiful sunny morning he saw the golden-haired girl standing at the window. She was grown up, taller than I am, so he saw her from her lovely hair down her body to her waist. Supposing she was a mermaid below? It would have been a different story…. But she wasn't a mermaid, she was a beauti-ful girl and they practised him climbing up her hair into the tower. My days how that would have pulled if it was real life! But it's a story so in the end he got her out and they rode away on horses happily ever after. (There are some other bits but I don't like them, about witches and eating something with roots like a radish which is horrible anyway. When I retell it I'll leave those bits out.)

Nani and Nana and Mummy and even Dad and Sunil when he's in a good mood – everyone I know in fact – all say I have beautiful hair. It's longer than anyone else's in my class. I prop my chin on the Velux edge and lean forward as far as I can, and I measure with my hands how far over the ledge I can make my hair go. But the wooden ledge is thick, and even my long hair hardly reaches down the slope of the roof tiles at all.

The street is quiet. It's called a close because it's closed at the end and all you can do is walk round the pavement to get out again. Or do a turn in your car. Sometimes people use our driveway to turn round if one of our cars isn't here. They come too close to the front windows and make a petrol smell in the house. It makes Dad cross, but I don't see what people are to do otherwise. If people had horses like in Rapunzel the smell would be different and you could hear them trotting.

There's a trotting sound now but it's a lady with high heels doing that funny run grown up ladies do that doesn't make them go any faster. Maybe there's a bus coming on the main road. I follow her with my eyes down to the turning, where Nathan and his dad are just coming into the road, very small, back from the after-school club he goes to while his dad's at work. I can see them talking to each other but from here you can't hear anything. It's like having the tablet on mute.

Nathan. He's quiet and doesn't get noticed, except on Monday when he had new glasses, and he feels like my friend. Only it's a bit funny to have friends who are boys now I'm in Year 3, except Sunil. Nathan lives in the flats. There were tall white sheets of wood with signs on them and then when I was really little we came back from holiday and the wooden walls had gone and we could see the flats. My dad whistled when we turned into our road at the end of driving back from the airport. His whistle means he's surprised. "I bet they cost more than our house!" he said. Well, of course they'd be more money, because it's a great big building and our house has only two parking spaces. But they only have one garden between them all. Nathan and his dad can go in because they know which numbers to press, like knowing a magic spell.

The other children would laugh if I made Nathan into my prince, but the reminder came to get on with the story, and if I can't have Nathan I must have *somebody* – unless I could get ideas from some of Nani's gods and goddesses? They have hundreds of stories to tell.

No one's in my room for a change so I find my tablet and Google "Indian gods" but there's so much writing it's hard even though I'm a good reader. So I search Google images – there's loads! Gods with bright colours and four arms each side with lotus flowers like Ganesh and riding on tigers like the pictures Nani puts downstairs sometimes. Could Rapunzel's prince bring her a tiger to escape on, not a horse? Then further down the screen I see photos of statues that look like they're made of gold. This one makes me laugh! No one would do puja in front of her! She doesn't have enough clothes on and she has big round boobies, bigger than Mummy's with the middle bits standing up exactly in the centre even without a bra to help them. They're like great big marbles; you could cup your hands round them. The statue's body is all gold, it would be too heavy to hold for long – and she has a huge head and hands but her waist is tiny like a Barbie doll. Her tummy button points up as though it's trying to catch up with her boobies. At least she has trousers on, a darker gold, but she has to have her hips stuck out sideways like when you're hula hooping so they don't fall down. The label on the picture (I think Miss Patel said they're called captions) says she's Shiva's wife ... I think he should tell her to put more clothes on.

Someone's coming upstairs. I'm not sure they'll think I should be looking at these pictures. I shove the tablet under the bed, but for the rest of the day I can't stop thinking about the half-undressed stone goddess and although it was funny at first, it makes me feel uncomfortable with the grownups downstairs having those pictures going round in my head.

Thursday 22nd September 2016

Mr Chan

With Nathan in bed I catch up on office work, overspills from the day. Deleting emails, running my eye over tomorrow's tasks, the TV on for company. I finish updating a spreadsheet and I'm all done till morning, so I pour a small whisky for another kind of company, partly to celebrate a successful deal today and partly to demarcate this as official leisure time.

On TV there's a documentary called "*Someday my prince will come*", about women who use dating sites. It's not an idea I like, but the programme catches my fuller attention because – well, precisely because they are *not* eye catching, most of these women. The men they find look ordinary too, but respectable. Some of them are interviewed in their workplaces – I would severely reprimand any employee I found using *my* premises to give an interview on such a subject! Some speak from the homes they now share in the suburbs or where they're living the dream out in the wilds. They all seem sublimely content, on high stools in their bright kitchens or leaning on forks by their lettuce plots. Clearly, I must revise my idea that only loners and the desperate use dating sites. It seems to be the accepted thing. There's even footage of a wedding, and the groom's speech begins "When I found her in the catalogue..." and people laugh but in a kind way.

I wonder which sites they used...Really...! In the kitchen I swill out my whisky glass. One is enough. The homework reminder from the school is pinned to the notice board – this weekend we must do something about that. I take a quick look in on Nathan who's fallen asleep with his glasses on. He gives a small sigh as I use both hands gently to unhook them and place them safely on his bedside cabinet. When I need to feel everything is in its right place, I find it helpful to stand guard in his room, with his calm sleep breathing health and possibility into the air before me.

I consider how we are.

He's growing up and becoming more separate every day. Who knows what lies ahead for him? Life is what we make of it...for me the transition from my English colonial style school in Hong Kong to private school here was the least of the changes I experienced at fourteen. We had to stay long enough to get full UK passports and for however long my studies would take, then maybe for ever if such was God's will.

"Ah, perhaps if we'd gone to Canada..." my parents would say. It was a question of choosing between fearsome winters and London prejudice: they had to find a discreet niche and I had to excel over my

English classmates. Excelling was no trouble for I had been brought up to chase grades, aim for the top of the class. I settled in, I made one or two friends among the boffins in the maths stream. I studied business and applied all that I'd learnt. I have made money and I slide silently around UK society and no longer do I hear anybody question my right to be here. I have known sneers, but I can disappear inside myself and bear that. For other arrivals it was harder: they had no transitional arrangements when their countries suffered less predictable political changes. They hadn't already started a sound English education, or they were perhaps already too old or too fixed in an ill-matching set of beliefs.

Where I could shine, my parents' only option was discretion. They soon realised their role would be to lurk quietly in the hard-working corners of immigrant life; make no trouble; deflect the 'Chinky' jibes and dole out the sweet and sour chicken. What their Buddhist forebears would have accepted, my Christian parents knew would rob them of their self respect, and that rattled me. Just when I needed their confidence, their answers and guidance, they were investing their hopes in me, so I studied and studied for their sakes as well as my own.

They were right to return to Hong Kong: I should not have liked them to continue cooped up like my aunt and uncle, closed into their tiny flat above their dark store room, shielded – or was it trapped – behind their waist-high takeaway counter with the television high in the corner to discourage conversation from the customers. For years, my aunt has shuffled between the kitchen and the shop, speaking only Cantonese. My uncle's trips to the wholesaler extend his horizon a couple of miles, but it's poor compensation for the bantering life of the Hong Kong streets and markets. For my uncle and aunt, it soon became clear the future belonged to the customers of all colours and races who carried their syrupy Anglo-Chinese food out into the wider world. They have fused together in their isolation, news from the wholesaler fed in scraps by my uncle to my aunt.

My parents fitted in with a similar life here no longer than they needed to assure my future. My uncle and aunt remain, smaller in mind and body on each of our fortnightly visits, displaying the same menu but with fewer dishes available, reducing opening hours, even the flatter TV looming less from the wall. After my parents went home, I had no other older relations to turn to for the wisdom I still sometimes sought. It wasn't until university that I found the Chinese church whose belated welcome built on the God Speeds of the congregation back home in Hong Kong.

If, occasionally, I miss study for its own sake, the greater beauty of Maths over Money, I consider Nathan's needs and I think, in occupational terms, things have turned out well. The foundation I am providing for Nathan is less tenuous than mine was. My upbringing trained me to stay present, accept circumstances as part of a larger whole, take the hand fate dealt me … I have certainly provided for Nathan materially, but in Hong Kong would I have accepted his mother's death more philosophically? It's futile to think about it: in Hong Kong, I would never have met Maxine.

In another life she would have cared for Nathan and there would no doubt have been brothers, sisters. But now we are one man and one boy, alone together in our snazzy London flat, working through the practical requirements of each day. Both of us have more reasons to say "I" than "we", and English suits that better than Cantonese. Unless he leaves the UK he will have completed the process I started, and his children may be more British than Chinese.

Sometimes, late, I dust. Our cleaner is good and I keep us free of clutter, but here by the main road there seems always to be dust on the shelves and dust on the mirrors. I sleep better when it is gone. Today I find it on the only ornament I display, the black painted wooden bear cub my grandfather left specifically to me, along with its mother who was big enough for me to sit on as a child…. The great mother bear remains in Hong Kong – people who change their lives with one aeroplane trip do not heave such items around with them. But the cub is here, for Nathan to stroke and me to dust, and as a reminder of my grandfather. I wonder what he would think of our lives here.

Now I am old enough myself to be disconcerted by how fast the world changes. When I first came here I ran exhilarated with the whirlwind, grasping new knowledge and opportunities in excited, adaptable hands. But now we've settled, with a pleasant home, an established routine, and an income as secure as I can make it in a business where I must often run on the spot just to keep up. Nathan is still so young. I swallow a homeopathic sleeping aid, but asleep I encounter a screen-shaped parade of long-haired women and flat chested little girls straddled provocatively across the mother bear cub. In the early hours I wake with a start, appalled that such ideas could occur to me even as dreams. For some time I lie, deliberately calling up the reassuring memory of my wife before Nathan was born.

24TH – 25TH SEPTEMBER
2016

SAFIYA

What a beautiful day! My parents could never understand English people saying that. For them it was always cold, always chilly, the light was never bright and the colours were too green. But I grew up here, my feet on these pavements, my hand, occasionally, in this soil. Sudan was beautiful in a different way, but I was ill: everywhere was dry and dust-gravelly, my throat was hoarse and I was sore. For a long time I was feverish. To me, a child, our stay seemed to last forever, but it was probably just a few weeks. They called Sudan going "nearer home". When I was beginning to recover they brought me "back" again. But for me this was as close to home as anywhere.

For Xoriyo England has always been home.

We have said no more about the language she speaks at school. There will be a parents' meeting sometime, and I'll discuss it with the teacher then. It's she who has to experience settling into a new class, not I. She who is the outsider, who must find a route through to people's understanding. I am often in that position. The most obvious way forward may not be the most successful.

"I was thinking—"

"Can we go to the park?"

"My sweet, you interrupted me when I was just going to suggest that!"

I'm sure Xoriyo is secretly bored with her stand-off. It must be exhausting keeping silent at school, and her efforts to sulk at home disappointing, with me not taking the bait. No room either to burn energy in our small flat. She scampers for her jacket.

In the park the London autumn is beginning to take hold. Lurking clouds may blot out the blue sky, when the wind changes. The huge trees lining the paths are still mostly green, but a few brown leaves already lie defeated on the ground. The smaller trees have turned: bright yellow all over, their luminous branches splay like male peacocks. Today may be their last chance before the forecast gales.

Xoriyo skips beside me chattering to herself. Breaking away she runs fast to a big horse chestnut tree; she tries to wrap her arms around the trunk, but even when I catch up and add mine we can't join the circle. She lays her cheek against the rough bark.

"Don't worry, he won't scratch me if I talk to him gently."

She's murmuring mixed English, Somali, and Arabic words, too quiet to hear clearly. If she wanted me to listen she'd speak louder so I wait until she's finished.

"He says I can have this."

She bends to pick up a spiky green shell, two halves peeping apart reveal the shiny brown chestnut inside.

"If you put it in your pocket it will hurt," I tell her, but Xoriyo is not a greedy child. She only wants one, and she doesn't mind carrying it around in her hand. Today is not cold, although in the evening we'll need to pull my shawl around us. For now she has no gloves but her bare hand is fine. She puts the other hand in mind. Her chat with the friendly tree cured her of standing apart from me. We're friends again.

"Talking of things with stones…" she begins and I smile because the expression sounds so grown up, and we weren't, or not aloud, "…may we buy another peach?"

"More than one, I think," I answer. "Tomorrow Fawzia is going to come to show us her baby."

Xoriyo's face gleams with new happiness!

"Is the baby my cousin too?"

I have to think. Fawzia is my first cousin, so what does that make the relationship between my daughter and her child? I can't work it out.

"Isn't she still in hospital? I thought mummies had to go to hospital when they have their babies."

"Not Fawzia," I tell her. "Fawzia is a tough young woman. She has a baby, next day she is out and about again. The baby is only a week old and already she wants to bring him on outings."

"How will she fit his pram in our hall?"

Our "hall" is not a hall. It's a flat square that the front door opens into, only because a door has to open into somewhere. It was difficult when we moved in, even with our few possessions, to squeeze them round the corner and up the stairs. I remember all day Xoriyo worrying the bed and the table wouldn't fit, but we took the bed apart until it was just wooden slats, and we unscrewed the table legs. Later she told me, ever since when she looks at a piece of furniture she wonders how many pieces it would split into.

"She doesn't have a pram. She'll carry him in her arms or on her back."

"Perhaps she'll come on the magic carpet!"

"I think today the magic carpet is red, and it has two decks and a number on the front," I say.

"…and someone kind to help her hold on tight when she wobbles with the baby on her back!"

Yes, let's hope there is a kind person on the bus.

I am pleased and reassured Fawzia's come to visit. She's always cheerful: "This is a nice flat! You can watch so many things from this window – hey, you can even run for the bus if you see it from here!"

It's easy to believe Fawzia, already adept with a baby sling and all her bags, would run, but I, less confident, would be early and wait shivering at the bus stop. She enjoyed her bus ride, as I do sometimes, when it's light and the windows are clean enough to see through. Why do buses feel kinder than tubes? The passengers often speak to each other, budge along with their shopping, make funny faces for little children. But I remember a long wait for the tube to this branch of the line and when it came Xoriyo and I stood like sardines. Across the carriage a man's nasal voice sneered: "It wouldn't be like this, folks, if we hadn't let all them immigrants in." Xoriyo didn't hear, she had my earbuds in, but I stiffened. A middle-aged woman next to me muttered, "Shut up!" in a stage whisper and people around giggled or ignored both of them. Ignoring people is an art form, on the tube. This woman broke ranks. She craned her neck to see the culprit and spoke wearily to me. "The worst of it is, he's wearing Transport for London uniform. I'll report him when I get off." I felt a bit better, but I don't expect she did report him. It would have gone out of her mind as soon as she left the train a stop before ours. It wasn't her problem.

Fawzia's son sucks intently with miniature gulps like a fish. He and his mother could survive anywhere; she gives as good as she gets. Now he's so firmly latched, she wants to chat. She shifts him against her body and Xoriyo, daring, picks up a corner of her shawl and covers him more snugly.

"That's better," smiles Fawzia. They exchange approving looks. But my cousin's skin glistens.

Xoriyo puts out a tentative finger and feels Fawzia's cheek, asking: "Does it make you hot, feeding a baby?"

"Maybe … my God, there are many new feelings."

Xoriyo gets up from where she was kneeling before them. She pads into the kitchen, staggering back with the huge bottle of Pepsi and the stacked beakers. Maybe the top wasn't replaced too well last time since she can open it herself and we're all disappointed when there's no whoosh of gas escaping. I lean to help her pour but she brushes me away. Carefully she positions the beakers on the carpet, red for her, blue for me, green for our guest. She grasps the bottle with both hands and steadies herself as it changes shape with the shifting liquid. We hold our breath but she spills nothing. Honour satisfied, she passes a beaker to each of us and sits back on her heels to drink.

Fawzia drains her Pepsi so quickly she burps, and that sets us laughing. Maybe there was some fizz after all.

"So thirsty!" she exclaims, wiping her forehead with her scarf. "This boy drinks so much he empties me!"

I can see the thoughts turning in Xoriyo's head, but she's sensible and says nothing.

"It's good to eat and drink, you'll need energy."

Without needing to be told, Xoriyo fetches the peaches, plates and a sharp knife to our dusty carpet. I'm told children shouldn't be allowed sharp knives but how is she to learn if she doesn't use them? We watch as the pressure of the blade squeezes out the juice and the peach skids on the plates. She passes Fawzia evenly cut slices, one at a time, and a tissue for her fingers at the end. In a ceremonious way she does the same for me, to show we're friends again. Her own peach must be the best one, as when she halves it the stone tips clean from the rosy hole on to her plate. She examines the intricate surface and sighs deeply.

"What is it, sweetheart?" Fawzia and I are almost in unison.

"I just want the baby to hurry up so you do his nappy."

Fawzia is doubtful. "He may go straight to sleep…" but on cue, the baby's face darkens and he strains and grunts. The three of us are helpless with laughter, as Xoriyo exaggerates holding her nose and running to the window for fresh air. Finished, the baby's face relaxes on his mother's shoulder.

Fawzia spreads a towel on the floor. Xoriyo brings a bowl of warm water She's had less time around babies than most Somali girls her age. She seems childish, watching with pursed lips as Fawzia cleans the yellowish goo the baby produced, and she averts her eyes from his tiny penis and scrotum wrinkled like the peach stone. That's fine by me as I don't feel like explaining. I wonder if I will ever feel like explaining.

When his nappy's on I think we all feel better. Like any clean, fed baby he's happy now. He kicks with surprising strength and Fawzia shows Xoriyo how to play bicycle with his little legs. He makes funny humphing noises, and there are bubbles on his mouth where a white milk blister shows his greed.

"He'll get cold, I should dress him." But she can't resist a longer look at his healthy chest and the darker brown circles of his nipples, the indents of his neck and his chubby knees as he lies freely on the towel. I nod when Xoriyo picks up my phone. It amuses me to watch her circling him paparazzo fashion, sniping pictures from different angles. He offers a series of miniature sneezes and Fawzia picks him up. Now Xoriyo zooms in on the peach halves, with and without their wrinkled stone until I hold out my hand silently for my phone to be returned. Goodness she has taken a lot of pictures!

"May I read him my book?"

"Sure. Why not? Never too young for a story," Fawzia agrees. All three of us sit ready and Xoriyo clears her throat importantly. The baby is the most attentive. His domed forehead creases thoughtfully, and his swimming eyes wander over the pretty pictures of Momataro the peach boy. "Wish I'd had this one like that," grumbles Fawzia. "Much less hard work," and she grins at me but I don't react. I will not explain to Xoriyo yet and anyway, she acts oblivious. Perhaps she is colluding with generations of Somali women, knowing there are things it's better not to know.

We see them off at the bus stop and turn for our new home. It's good to see Fawzia and I miss her, but I was glad to move away from the disagreeing Somalis. The distance helps us be more polite with each other and the older people to accept my decisions. At least, they no longer voice their discontent.

I think towards the end my mother was beginning to see the rigid rules she clung to were not helping. They were rules from a previous place and didn't ensure my physical health, or make me happy in my mind. Going back never held even a trace of possibility, but even so my mother used to suggest it. We knew it would never happen: not in the sense that, say, my Afro-Caribbean friends' families planned to return. Two by two their grandparents retired from the NHS or from driving tubes and buses to paradise homes in St Lucia or Barbados. But my mother had nowhere to locate such a dream. Any "home" she envisaged dated back to memories of *her* parents, the spacious house and walled grounds, lush foliage tended by gardeners, the perks and influence of a high-status family. Already by the time we came to the UK when I was two, that proud status had diminished, under constant attack in the dusty refugee camps of Djibouti. It never meant anything to people here.

In London we lived close to other Isaaqs, who, although they were not always from the same subclan and spent hours debating our relative places in the clan structure, did chime with my family in constantly mourning a lifestyle they had not been born early enough to retain. Much of Hargeisa is rebuilt and calm, and people claim it's a happy city, and although it was too late for my mother, many Somalilanders *have* returned – but Somaliland isn't officially recognised. To live there, however modern and sparkling it may be, could be to return to a citizenship dilemma as precarious as when we were first here seeking asylum, the lurking threats of drought and hunger always nearby to pounce on our stability. Not to mention the collective survivor memory of genocide that's pervasive enough in London and must be overpowering there.

Now my parents have passed, peace be upon them. There is no need for the isolation they felt when we first arrived, for the diaspora is larger, but I fear for the women as much in this Western society as in the traditional one my parents yearned for. On the estates we hear tales of gangs and female children pressured into sex: our girls either run wild under their disguise or are trapped by what should be a religion of protection and care. For Xoriyo's sake as well as my own, I'm pleased to be in the suburbs, like another land though just a few tube stops away. Here we've found asylum for a second time, and relative safety.

Most Somalis don't come in this direction, on the tube. Only Fawzia comes by bus, unafraid to move freely, claiming all London for herself and now her son. I prefer them to come here than to go there again so soon after Eid, with the judging elders bossing over us and the languid children and the continuing pretence that our culture can move unchanged from the Horn of Africa to the maw of Mile End.

Some communities slough off collective memory with more resilience. They guard the good traditions but establish themselves here, set up businesses, bask in significance and safety. Families in this street where we now live are turbaned, speak Indian languages, drive nice cars and must own their homes or why would they be constantly extending the lofts and celebrating the house values? I'd like Xoriyo to achieve this – sometimes I wonder whether even I might one day attain such a home and such worries.

Removal from the muttering clan who were holding us in the past and threatening our future with their monstrous dogma is, perhaps, a first step. When I picked Xoriyo up from school last November, I remember every word and how clear it became that we must go.

"The teacher told us about Guy Fawkes. He was a bad man. He had gunpowder, hidden in barrels under the Houses of Parliament – enough to blow up the whole building and everyone in it, including the King!"

"And why would he want to do that?"

There is such pleasure for children in telling their parents what, to them, is a new story. And to be honest I'd forgotten the reasons behind all the noise and clamour of November 5th. It's a celebration I never enjoyed because my parents were so frightened by the bangs that for them brought back the sounds of street battles and lawlessness.

"The teacher explained but I don't really understand. Guy Fawkes was one kind of Christian and the King was another. Like, you know, different kinds of Muslims. The King wouldn't let Guy Fawkes pray the way he wanted to. So Guy Fawkes wanted to blow him up so people like him could do their religion without anyone stopping them."

"It sounds to me as though you've understood very well. What happened?"

"They caught Guy Fawkes and killed him. They cut his head off and put it on London Bridge to stop other people doing the same thing. And now people burn dolls of him on bonfires, but not as much as they used to, and we have fireworks to remind us of the explosion he'd have made and celebrate him getting caught. Because people think he was a bad man."

"He *was* bad, to want to kill the King."

I was remembering now, and having the same trouble I'd always had with the morals behind the story. "Although he wouldn't have wanted to kill the King, if they'd let him pray the way he wanted in the first place."

"Anyway," Xoriyo said, "*I* don't think he was bad. It's a wonderful thing, to die for your religion. Even if for him it wasn't Allah but another kind of God, Guy Fawkes was a good man to be ready to give up his life for him."

My blood ran cold. Even as I applauded her intelligence for making the connection – it had never occurred to me and I'm sure most six-year-olds couldn't see it! – her glorying of martyrdom terrified me.

"Who's told you that? Allah gave you life, it would not be obeying Allah to throw it away before your normal time."

"Oh ... wouldn't it? Anyway, I don't like the noise of fireworks. Can we just watch from the window?"

That night, each explosion mocked the "wonderful" martyrdom for me, with colours and celebration, laughter, screams. I never did find out who put such ideas into her head, although I questioned her carefully when she returned from the madrassa, and I listened, all the time, to what people were saying. So much posturing, so much strutting, each hysterical claim taking us further from the intermittent charity and tolerance we received and tried so hard to return throughout my own childhood. Here, away from that hotbed, we can breathe again and maybe, if I don't think about it, the passions and fanaticism will one day burn themselves out. It was only a small core; most of us do not agree with it. Unfortunately we do not say so often or loudly enough. We do not speak our thoughts.

But we have a more powerful culture, a heritage stretching back centuries. If we remember and celebrate it, our rich history will outweigh these recent obsessions. We have our language, which I am teaching Xoriyo to write; we have poets and storytellers and musicians and the greater power of a kinder Islam. Of course, at Eid, we took the tube to see our people, with gifts of food and other presents; all year round we give to Islamic charities and others. Even living out here I find ways to support our older people with gifts and some hours of my time. I teach Xoriyo all this, but I also want her to be a happy British child, as I, perhaps, could have been. I believe these hopes can coincide. My cousin believes it too, and so she came to see us with her baby.

After Fawzia's visit I wait for a flood of questions but none come. Instead, Xoriyo takes an empty exercise book she's brought from school, and spends the next hour trying to copy her favourite photo of the baby. Glancing over, I'm moved by the detail of his black curly hair and round forehead and it's only then I remember I wanted to ask Fawzia what she thinks about Xoriyo refusing to speak English at her new school. The baby boy had taken all our attention.

Xoriyo looks up: "Did Fawzia like our new flat, mummy?"

"You know Fawzia, my love. She always says kind things."

Xoriyo looks at the sagging sofa and the scratched table, the dado rail that was the fashion when I was her age and the carpet with the dull, tired flowers. "I think you should make it smart like the other houses here. Outside so people don't sniff and inside to make it home. Could you, Mummy? If I help?"

I cannot tell her some people will sniff whatever we do. "We'll have a go, my love. Then perhaps when it's nicer we can invite some of your new school friends to play?"

She has hunched back over her drawing.

"And yours," she says.

MONDAY 26TH SEPTEMBER 2016

Mrs Kaur

Here's a "fairy tale project" reminder to all children in __Year 3__ (Classes 3S and 3P). If you need any help with materials or ideas for retelling your story with your family, just ask your teacher! The closing date for entries for our festival is __Tuesday 11th October.__

Only my husband is at home at this time of day. I come back from taking Mandeep to school and he is finishing his meditation before our tasks begin.

We sit in our armchairs in the lounge – armchairs for our old backs, with recliners and footstools, specially bought by Suki and truly it was kind of her, for they do not match the other fittings in this sleek room. We are sipping our chai and thinking our thoughts. Later I'll go to the langar for my turn cooking. He'll go out for the newspaper and maybe to visit his friend whose wife passed away last year. The sun comes in through the front window, so bright! My husband gets up very slowly to draw the curtain across and as he returns to his chair I see how his hips are bent. He doesn't move so well nowadays.

"You should walk with me to school, then you will not be so stiff."

"No doubt. And then I will be caught with all the gossipy mothers and the children running round my ankles…no, I prefer to go out later, when the streets are clear."

"Some Babas there too, today, at the gate. Nice to see the old men with their little ones. And meeting their old girlfriends!"

We laugh now about the time when suddenly across the playground an older lady was calling him, a big beaming smile on her face. We had gone together to the school, taking Gurdeep, so it must have been five, six years ago now. I didn't know what was going on, but slowly my husband got a big smile on his face. This lady had been at his village school, in Punjab, fifty–sixty years ago! And she thought she recognised him, across the wide playground, and asked someone his name and said omigod I know that man! Even with a big white beard and grown up turban and fat belly! We all came home and had chai and a long, long chat. It seemed very important, that day, to meet someone from such a time ago. Of course I was a little bit left out because I did not grow up in that village or go to that school, but for a while we saw her often and they talked about the past. Then I think he saw I was a little bit jealous, or maybe they ran out of memories to say together. Her grandson finished at the primary school and we didn't see her again. So it's just a coincidence story now, no hurt feelings for anyone. But my husband does not come to school any more with me and Mandeep.

"Mandeep is happy, this year?" he asks me.

My husband sits with Aman to watch football sometimes, but mostly he reads his paper in our room and he does not come out except to eat with us. So information about the boys comes to him through me, all news good and bad, unless we talk about it at table.

"Mandeep is always happy," I tell him. "Most happy child I know."

"Sometimes lazy, they say to me. They ask, 'Baba, what to do with this boy?'"

"He's not so lazy now, he wrote a lovely story."

I pour more chai to make him pleased, and I pass him the exercise book Mandeep has left at home. He frowns at the handwriting but I tell him "Never mind untidy, don't you think it so funny what he says?"

"You think it is funny? To be stuck ironing forever? I thought you wanted to enjoy yourself more?"

He gives me a lovely smile and wink like when we first met. He is thinking about when I was a young bride in India. We moved from his parents' house to our own place, very modern thing to do, and he found me weeping when he came home from his office because the sheets were so huge and there was nobody to help me fold them. I was going to have to iron them all over again. He put his arms round me and held me warm and close. *You know, today, it is not important if sheets are ironed because we are going to make them crumpled again,* he murmured, and I giggled and he said *yes?* I agreed and we went to crumple the sheets, had a lovely lovely time. Next day someone knocked at the door and it was the neighbour's daughter come to help me. One morning every week, she said, your husband has paid. And do you have ironing?

"So we must make you a happier ending," says my husband.

We talk about what to put in the story, what I really like to do – grow plants in the garden and vegetables on the allotment, but not too much, not so it makes my bones stiff – and chat in the langar while we make the food, then sit to watch while all the people eat.

"But that is all things you do now," he says and for a moment he looks a little bit sad. "If you could do what you really really want?" We smile together because this is a silly song my husband liked when it came out and he always says "What you really really want?" like a question, and then if he can he gives it to me and he says "What you really really want!" like a statement. This is a joke between us, other members of the family do not know.

I don't know…I am lucky, I think, have a good family, a nice home. What I really, really always wanted was a daughter. We had three fine sons, Aman now here, Dilraj in Canada, Sundeep in New York. In my day the daughters went to live with their husbands and a mother was more likely to live close with her sons. But if I had had a daughter I would have kept her near to me, even when she married. No granddaughters, either, no sign of more grand-children both sides of the ocean. I should be content with all the healthy young men and boys we have produced; I am a lucky woman.

"I tell you what." My husband's eyes are twinkling. "When you were a little girl, you used to dance…"

"Yes, but it is not respectable for a woman to dance."

"Aha, but in *this* country, women may dance, old as they like. Anyway, this is a magic story. You dance in the magic parts, then you sit quiet and polite the rest of the time."

And he puts me dancing at the end of the story, young again and strong. I was a good dancer when I was a little girl, with a lot of energy, and good with making my hands talk to the audience – it was only my little friends and the servants. The dance was a story, with my hands twisting and my expressions changing with the mood. Many years later when I saw my husband for the first time and I didn't know he would be my husband, he was playing a *Kacchi dhol*, lost in the taps and rhythms; I was too old to dance by then but standing by the wall my strong feet slapped down on the floor to the beat getting fast, faster until my mother saw and signalled stop … Ah, it was a long time ago!

"Look, I am writing you dancing down the sun-flower with one hand holding on. With your other hand you're making dance moves, and your feet arch to hold tight to the leaves. You are very young and beautiful!"

He writes me reaching Mandeep's story house at the bottom of the stalk. Inside I go to look after him, but there are many people to help so I have time free to dance behind the curtains where no one can see.

We find more paper, so as not to spoil Mandeep's book, and sitting together we write our stories. My husband's rumbly voice reading aloud sounds so different to Mandeep's! We choose the good bits I did and the good bits Mandeep did, and we put them together with the best ideas from my husband. I copy it out in my neat Punjabi handwriting and he will make an English version for the rest of the family.

The drums stayed in India when we came to live here, but when we finish the story my husband says: shall we give the boys lessons, for Diwali? Then if they like it and they work hard at school, we can buy drums for this house?

It seems a good idea to me.

WEDNESDAY 28TH SEPTEMBER 2016

SAFIYA

"Hallo, my love, have you had a good day today?"

Large eyes look up, a wide smile grins at me – it seems she's happy with it so far.

"I've asked if you could go into the after-school club – that'll be fun, won't it? – while I see Miss Patel. I have a question to ask her."

Xoriyo has wondered what happens at the after-school club so, as I hoped, her curiosity outweighs any apprehension about why I'm seeing the teacher. Off she skips happily enough down some internal corridor, while I leave the playground and jump back in to the reception area through three security hoops: the entryphone gate, the office window and the visitors' book.

My daughter is mischievous: she gets it from me. I'm tempted to play the same trick and pretend my English is poor. When Xoriyo entered the school in September, I was working, so Fawzia brought her. It was Fawzia too who made the original application and did the paperwork in the summer, when I was preoccupied with moving in. Nobody could be in more capable, caring hands than Fawzia's. She stands no nonsense! I trusted her absolutely to start my daughter off well. And until last weekend I thought Xoriyo was happy, so I waved her goodbye in the morning and collected her in the afternoon without lingering. Some parents, I notice, speak to the teacher every day: special requests for this and that, wanting to know the last time their child sneezed or passed water. Today I have my first, small request. I hope it will help Xoriyo tell her story.

This school has been designed to be quiet, so now, with most children gone, it's even more so. The carpeted floor helps, and, in the small foyer, the soft sofa is a cocoon that enfolds my waiting body. I notice the examples of children's work hanging on the walls have been framed as though they're particularly prized. In this, Xoriyo's third school and my sixth if you count my own childhood, the usual rack of leaflets tells us of child safety hazards, English classes, library opening hours and what the children are learning this term. "Welcome!" blaze the colours of the multilingual poster I see in every school. From my nest of cushions I consider this. How will the welcome feel if I present myself as somebody who doesn't speak English? I'd like to receive the place through my daughter's eyes. I'll be discreet: I'll respond with understanding but I shall not offer information.

"Mrs Ahmed?" A young Asian lady in a business suit stands in the inner doorway, that remained locked when I was shown in this far. She holds out her hand.

"I'm Miss Patel, Xoriyo's teacher. Pleased to meet you. How can we help you today?"

I want to giggle because it's like Virgin Media when I phoned them about the bad broadband. How can we help you today? But the product here is children. Press 1 for children; press 2 for trouble-shooting; hold to speak to an operator.

I spring out of the sofa as an older person could not. I hold out my copy of the school's letter and point to the sentence about helping us with materials.

"Xoriyo took photos for the story but I have no printer. Would you be able to print them for us please?"

The teacher looks surprised and she doesn't move from the doorway.

"Yes, I think I could. Some, anyway. Do you have a memory stick or … something? I'll print them and give it all back to Xoriyo tomorrow."

"No … they're on my phone. Also, I want it to be a surprise for Xoriyo. She's been copying them with crayons but she doesn't like her drawings."

"I'm sure her drawings are very good—" begins the teacher.

I interrupt: "The letter says the school will help us and this is what we need you to do. Please."

She inclines her head. "Please, come with me."

She holds open the inner door and I follow her past boards with jolly children's artwork of autumn leaves and silver moons shining over mosques and minarets. In the computer suite she enters a pass-word, scrabbles around for a lead to connect my phone and sits back while I upload the pictures. She is careful not to look across at anything else on my phone. I flush when I see a photo of the baby before his nappy was back on: quickly, hoping she has not seen, I delete it.

"What size would you like?"

I haven't thought. "May we have different sizes, to see what works with the writing?"

She frowns. I do not warm to this young woman with her crisp striped shirt.

"Unfortunately we have a budget for printing. I can only do so many colour pictures every day. But yes, if you choose what you want, I can do a few."

I don't know if that's the only reason she's frowning. She may also be wondering why I haven't taught my daughter to speak English as well as I do. Does she think me a bad mother? I want to reassure her.

"Xoriyo is so keen to do well in this, I'd like so much to help her."

Another teacher looks up from across the room. She's older, with a flowery skirt and fat legs tipping over the top of her shoes. I can't see where her ankles end and her feet begin and I wonder as always why white women think it is we who are constrained by our clothes. But she has a kind smile.

"I haven't used all my printing allocation today, Miss Patel. Use mine if you haven't enough."

Miss Patel nods at her and gives me a first smile. "This baby boy" – so she did see the picture without a nappy – "these are family photos?"

"Yes, my cousin's baby. But we want them for the story because it has a baby. And the ones of the peach. With the stone and not with it."

"I'll be interested to see what you do. I thought I gave Xoriyo a story about a magic carpet."

I'm saved by the same warm voice:

"Was that your cousin who brought Xoriyo in when she started here? I remember her – she was quite far on then, wasn't she? Do let me see. Oh, isn't he a darling?"

Miss Patel's face softens too. How could you not, looking at this little hero, all chubby limbs, round face, curls on his dome of a forehead. The pictures crunch slowly from the machine, colour gleaming. I think Xoriyo will be delighted. The peach almost drips off the page and the baby blows happy bubbles.

"And how is Xoriyo finding us?"

The other teacher again. I wish Xoriyo was in her class. She seems genuinely to care.

"She doesn't join in. Except in PE, she's keen on that. But even then she doesn't speak. Not at all," comments Miss Patel before I can say anything. "I must admit I'm a bit surprised, because your cousin's English is excellent and yours, too…"

"Oh, she'll settle in," says the older one. They talk across me as if I wasn't there, but actually, that saves me from thinking what to say or do, and I can see why my daughter acts as she does, now. It's easier, to say less than others say.

"I'll talk to her about it," I tell them.

165

"Will you be telling the story in English, or ..." I sense Miss Patel trying to remember what languages we speak and then she gets them right.

"You'll have to wait and see," I say. "Thank you very much for the photographs. I shall tell Xoriyo what a lucky girl she is to be in such a lovely school."

THURSDAY 29TH SEPTEMBER
2016

TERESA

I'm so late, won't get to school anywhere near in time to pick Sky up. I'm cursing … if I want to start childminding again the school staff would be my best referees; I can't be giving them a bad impression. But a helpful secretary answers the phone.

"Don't worry, Mrs Perry. We run an after-school club in the hall, with a few drop-in places. As long as you don't mind paying when you pick her up, and signing permission forms, I'll nip along to her class and tell her to go straight there after school? If that's ok?"

Phew!

I'm all hot and sweaty with rushing about. Now I've time to run home and freshen up. In the shower, corny as it may sound I feel the warm water washing away so much more than just the stickiness of the day. I bother to moisturise. I treat the dusty bottle of Christmas present body lotion to a wash down too: not only I but my bathroom too will be smarter from now on! The lateness thing was solved so smoothly; perhaps other problems will turn out to have easy, practical answers as well. I wash and blow dry my hair carefully, achieving something worthy of the word hairstyle. When Sky's around she's critical, or we're in too much of a rush, so what a treat this is! The counsellor said if I don't take care of myself I won't be able to care for others. I don't know what he'd make of me doing it in what should be Sky's time with me – oh! More pointless guilt kicking in! He also said guilt only leads you round in circles… Go away, guilt.

Today I like what I see in the mirror. I can hold my tummy in and it stays there, my hair's gleaming with a hint of the highlights from months ago. The September weather's still gorgeous but not so hot I have to squeeze my bulges into the tiny summer clothes I think the other mums sneer at. I choose a green knee-length skirt with ankle boots and a long-sleeved tee shirt that matches it exactly. I'll be bored with these clothes by Christmas but it's always refreshing the first time you get out autumn clothes, when the summer stuff's gone limp and your feet ache with flip flop fatigue. I add a warm cardi just in case. I'm hoping Sky will have found the after-school club a nice surprise: she likes having other children around and she's not the kind to be worried by a sudden change of plans.

It's a satisfying walk, not dawdling, not hurrying, feeling presentable. I swing my arms evenly in a fitness technique. Crisp fallen leaves are scattered across the pavement, scraps from the glowing trees that stand out golden against the heavy sky. Perhaps the rabbit did survive? We could invent a story of escape to a burrow full of harvest hay for warmth with stores of grass and twigs for winter days. The school gates aren't open yet and I wait, vaguely wondering what wild rabbits eat in winter.

"Good evening! I do find it hard to get here on time every day...You are not usually here, though, are you?"

It's the Chinese man from the smart flats, panting towards me from the direction of the station with his briefcase swinging. As I'm smiling an answer the children start coming out. Sky's pink and rosy with excitement.

"Brilliant!" says the teacher. "Joined in with everything and couldn't get enough of our toys. There are so many things here they never get a chance to use in the classroom, you see. Would you like to come again, Sky?"

"We'll have to talk about it."

There I go, spoiling things again. Sky's pleading immediately and I'd like it too, to free me up and give her playing time with other children. But although it's cheap it's still money flowing out. As we turn to go we see the Chinese boy and his father have waited. I'm anxious she'll sulk but the shared after school experience must have wiped away her hurt feelings. The children fall into a natural run ahead. The father's breathing has eased but I feel it's my turn to speak.

"That was a one-off – I was late. But she's certainly enjoyed it! Does your son come every day?"

"Every day, yes. He likes it too but the six o'clock finish is inconvenient for my work." He sighs.

"That's tricky…" I sense an opportunity. "Have you thought about a childminder?"

He walks straight ahead, perhaps not hearing me, the sun glinting on his neat hair. I decide to push: "Does your wife work too?"

"No, my wife died in an accident. We are a household of two males, one very young and one I fear getting steadily older."

I can't tell what age he is; he's slim, and has smooth skin, but compared to white men Chinese men usually do. As for the wife … "I'm sorry…"

The small smile remains on his round face.

"You weren't to know. I've brought Nathan up myself. For many years I worked from home, and he was a good boy, even as a toddler. He slept well and I could do a lot in the evenings. But I'm office-based now and having to leave earlier and earlier to be sure of being here on time."

I suppose he must have trotted their story out so many times it seems neutral information to him now. As he walks his chin juts and the bright trees are reflected in the dark of his glasses. He must have old lenses. They always take a long time to clear when the sun goes. Everything else about him is smart: polished shoes, neat bag and a light raincoat folded over his arm. Sky thrust her rucksack at me as soon as she saw me, but he doesn't carry his son's. It bobs neatly along on the boy's back as the children kick along the road crushing the leaves.

"I'm a childminder. I could pick him up from the club for you and give him his tea with Sky so you could collect him later. Since we live in the same road..."

I've always been impulsive, but this seems too easy a potential job to let it pass unclaimed. A pleasant child and father, very local, maybe not every night. And perhaps Sky could go to the club too, because the money from Nathan would cancel out the fees. His father hesitates, but I can't miss how his face brightens at my suggestion. As I finish speaking a line of motorbikes roars by so he can't answer immediately.

We turn into the close and on the pavement outside the flats, just as I'm wondering if I've gone too far, he turns to me.

"It's a possibility..."

I suppose I shouldn't expect more enthusiasm for such an out of the blue suggestion. But perhaps he's worried he's hurt my feelings, for he adds: "May we visit you then? Perhaps, Saturday afternoon?"

As we shake hands we are both smiling broadly. I notice he doesn't ask Nathan what he thinks of the idea, and I haven't asked Sky – but my goodness, that was a committed handshake.

Friday 30th September 2016

SAFIYA

"Hallo, my sweet, how was your day?"

When the main doors open I step forward confidently. I no longer hover at the edge of the crowd waiting until Xoriyo dashes over to me. Miss Patel and the older teacher are both standing at the door and wave simultaneous greetings and goodbyes.

"Another letter? So many letters this school sends out!"

We never have to buy paper at home; we always have these to be used for stories and shopping lists and drawings on the back. Some careless children have already let their letters blow away across the playground. The caretaker is picking them up and holding them out hopelessly, but nobody wants them so he has a big handful. Instead the children are happily showing their mums and dads big flappy paintings they've done, and Xoriyo is laughing: "Yes, but look! Aren't I lucky? I got a red sweetie because it's that boy's birthday!"

And she points to a grinning boy with a huge badge, the red and yellow number eight obliterating most of his chest.

The adults on their phones notice nothing, but it's good to watch the happy reunion of children and parents as their separate days reattach. Xoriyo's unwrapping her sweetie and as I'm putting her letter in her bag to read later, my eyes meet those of the lady who came to ask about her rabbit at the weekend. We both shyly smile. Her daughter's cheek is bulging like Xoriyo's and she's also had to rescue a letter. She was glancing at it with a frown; she folded it quickly away when she saw me.

If she talks to me we can walk back together. But English people take friendliness in small steps: today a smile, tomorrow a word perhaps, in a month, a year – or never – an invitation home. Despite growing up here, I can still count on one hand the English homes I've been inside, even when I was at university.

"Let's go, Mum."

Xoriyo's voice is indistinct with sucking so she pulls my hand, three twirling steps for every one of mine. When we reach the gates even she has to shuffle in the dense crowd. All along the main road I sense the rabbit neighbour behind us, not friendly, not unfriendly. A long line of parents and children walk back this way, chatting or lost in thought, in the daily company of grumbling lorries and thumping music from the cars. Some mothers look like they've just come from the beauty salon; they toss their hair and brandish their bright nails so everyone can see and they laugh extra loud, oh my days, wow. The Asian mothers in shalwar kameez are more elegant, to my mind, than those in tight English clothing or me in my plain long skirt and top ... How they sway as they walk! The bright colours and thin fabrics float with them, and their shiny loose hair shifts in sympathy or their plaits thump so heavy you could make a rope. Xoriyo likes to point out the "diamonds" on their strappy sandals, but it's colder today and some have swapped them for trainers. The practical thick rubber is clumsy against their silky outfits.

As families peel off down side turnings the line gets more strung out. The children on bikes and scooters wheel back and forth with more daring, tangling with pram wheels and dog leads. I know Xoriyo wants a bike and now we're so close to a park she could learn to ride it there, or perhaps in the close behind our flat because there is so little traffic. Only I'm never sure if our house is part of the close or not. Our address is the main road, which we face, and our landlord does not keep the outside smart like the other houses. Would people mind her riding on the pavement? Would it interfere with the complicated English process of becoming friends with your neighbours ... although so many people in the close are not, apparently, English.

We had English neighbours where we lived before. My father and I knocked on their door to give them boxes of chocolates at Eid and at Christmas. They were surprised, and politely thanked us, and at Easter they left me an egg on the doorstep with a card. But we never spoke at other times.

A lorry thunders past gusting fumes and chill wind.

"Brrr! Aren't you glad we're nearly home?"

"Hmm … Can I go up here?"

Xoriyo lets go of my hand to climb on the low wall she loves to balance along. I wonder how many more years – Oh! Pain smacks on my arm, freezing my view of her face gone sharp like a photo, her eyes wide and mouth open. I'm on the pavement, bags and papers everywhere, skirt high above my ankles, back jarred. Through receding shockwaves I see my child's round handwriting on her spilled exercise book: it's Friday 30th September and we're in an incident. I assess the pain, harsh on my shoulder, then an acid thump in my stomach.

"What—?"

"It's all right, it's ok …" The rabbit lady's bending over me, her face much too close, her teeth yellow and a smoky smell.

"Go away, piss off!"

Shouts from somewhere in the lined up traffic, and other dark voices of menace shout too: "Go back where you came from, fuck off home, foreign vermin, fuck off!" But engines rev, horns sound and their noise covers the ugly words. Some people are making a surround for me and others are walking away as fast as they can, pulling children who try to look behind them as they trot to keep up. Xoriyo is in my arms saying *mummy mummy what happened are you ok* very fast and I soothe her shaking all the while and say, *yes, ok, I'm ok,* because I realise, actually, nothing too bad has occurred to me, on a physical level. The stone glanced off my upper arm and I fell from surprise, not from any direct blow.

The rabbit lady has a large face. Her hair straggles around blotchy cheeks and her smile is huge and kind like an ogre from one of Xoriyo's books. Is it safe to go with her?

"Vermin. That means rats. Like in the Pied Piper of Hamelin story Miss Patel read today," says her daughter. Her plump face is scared and excited.

"Be quiet, Sky," says the ogre in a firm voice. She reaches a hand to Xoriyo but Xoriyo cowers against me. With an effort I stand to show I'm in control, but as I do so I go dizzy and lose my balance. The rabbit lady plants her feet apart on the pavement and receives my body against her own until I'm more secure. She's trying to put her arms around me but I'm shivering away from her.

"Ok, ok..." she repeats. When she thinks I'm steady: "Shall we go?"

I take Xoriyo's hand and slowly, invalids limping from a battlefield, we start moving towards our close. We have people murmuring all around us and I'm not looking up. Like a baby, I hope if I can't see them then they can't see me. I don't want them to, kind or not. A man's deep voice says, *just stay still a minute,* and the rabbit lady guides me to a halt saying *why,* and the man's voice says, *we don't want them to see where we live. Give them time to drive away completely, they are cowards, the lights are changing and they are going already, but don't look.* His voice is old and slow and wise. I think, he has seen all this before.

These people are kind – yes, they are, and the shouting men who threw stones have roared off through the green traffic lights, but I want to be alone with my child. The most important thing now is to show her I'm all right. So at my door with chattering teeth I thank the rabbit lady and the old man, who is a Sikh gentleman with tiny yellowing eyes. I try to get my key in the lock but my hands are shaking. The rabbit lady helps me, I push Xoriyo up ahead of me and she waits at the top of the stairs as I lock us inside. Tomorrow is Saturday, we have food and plasters in the house and we can ask Fawzia to bring more. For now we have to get through one minute at a time and by Sunday night I shall know what to do.

SATURDAY 1ST OCTOBER 2016

ALKA

I'm trying to remember how things were before Mummy was ill. Now her skin isn't so grey, and the ugly red in her eye has almost gone, but she doesn't seem better yet. She doesn't like me touching her face so maybe it still hurts.

I heard Dad say to Nana: "You don't need to stay anymore."

"Oh yes," answered Nana, "We do."

Mummy is always in the bathroom or my old bedroom and it's just Dad and Nana in the lounge. Nana's legs are crossed but Dad's are making a wide triangle. Dad's chewing something and a drop of gob falls on the sofa leather and Dad wipes it off quick with his hand. The way Nana watches Dad is closed and patient like the big animals waiting for prey on the wildlife programmes. Then Dad sees me standing by the lacy glass doors. He puts a big smile on and clears his throat.

"Yes, of course you and Nani must be here. I expect you'll want to tell the children all the Navratri stories and go to some dances."

Nana's voice is stern. "We would stay whether it's Navratri or not. I know you don't pay much attention to such matters, but have you thought how ironic this is? The festival of women, of their strength, their fertility, how they protect us... We can worship the goddesses anywhere, but for now it is only if I am here that I can be sure my daughter is safe."

He's using too many words I don't know: *fertility, ironic*... Dad coughs too loud for a real cough. "Of course she is safe. We are all safe, aren't we, Alka?"

Now Nana sees me.

"Oh yes, very safe," he says, too quickly. "Safe as houses. Come, Alka, come and tell your Nana what you've been doing at school. Have you any homework for this weekend?"

Now maybe he will help me with my story! When I get my bag I see none of the grownups have looked in it for ages. There are letters, finished and unfinished work, Janki's party invite that I haven't asked them about yet... if I go someone must take me and collect me. Nani is doing so much cooking and housework, and Mummy still sits most of the time in front of the TV. Before she was ill I'd have asked her straight away. She'd have been excited with me, chosen a dress and what to put in my hair, and the present we'd buy. As long as I don't show her the invitation I can imagine us getting ready together for the party like we used to. But now she passes everything on to Nani and Nana. Nani is too tired and Nana wouldn't know how to deal with a girl's party because he's a serious old man.

Actually I wonder if Nana is too old to keep us safe?

In the living room Nani's put up bright pictures of the nine Durga goddesses with the tiger picture in the middle. They must have brought them from Leicester, just little ones on postcards, smaller than they had at their house the year we stayed with them for Navratri. Each goddess is an *avatar* of Ganesh's mother. *Avatar* means she was born lots of times, all different, like on a computer, and each time she had a different power and different mad adventures that show her strength and how she protects us. Last year Nani told me stories of all the goddess's adventures, one for every night of Navratri.

I was going to change Rapunzel's prince's horse into a tiger. But it was a silly idea. Now I see the Durga goddesses again I realise Rapunzel's nothing like them. They do more rescuing than getting rescued, for a start. That's why Nani likes to do puja for them even if she can't get to the temple, and why she has pictures here and offers them Prasad.

Nani's hung a garland of flowers above the pictures and there's a special lamp with holes in it and a diva inside sending stripes of light out all around it like the rays of the sun the way I used to draw it when I was littler. She's put a small bowl of food in front of the goddesses, which I used to think they would really eat. Tomorrow the bowl will hold sugar, and the next day sweets made of milk, I think, then more different foods for nine days. Last year Daddy said, *why do we have to have food in the living room, it is not very clean and the next thing we know we'll have mice again. At least just keep it to fruit and water.* But Nani explained all the different foods the goddesses must have for nine days and Mummy said, *yes, leave it, it reminds me of when I was a child.*

I think one of the grownups eats it themselves when we're in bed. They've mainly put it high up to stop that naughty Sunil helping himself.

I don't think Daddy knows Nani and Nana have a mandir in the loft too, with more food.

The food means the goddesses can eat all day if they want to but Nani wants to fast. Poor Nani is so tired this year doing all the housework and looking after Sunil, I wonder if she will be able to? Nana doesn't do the housework, or fast except on Fridays.

Nana holds out his hand for my homework, but there's nothing to show him except the reminder about the story on the Monday newsletter. School letters always have a picture of a farm at the top for "Home Farm Primary School" and lots of badges that mean how good the school is. I find the piece of paper with that picture on it and pass it to him. It's only a school letter so I'm surprised when he frowns at it.

"Excuse me, Alka."

He heaves himself out of the armchair where he'd only just settled. Taking the letter with him he goes into the kitchen where Nani is and shuts the door. That leaves me with Dad. He's hunched over his phone texting fast. I don't like being alone with Dad anymore since whatever it was he did to Mummy. Push, tap, rest, push go his strong thumbs and I creep out of the room and climb the stairs to the loft, up the soft carpet with my fairy steps no one can hear.

Mr Chan

"It's pleasant here. And the upstairs neighbours?"

I am making small talk to keep us a little longer. I need time to come to the correct decision for Nathan. Much in Teresa's living room is dated, but still it is bright and clean with no visible dangers for children. She has settled Nathan and Sky on the floor with a Harry Potter Lego set and they are constructing a complicated spiral staircase for the castle. She offered me tea in a thin bone china mug, more delicate than I'd have expected. I admired her care as she carried the hot drinks past the children who are concentrating too hard to be aware of her and could easily have jogged her.

"Upstairs is a young couple, but they're away a lot. My grandmother bought this maisonette, and when she died she left it to me. I'm doing it up bit by bit, but you know, it's expensive and takes time. But I've done this room."

"It's just you and Sky living here?"

I ought to know which other adults Nathan may come into contact with.

"Yes. Sky's father left three years ago and my divorce came through last year."

"He visits her?"

Teresa frowns and stands up. The hand that's holding her mug waves it to indicate the kitchen, and once there we lean against the worn pine cupboards, placing our drinks on the counter. Her tone is low.

"He doesn't visit, no. He's supposed to, but he doesn't. We sometimes go and meet him in town but that's less and less frequent. I appreciate you need to know, but I prefer not to talk about it in front of Sky as she used to get upset."

"I'm sorry you have to tell me, but you understand why I have to ask. Sky is no longer upset?"

"Well...we've got used to it. Of course, if he was ever likely to come here when I had Nathan, I'd let you know. But in any case, he's not...violent or anything."

"I see."

I do not really see, but I cannot think this situation could affect Nathan, who would only be here for short periods. Teresa is twisting a straggle of hair nervously round her finger, so tight it must be pulling. It's embarrassing for me and awkward for her. Glancing away through the window I receive a pleasant surprise.

"I didn't realise the gardens were so long at this end of the close. I'd like Nathan to have more opportunities to play in the fresh air. Is it shared? May I see outside?"

"Sure. It's all my garden. Upstairs have the front. There's such a squeak on this door, Sky'll hear and know where we are."

She's right, the door needs a good wrench. The frame must be swollen after the sudden downpour last night. She braces her feet against the floor and suddenly the door does as she wants and she's thrown backwards against me.

She's planted troughs and pots with bright flowers, and there's a bench.

"We put the bulbs in last week with lots of pansies on top to stop the squirrels," she says, as though I would know what was or wasn't good gardening, having never had more than a window box and that fiercely guarded by my mother for her cooking herbs. I note the empty rabbit hutch and raise one eyebrow: *no, we didn't*, she says. That's fine by me. I've had to try to sell enough smelly properties where pets have been indulged as family members in the British way. The obsession with pets is one I've never understood. This hutch, with no occupant, is cleaner than many I've seen, and the patio tidy, apart from the cigarette ends in the flowerbed.

"Only outside," Teresa says quickly, "after Sky's asleep. Only two or three a day. A night, I mean."

"It's ok. If I had more outside space I might do the same."

"I wouldn't – of course I wouldn't – when the children are here."

There's a noise behind us and Nathan and Sky appear in the doorway, shoes back on – I always tell

Nathan to remove his shoes in the house as I was brought up to do. They race past down the long squelchy grass to the basketball post on the wall at the far end. Nathan runs round with helicopter arms and Sky, plump and clumsy, cannot catch him. I hope she won't become frustrated with him, because I find myself keener and keener that this arrangement will work. He slows to a halt and bends down in close inspection of the ground.

"Look, you have mushrooms." He's fascinated.

"Oh, they always come after rain. Come over here, there's usually a big patch." Nathan straightens up and turns to follow Sky but something catches his eye, high up in the house next door. Immediately he's waving excitedly:

"It's Alka! Hey Dad, it's Alka, the one I told you about. I didn't know you lived next door to her," he says to Sky. It sounds close to an accusation. "Does she come here to play?"

Teresa has started walking towards the children, and I follow despite the wetness on my good shoes. We stand in a row at the end of Teresa's garden, looking up at the dormer window of the house next door. Very small, peeping above the window sill is the top half of a child's pretty pale face surrounded by black hair, watching as Nathan waves and waves. Next minute she disappears and Nathan is bereft.

"Alka's always doing that! One moment she's there to play with and the next she's gone. I want so much to be friends with her but she won't let it happen."

"You have Sky, here, now," I reprove him gently and he looks up.

"Yes. But it's not the same." He considers. "Hang on, though – hey Sky, do you think you could get Alka here and we could all practise my Midas story together? Your mum's got some good things we could use – that goldy coloured carpet and your shiny curtains and there's a gold bowl in your living room—"

Fortunately it seems Teresa's daughter is so happy with this idea she's missed the implied criticism from my son. She's nodding with such an exaggerated motion I fear she may hurt herself.

"She's back anyway, look!" shouts Sky.

Off they go waving again like mad things at the little girl in the window. She must have found something to stand on now, for we can see almost her whole body down to the knees, precariously framed in the window and waving back as if her life depended on it, calling something we can't grasp and hoping for replies she couldn't possibly hear. Nathan's jumping up and down and Sky's doing some great galumphing dance which involves a most undignified leapfrog action – and then the girl falls backwards away from the window.

"Inside, you two, if you want to get that castle finished before Nathan has to go." Teresa's voice is firm and I respect how she makes them obey her straight away.

Walking behind them back up the garden, I see no further sign of the little girl in the dormer window.

MRS KAUR

"There will be more of that sort of thing if that fellow Trump gets in." My husband rustles the newspaper.

"Trump? That's a funny name. Who's Trump?"

Mandeep comes up behind the armchair and rests his chin on the back. My husband points and Mandeep shrieks with laughter.

"He's like the ogre in my book – look!"

It is true. When Mandeep fetches "Jack and the Beanstalk" there is Mr Trump, sitting in an enormous armchair with massive fists round his carving knife while his ogress wife bends to the hot oven. On his red face his cheeks bulge and hair sticks up from his head like hay.

"Needs his hairdresser to come, in this picture," chortles my husband. I am pleased he is laughing again. When he reads the paper he is often depressed.

"At the end when Jack cuts down the beanstalk he'd go bump! Trump goes bump! No, thump! *Bump, bump, Trump goes thump!*" Mandeep crashes onto the carpet and bounces straight up again.

"In your story it is sunflowers, not a beanstalk," I remind him. "Look, your Baba and I made another ending for it."

"Yes…what do you mean, what Trump Goes Bump'll do if he gets in, Baba?"

I bring the exercise book to distract him, with the story we invented about me dancing down the beanstalk away from my ironing. He snorts a small laugh at his Baba's clever drawings, but he doesn't admire my beautiful handwriting I took such pains with. I suppose since he can barely read Punjabi it's as meaningless to him as English writing is to me, but inside my pride shrivels small.

"More of *what* sort of thing. Baba?"

Please don't tell him, I say quiet in my head. My husband was so shocked yesterday after school. He walked there to please me and got a big fright. It took him back to the early days, when we used to visit the UK and they tried to pass a law to stop Sikhs wearing turbans on motor bikes and everybody in the street called us Paki. It's a long time since all that. When we came to live here permanently with Aman and Suki, we worried but there was no need. People in this neighbourhood are good – they check your letterbox if you go away, put up posters about lost pets, that sort of thing. Aman works in the City, no problem there. We spend a lot of our time at the gudwara, cooking for the langar, studying the scriptures, organising charity events. The gudwara committee organises outings, and we go with our friends, like last month to the battlefields at Ypres.

So many Sikhs died in World Wars for the UK, I'm not sure if UK people know; I didn't know the great numbers myself until that outing.

But UK people are good to us now. The teachers and the other children are kind to the boys, and we have nice neighbours both sides. When the referendum came my husband and Suki and Aman argued: my husband voted stay, he said we are all friends now, all races together, look it's working better than we thought it would. Together is strong and good for trade and better still there will be no more big wars in Europe if the countries are together. Aman agreed and voted stay too, he said in the City everyone wants stay for finance and the markets, but Suki was fed up with rules and regulations, finding money to pay maternity leave for shop assistants and high prices for stock because the garment factories have to keep the European laws. I was confused. My husband said I must vote, you must always vote or you have no right to complain when you don't get what you want.

I went to the polling station with my husband but when I was there, for the first time I did not vote exactly the same way as my husband. I did put a cross for stay to please him and Aman, but also a cross for go to please Suki. When I told them what I did they said that's no good, your votes won't count. Suki gave me a kiss when we were washing up, to say thank you, but I was sad the men were laughing at me. Mandeep was the happiest that day, on holiday while his school was a polling station.

"*What* sort of thing?" insists Mandeep.

I wait. Yesterday, walking with the big group when the car came with the man throwing stones, I pulled Mandeep behind a big tree on the pavement. I pretended I was looking for conkers so he would look down at the pavement with me. When my husband turned and waved, we continued home with him, and I think Mandeep didn't see or hear the men with their cans of beer and their tattoos. Quickly I started talking about something else. Now in his armchair my husband has gone deaf. Luckily something clunks through the letterbox and Mandeep runs off to see what it is.

"I will take pakoras to that lady and her daughter," I say to my husband.

"Hmm … I wouldn't open the front door, if I was her. If I wasn't expecting anyone."

"Then I will bring them back. We'll just have more pakoras, not a problem!"

Very slowly my husband puts down his newspaper and creaks up from the armchair. He comes to me with a sad smile of his old eyes. He looks at me like he's thinking hard and he puts his arms round me carefully like I'm broken china and he wants to stick me together with such care the cracks will never show.

"Are you keeping Bibi's cardigan warm, Baba?"

Mandeep runs back from the hall to join in with the hug, dropping the leaflet that came through the door, and my heart is full to breaking because my husband is so sad and my little grandson doesn't

understand anything yet of the world. When my husband sees my tears he says:

"Come here, Mandeep, and I will tell you the
story of the dancer and the bhangra drums. We
need some saucepans and we need your Bibi and
you will see what fun it will be to tell the story we
have written for you."

Then he puts wooden spoons in Mandeep's
hands and holds his thin wrists to show him how to
keep the beat on the upside-down saucepan. They
go slow and quiet to get it right and stop it scratching
the floorboards. When I was a little girl the house
servants taught me to dance, taught me many movements, and I practised them soft and small so no one
saw me to tell me off. On the sofa now I remember
those steps. I extend my arms under my big cardigan
sleeves, slap my feet down gently ... keep discreet, just
clapping the rhythm with my hands. It's all my old
body can do now anyway, but when I was young my
days what trouble I would have been in if my parents
had seen me dancing like poor girls dance. Mandeep
is so busy with the saucepans he doesn't look too hard
at me. Why would he want to? I'm all old and wrinkly
now, but I notice even so he gives me little smiles now
and then like he knows my dancing secret.

My grandson's eyes are shining and he says
"What about the ogre? Trump who goes thump!"

Now my husband surprises me. Crash on the
saucepans! Bang, thump! Fast, hard!

"We'll chase him away, like this, we'll frighten
him so he never dares tell us what to do again." His

eyes are yellow and tired. "And I'll teach you how as well, Mandeep, so all your life you know how to chase him away too."

Bump, bump, Trump goes thump! Bump, bump, Trump goes thump! Bump, bump, Trump goes thump!

Aman comes down the stairs, picks up the leaflet from the mat, shakes his head and stuffs it in his pocket. Now he stands in the doorway tapping his feet, clapping and moving his body like a graceful serpent, just as I could when I was a happy little girl.

TERESA

Did Alka take a tumble? My selfish head wants to seal the Nathan deal so it's telling me she just got down from that high thing she was balancing on because she'd had enough. But in that household, she may have been pulled down, backwards. My racing heart says go and check.

Mr Chan won't know what happened next door last month. To him there's no cause for alarm.

The children stamp their shoes clean on the kitchen mat and take them off, racing back to the Hogwarts Lego like that was the only thing on their minds all the time. How quickly children switch attention! Sky carefully balances a big-haired Hermione, wand outstretched, on top of the mauve castle spire ... it may be the hair that reminds Nathan. He looks up, glasses flashing like the boy wizard himself and asks: "Do you think Alka's all right? She looked like she fell."

Bless him. Sky's impervious, trying to balance tiny Hermione on her pinnacle.

"Would you mind ...?" I glance at Mr Chan, who seems unsure what I mean. I'll have to spell it out.

"Would you keep an eye on these two while I nip next door and check the little girl's all right?"

Surely my concern for another child's welfare will be a mark in my favour anyway. Mr Chan seems surprised and of course – I grin inside – he may never have been left in charge of two children in a stranger's house before, whereas for me it's my bread and butter. Or used to be. I make an assumption: he's such a polite, sensible man, surely...

"Put the kettle on again, if you like..."

Because some instinct is propelling me, almost whether he agrees or not, to fly next door as quickly as I can and check on the little girl who's fallen backwards away from the window of her tower.

SAFIYA

It wasn't so hard, last night, when we'd locked the door. At the top of the stairs I pulled up my sleeve to check my arm. No bandage needed. There was a red mark. It will bruise and go. Nothing serious.

But the abuse monster squatted in the room between us. Xoriyo and I colluded, trying to cut it down to size. Gently she asked me: "Are you ok, Mummy, are you sure?" and I said yes and we both accepted what I said. We turned the TV on. Xoriyo offered to make us a drink but I did it, to show her everything was normal. I closed the curtains and said it was to see the TV better and although we never do that usually, she believed me. She was quiet, and so was I. We watched TV. I don't know what we watched.

Xoriyo asked: "Is it time, Mummy?"

We prepared thoroughly for our prayers, last night. Preparing and praying together was calming, familiar. The slow rituals lessened the churning of my stomach and passed more time for us. Afterwards I had no appetite but I found leftover pasta and salad in the fridge for Xoriyo and we were silent again until she said:

"I want a long bath tonight and you can come in and talk to me."

Like when she was a baby. It was her offering to me, so I wasn't left alone and brooding. For a while now she has shut the door, she washes herself, maybe she plays a bit, I don't know. She's in the junior school now, no need for me to do those things with her. But last night she asked me to be there.

My heart ached when I saw her thin body. Such a slight girl, flat chest, straight legs, angular shoulders. Not a curve on her, and at the end of her long fingers even the nails quite square across. She is the same age now that I was when I was taken in the aeroplane to what they called home. One day she will have breasts, a waist, hips and calves, and her innocence will be gone, but at least she will never sit as I did in a bath of warm water with the canister of salt shaken into it making me sting like nibbling bites, wincing and shifting to wriggle away the soreness. The salt kept me clean and helped me heal, but even so I used to moan and cry by myself in the bathroom where the women couldn't see me, and then if they came in I would pretend I was singing. Last night Xoriyo sang a song to herself in the bath, a comforting song for English babies she must have learned at her nursery school. When Fawzia brought her baby, Xoriyo found a rubber duck for him that I thought I'd thrown away when we moved. Last night she pushed it up and down in the water making waves, first gentle, then violent until I told her it was time to get out.

This landlord's bath is a horrible colour, a dingy, greyish mid green – one day I will have a gleaming white china bathroom! – and Xoriyo's light brown skin in the electric light blurred against the bath sides and the water. How beautiful she is! It was soothing and sad at the same time, after our "incident" (the English always call unpleasant things *incidents*) to sit quietly on the bathroom stool and watch her. But when I told her to wash she scrubbed so violently at her own skin that I took over for fear she might hurt herself. I didn't ask why she scrubbed so hard. Instead I praised the soft smoothness of her skin, and showed her gentler ways to clean and care for it.

Later we had bedtime stories together. I read one to her and she read to me and then I stroked her little body until she slept and I was surprised this morning to find I had slept too. In the house, Xoriyo and I, just the two of us, we feel safe.

Xoriyo is only little, and so if something bad happens, the next day she has forgotten about it. This will not last much longer, but she is young for her age. So she has another year or so of such innocence, I hope, and I was not surprised when I woke this morning to see her quite happy, trotting round to make me breakfast and talking about going to the park again.

I don't want to go to the park. Soon I will go – I will not allow anyone to stop me taking my daughter to school, or the park, or the shops or anywhere. But just today, I want to leave it. Like when you are recovering from a wound and you become more active little by little, bit by bit.

"Maybe we'll go tomorrow, if Fawzia comes."

But Fawzia may come on Monday instead, for the first day of Muharram. She knows it's good to have company on the day for stories of the angel who stands on the boundary of earth and paradise shaking named leaves from the tree, a leaf for each person who will die in the coming year.

Xoriyo pouts when I say no: she is disappointed.

"It's long here, with just the TV. I want to take a ball."

"I know, sweetheart, but just today… Oh, look, how beautifully you've prepared our food!"

How well she has laid the cloth! How clever to heat the milk just right without it boiling over! Look, here's some jam, a new kind we haven't tried before. It isn't hard to return Xoriyo to a good mood, or pretending to be in a good mood. We've been through many things together and we are kind to each other this way. But today she is not quite herself and so I decide to show her the photographs I asked the school to print.

She is delighted! Watching her pleasure in the peach and in the baby photos, all different sizes and tones, helps me begin to put aside what happened last night. She sorts them on the floor, thinking how to use them together.

"Can I use your good pen, to write it out again?" Her voice is serious with the weight of her project.

"I'll write the story again in – Miss Patel said they're called 'episodes'. Then I'll stick the bits next to the right photo on a bigger bit of paper, and last I'll add a border."

My good pen that we keep for special occasions – of course she may use it. For the moment we have no larger sheet of paper, but she can get started with her "episodes". I'm happy she takes such care choosing her words. Her thin fingers are so delicate, plotting her careful handwriting. She uses an edge of the newspaper to try out difficult letters, the f's and the k's until she's satisfied she can join them handsomely. Sometimes she asks me a spelling, but Xoriyo does not need much help, and I chuckle to think how she has deceived her teachers and how this beautiful work will surprise them.

"Is there any more paper?"

She's made so many fair copies she's used up all the old school letters. "There was one yesterday. If you read it quickly can I have it?"

She rummages in her bag and hands it to me.

Home Farm Primary School
*September 30*th *2016*

Autumn Census 2016

Dear Families,
    PLEASE READ CAREFULLY
    The new school census for Autumn 2016 requires us to hold the following information:

Nationality of Child:
Country of Birth of Child:
<u>*You do not need to respond if your child was*</u>
<u>*born in the UK and is a British National.*</u>
All information is confidential. It is used only
by the DfE for data purposes.
Information should be returned by Wednesday
*5*th *October 2016.*

Thanks in advance,
Mrs DasGupta – Head Teacher
L. O'Hara – Chair of Governors

My stomach grips with the same acid shock I received yesterday in the street. There were never letters like this from my daughter's previous schools. Why do they need to know?

I read again. Xoriyo waits patiently. She knows from my face something is wrong; she doesn't want to ask what it is and I don't want to say. Only – but it isn't only, it is huge – a sense of foreboding, an adding together of "incidents" like the one yesterday along with the graffiti near the corner shop and the man on the tube and the front of the newspapers since the referendum and this letter...

PLEASE READ CAREFULLY. In capitals, like shouting. It seems to me some parents read carefully, others do not read at all, and why should I read carefully when all these letters do is hurt my feelings? The one that told me I may keep Xoriyo out for Eid, but would I consider carefully as they would prefer if I didn't. The many since nursery asking for money,

for outings, for extra this and special that, or the last
school always telling me about Christmas dinner or
sometimes to dress her up in clever ways as though
I have a stock of costumes just sitting here waiting
to be used one day a year. Then this school asked
for food for their poor people at harvest time – *their*
poor people! Don't they know I already give as the
Prophet (peace be upon him) requires? Don't they
know I am poor myself?

"Mummy?"

PLEASE READ CAREFULLY. I swallow my
rage, but it surges back, swelling high in my throat.
Is this so different from a stone thrown in the street?
A stone that could have hit my daughter's bobbing
head as she balanced carefully along the wall? A
stone that barely cut my flesh but shook me and all
the people around and I saw, I saw how they divided
into those who would check if I was all right and
the bigger group who hurried away. People from
all backgrounds in both groups... I push the lump
of anger back down inside and read again, more
carefully, as instructed. I do not need to return any
information because Xoriyo was born in the UK.

Does that make it ok to send such a letter?

I would not fill it in and return it even if she had
not been born here.

If people do not want us here, we cannot go
home. What they think is our home – if indeed
they think at all – was war torn for years, beaten by
drought and hunger and trade embargos and anar-
chy and the rule of violence. Even now, with some

elements of peace returned, what my parents called our homeland is not a recognised state. Once back in, we would only be trapped at the next heave of our unsettled history. Online I see smart green and red flags and uniformed processions, gleaming buildings and government edicts – I wish the Somalilanders well but they do not convince me!

I was only two when we came here. Xoriyo was born here. So the UK is our home, whether "they" like it or not. Do they think *we* like it, so much? It is better than what has become of my parents' home. But it is no more perfect for us than it is for those who hate us.

"Mummy?"

"Here, have it."

"Is there something bad in the letter?"

I shake my head, I put my arms around her, and she doesn't understand but she allows me to rock her, rock her and it is not Xoriyo I am trying to comfort, it is myself.

I must not frighten my daughter, who has only me to make her brave and confident.

"Let me see what you have done – oh, look, sweetheart, this is wonderful! Your beautiful writing!"

She glows with pride.

"I want to stick the papers back to back, to make a book," she explains. "So only my writing will show and none of those stupid letters."

Her dismissal – "stupid letter" – gives me quick comfort. She is allying herself with me even though she doesn't know what the battle is. My clever daughter! When she sticks the letters from the school together, all their messages will be hidden. The good ones about the fairy stories will blot out the bad questionnaires. The only thing these pieces of paper will represent is a child's happy story of a baby and a luscious peach.

I draw her into a new hug, with a hearty kiss on each glowing cheek.

"Because I did beautiful work?"

"No, my sweet, because you are my lovely daughter and yes, because you do beautiful work too."

But now she's anxious. "Is it ok if I don't stick them straight away? The paper will wrinkle if I don't wait for all the ink and the glue from the pictures to dry. Then the colouring wouldn't work."

So many times when children begin things well they go on to spoil them because they do something in the wrong order or they use the wrong method. My little Xoriyo is learning this and making decisions accordingly. She will be a strong one, like Fawzia! But until she is old enough to care for herself fully, I must keep us both safe.

"You may do as you wish, my love. But maybe show me first so we can try a bit together and not spoil any of your beautiful work?"

Sometimes children and glue don't mix! Too little and nothing happens. Too much and there is mess everywhere. My anger over the letter has dissipated. I think of the kindness of those who stayed with us on Friday. The man in the turban, his own foreignness that could have brought down more anger upon us, the rabbit lady with her own child to protect. If we go back to our old estate, Xoriyo will run other risks – of bad ideas and worse practices, and if she can grow up here she will have her birthright: education, and a better marriage than mine…So we must stay, and to be safe we must become friends with all the neighbours in this close to have their support if we're threatened. It will be two steps forward, one or two steps back, but we have no choice.

I wonder if my wise daughter is thinking the same. If she doesn't speak English at the new school, is it because she wants to see how the land lies before committing herself to a particular group of friends? Well, let her do that for a while, but the best way forward is for her to impress and become popular at school, so she too will be embraced by this community and they will care for us.

That puts a lot of pressure on Xoriyo! In the short term, it means doing something brilliant for the fairy story festival, to impress everyone and make them value our contributions to their world. In the longer term, it means blending in and standing out at the same time.

The room is stuffy with the smell of glue and outside there are tired patches of blue sky. A bird perches on the tree opposite and it reminds me I have seen no flocks migrating yet. Yesterday was chilly but this first day of October seems mild. Perhaps we should take our jackets and go to the park after all.

ALKA

The door opens suddenly behind me and I twist so quickly to see who it is I lose my balance. I land on my bottom on the carpet, my palms flat behind me and my knees crooked up. Mummy looks at me for a moment. Then she holds out her hands to pull me up.

"You ok?"

She doesn't hug me but there's some caring in her eyes.

"Why have you put the stool here? Didn't you hear me coming upstairs?"

I don't know which question to answer first so I don't say anything. We stand fixed, her hands stretched out still holding mine and her eyes checking me closely.

"You looked like a spider, legs and arms all bent like that. You should be more careful."

She can see I'm not hurt so she can be stern about me standing on the stool instead.

"And you should not be moving the furniture. In fact you should not be in Nani and Nana's room at all."

All she's done is tell me off. I'm not hurt but I'd like her to be comforting. She used to comfort me when I fell. It makes her seem so far away nowadays. I want to close the distance. I lay my head against her chest where it just reaches to the sticking out boobies she used to let me press in with my finger when she was in a good mood. We used to laugh so much she had to make me stop. I reach my arms round her silky waist and hug as tight as I can to show her I care about her, and I don't mind even when my hair gets caught on a button. She goes stiff and peels my fingers away and some hair is pulled right out. Ouch! I don't think she notices.

"Not now, Alka … what were you doing in here?"

"I don't have my own room anymore. You've taken it and I have to be with that baby Sunil. If I come up here I get some peace and quiet."

"But what were you doing?"

"A boy – some children from school were in Sky's garden and I was waving to them."

"You should not be waving from the window."

"Why?"

"You just shouldn't, Alka. Never mind why. Now you can come and help me. We need to sort out your clothes and see what still fits you. You look all legs and arms. And you need to tidy yourself up. Your hair is such a mess, I wonder if I should cut it."

"It's because you don't help me brush it anymore."

"What do you think this is, a castle and you a princess? You're old enough to take care of your own hair. Now, help me put this stool back and then come along."

In fact I put the stool back because when she picks her end up it must make something hurt so she lets it thump down again. She watches me push it over to the dressing table. The legs stick against the thick carpet leaving marks the way aeroplanes leave a trail in the sky. But now there *is* something to be cross about she doesn't complain.

"Come."

She holds her hand out which is kinder but I wish she would cuddle me like she used to. In my room – her room – it takes a while to go through my winter clothes. She sits on the bed and I make a pile of "too smalls" next to her. There's a cosy purple dress I love and I'm sad when it ends up there.

"You can keep it a bit longer, then. Just don't complain if it feels tight!"

I don't tell her about some other things that aren't comfy anymore but I like them. It's tricking her in a way, but it's not like she's offering me anything new. Now she helps me hang everything up neatly again. She's in a funny mood, not good enough to ask her about Janki's party, or if I go, could I have a new dress for that. But it's still nice to be just the two of us together concentrating on my things, no Sunil, no Dad.

The doorbell goes. It's Sky's mum asking Nani how I am and if I'd like to go and play with Sky and Nathan.

"Go and say we're busy sorting out your clothes," says Mummy. "Maybe another time."

There's something about Nathan that makes people kinder, even Sky might be nice with him there. I wonder why he's there … But Mummy's said no, and at least I'm having some time with her. I've found the costume Nani brought me from their trip to Gujarat last year for Navratri. It was too big and Nani was disappointed, but Mummy said it would last longer that way. I pull the garments off the hanger and hold them against me. The colours are brighter than my normal clothes: *shocking* pink, *luminous* orange, *vivid* turquoise. "The colours are so much more *vivid* on Indian clothes, we need special words," Mummy said last year when she was happy, and she taught me them. The Indian clothes made my skin look paler and everyone said I was beautiful. This year the *chaniya* will be the right length so I don't trip over and the *choli* will be tighter across my chest like it should be. I'm proud I remember the Indian words and I want to ask if the Gujarati school is holding garba dances again this year. I've been practising my dance steps and I could wear these clothes with all the beads and bangles and mirrors and they would teach me more new dance steps like last year. Mummy looks at me trying the *chaniya* against me before the mirror and although she doesn't say anything bad, inside my head I think she's not smiling enough to ask her, yet.

Maybe another time.

MRS KAUR

A man wants to take the boys for football in the park and it's chilly but we decide to go along. It makes me happy, watching my tall son and my skinny grandsons, standing with my husband knowing we produced these three fine young men. Mandeep's high voice shrieks with pleasure as Aman dribbles the ball for a long way. At the last minute he lets Mandeep outwit him. He pushes his dad's body, squealing, and Aman's out of breath, laughing.

"Time I taught you what a foul is! The ref would never allow what you do!" "Yeah," mutters Gurdeep. "Youngest one always gets away with things."

It's all good natured. They get on well, these three. My husband pushes his hands deep in his pockets and grunts, satisfied too. I take his arm and he turns to me with smiles.

Gurdeep has grown tall this year. Until spring he was thin, so thin I would feed and feed him, but now he seems stronger. He kicks the ball harder than he meant, it goes skidding over the grass nearly to the path with the conker trees. Mandeep dances about screaming at his brother and Aman says, *you go and get it Gurdeep* so off Gurdeep goes. He often surprises himself, my older grandson. Suddenly he's strong and his new muscles do things he doesn't expect. Then he has to put them right.

Someone's running towards Gurdeep, kicking the ball, a little thin person with a grownup trying to catch up behind. As they come near I see a young lady running with narrow steps to fit inside her long straight skirt, not like her little girl who is very fast! As Gurdeep goes to take the ball from her she laughs and dodges round him, keeping the ball between her feet with quick steps sideways and forwards to keep it from him. First he stops, and stands back, looking – *who is this girl who's got my ball?* He puts his hands on his hips, looks at my husband who laughs out loud, looks at Aman and Mandeep and when the little girl arrives at the goal post out of breath – Mandeep gasps!

"Hi! You're in my class!"

"I don't know about that," says Aman. "I think you've outclassed us!"

She looks confused and turns away, her shoulders drop, she looks for her mum who is still far away across the grass stepping small inside her skirt.

"Xoriyo! Say sorry and give back the ball now!" calls the young lady puffing towards us, but Mandeep grins.

"No, she's good, can she play? Me and her against Gurdeep and Dad?"

Finally the young lady reaches us and I see it's the lady from school on Friday.

"Good to see her in the park with her daughter," I say to my husband, and he replies "Good to see us here, too."

"No reason not to come, with Aman here to look after us."

"You think Aman could keep all that lot away, if they wanted to hurt us?"

I don't answer. I don't want to think about it. The kids and Aman have started off again, I know nothing about football but I see the little girl is good. She keeps the ball away from Gurdeep and Aman, changes direction, changes fast to slow to fast again, then passes to Mandeep when they're both going the other way and Mandeep understands her intention just in time to take it and kick it right in the middle of the goal! Mandeep and the little girl go running in big circles with their arms in the air shouting celebrations. The young woman is smiling, clapping, and we clap too. Gurdeep and Aman look a bit silly waiting for Mandeep and the girl to stop running.

We stand and watch, three of us smiling at each other without knowing names. But a big gust of wind blows a damp shiver through me.

"You want hot tea?" asks my husband pointing to the park café. The young lady has her arms across her chest rubbing her elbows: she is shivering too, I see.

"Come – you want hot tea too?"

We leave her clever daughter with our boys and enter the warm steamy room. We buy tea for the young lady, she is so cold she says yes but no biscuits.

"Not good like your biscuits anyway," says my husband. When we tell our names and the names of the children we find they're in the same class. We say, she's good at football, innit? I forget the names straight away, I'm not good with names now. We sit and smile while the children still play football under the falling leaves and we buy more tea, in thick white cups like all the cafés used to have.

"Nice not paper cups," I say, and she nods politely.

Later we walk home together, comfortable but still not finding what words to say. Aman is ahead with my husband, they talk politics and football, the boys are behind them and the little girl walks with her mother, humming. At their gate I take the young woman's hands, I press one warm on top and underneath with the other one.

"You need something, you ask," I say. "Number 14, innit?" and I point to our big rich house. Her eyes are wet inside, so I pretend like British people I don't see. It's better sometimes, if you don't see.

Gurdeep is sulking a little bit. "Beaten by a girl! Girl that can't even speak English!"

"You don't need English for football," says Mandeep.

MONDAY 3RD OCTOBER
2016

ALKA

P *lease note presentations should be a maximum of 10 minutes long. Shorter is fine!*

As soon as Nani and Nana brought us from school, Sunil was whining. It fills the house, behind every curtain, down every crack. He can go high, low, long and short. He whines about the TV being on, TV being off, not being allowed the same milk sweets as Nani's put in front of Durga because he'll spoil his dinner, toys he's tired of. Really he's just tired, after nursery. That's what happens, with babies like Sunil. When they're tired nothing's right and the whole family suffers.

Mum doesn't want him to go to sleep now or he won't go to bed at the right time. She gives him his iPad but he can't play the game properly to score any points. Nani and Nana don't know how to help and he snatches the iPad back when I try. Mummy's phone rings so she takes it to my room to talk. I give up with Sunil. While no-one's attention is on me I creep up into the loft to peep out the window. I can still can hear Sunil, faint whining turned to wailing, and I imagine him lying on his back on the floor with his heels drumming the carpet and poor Nani rushing out of the kitchen to plead with him to stop.

Every time I look out this window to the garden it seems more normal. The tepee would be a good place at the moment, with Sunil's whines covering the walls downstairs. Nobody plays there now: maybe the tepee too feels lonely. It used to wrap its light walls round us and the warmth came through them to stroke us as we played tea parties and cuddled up with stories. If Janki came she played there too and I wasn't lonely at other times, for I had my friend in my head, a clever, beautiful girl with the same birthday as me. I called her Kalpita … The shadows of the trees tapped against the tepee not to be left out, and once a robin came and looked through the doorway at us. Kalpita didn't stay in the tepee *that* night, once she saw I was reading Rapunzel. Maybe she was jealous, silly her. Then she didn't come because the real things that were happening were too big to leave room for her. She slipped away then but maybe now she's waiting in the tepee for me to come back. She may have been waiting all this time. I'm brave enough now to go back to the garden, especially if Kalpita's there. I won't take a book so she'll know she has me to herself.

I tiptoe my silent fairy steps down the loft stairs. My bedroom door's shut but I can hear Mum's voice on the phone. I stop to listen: *"… I'm telling you, Avni, I had no warning. He's always had a temper but this was like a guard dog you've kept in the family for years and suddenly it turns to savage you…"*

There was a dog on the front of the *Metro* and a horrible photo of a little boy Sunil's age with cuts and grazes all over, and his face not looking alive. I wonder if it was a dog like in the tinder box story we heard today at school with eyes like saucers. I'm glad I didn't get that story to work on at home. The dog idea makes me frightened but I've been practising a clever thing we were told about, also at school. If you do not like what you're thinking, you can make yourself think something different. I think, maybe Kalpita will help me with Rapunzel if I get her in a good mood. Maybe we'll surprise everyone with Rapunzel and they'll be pleased again.

"… they just gave him a caution … Excuse me …? Yes, he admitted he'd pushed me; it was when I fell against the table I did the damage. Not him directly. We were lucky to get away with it … You think so? And then what would happen to the house, his business, your and my business, our reputation, everything? No, this way is better, and he won't do it again, as long as Pretty Priti earns the money back, and we can do that, believe me … Well, that's as maybe, but I have to believe we can. As soon as my face looks okay we can pick up where we left off … yes, Av, you'll get your money back too. I promise … have I ever let you down before? Don't tell me you don't trust me anymore, just because I had an accident … yes it was an accident, we've already been through this …"

That thing that happened, it leaks into everything, like blood leaking through a bandage when you fall over and it doesn't get better and it gets that yellow stuff. I want to run away from it, to where the blood and the yellow stuff can't get me and my parents will put their arms round me again.

The kitchen's empty while Nani struggles with Sunil in the lounge. I slip through the side door into the garden. It's strange being outside the back of the house, I've only been outside the front since *that* night. One step. Two steps, along the side of the house. The little stones stuck to the walls will scratch me if I go too close; they're called "pebble-dash" and they guard the bricks of the house from damp and rain, Dad said, but they guard the walls from children too I think. I'm still doing my fairy steps in case anyone hears me, six…seven steps and I'm at the patio. It's a wide space, far enough for now. I stop to take it in. The patio has stone flags, not like cloth flags or flags that are flowers like irises. I like words that have many meanings. Dad used to tell me about words with many meanings and I gave them to Kalpita to remember for me because sometimes I have too much to remember already from everything we do at school. Dad hardly speaks to me now so maybe that's another reason Kalpita went away, because I gave her less to do. From the edge of the patio I look up at my bedroom window where the curtains are closed. Mum has shut herself in with her phone call to Avni. I change my thoughts. She has a friend like I have Kalpita. They're talking secrets and I can talk secrets too, with Kalpita.

"Alka! You're not cold, out here?"

Nana's deep voice makes me jump.

"Oh, *dikri*, I'm sorry. Did I frighten you? Were you far away in the land of the fairies?"

I suppose Kalpita *is* a kind of fairy. I'm cross if he's discovered her but it makes me feel safer with him out here and we can explore the whole garden together. Kalpita will have to wait again.

"I don't believe in fairies."

"No, of course not. You are a big girl now. I have been looking at this lovely tent of yours, getting all smeared. Does your father usually put it away for the winter? I think it's too cold to play here now, don't you?"

Poor, bad Nana. He's destroying the tepee and the fairies with his kind words. I hate him. He takes my hand and we inspect the tepee together. It's true, it does look sad. Big wet leaves are stuck half way down the outside walls, slapped over the pretty coloured pattern. The robin or maybe the blackbird has visited and left a black and white smear – "No, that must be pigeons," says Nana, "so much!" Inside the plastic floor is wrinkly wet like the paddling pool when we try to get it empty.

I watch Nana take down the centre pole. The strong plastic cloth creaks to the ground, making peaks like little half-size tents. He lays the pole on the grass and looks at the new shape. We both walk round it thoughtfully. He's made an earthquake and trapped my summer stories inside the ruins. When he takes an edge of the tepee and begins to spread it flatter some of my stories fly away and some are squashed until there's nothing big enough to remember. Far away Kalpita gives a tiny squeak of distress and from inside the house Sunil's cries rise louder. But the job is started so it must finish. Each of us takes an edge and pulls it as flat as we can, sunlit moments flying away like the moths in the autumn leaves or flattened forever. Nana's brought out a bowl of soapy water and now he puffs and humphs as he tries to pull on yellow rubber gloves and they stick on his knuckles and his wide gold wedding band. I watch him wipe away my stories with the pigeon mess, and some of the leaves stick but in the end it's all gone. We dry the tepee with an old towel and now Nana folds the heavy plastic and stoops with a grunt to carry it into the shed. When I try to follow with the pole it's too heavy and I let it drop with a clang. A squirrel in the trees freezes still.

The space looks even bigger without the tepee, marked with a yellow circle of sad flat grass, and I move to the shelter of the fence. It's high and I can't see over into Sky's garden so I watch the wet leather of my shoes darkening in the damp grass. Dandelions spread like spider webs in the border and there are real webs on the fence, a sign of autumn says Nana who's come to stand next to me. Mum hates spiders but I think they're clever, catching insects in their webs and decorating the garden. There's a famous book about a good spider that's on my list to read from the school library.

Nana points. A tunnel's been burrowed under the fence.

"The foxes do that, I saw under the classrooms at school."

"It's a small fox," says Nana. "If I hadn't seen so many foxes here, I'd say that was a rabbit. We should block it up, or we'll have little Sunil going down the rabbit hole like Alice."

"It's Sky's! We've found where it went! Can I go and tell her?"

"No, Sky's rabbit will be far away by now."

Nana shivers. He squeezes my hand. "Come inside, *mari dikri*. I'm sorry we had to put your tent away but in the spring we'll clean it up properly and then there'll be another summer after that."

TERESA

We leave five minutes earlier for school this morning. Sky helps by getting ready quickly. I do hope this new enthusiasm lasts! She's not yet good enough at telling the time to see the big hand isn't yet on the eight, and goes skipping along the pavement in her red coat so fast I have to call her back as we near the end of the close.

"Why do I have to stop? You know I won't go near the traffic."

We have endless discussions about keeping near the wall side on the pavement of the main road. I worry about traffic mounting the kerb; I worry about moped riders nicking my bag since I read about it in the *Evening Standard*; I worry even more about pollution. I don't know if it's logical to think every centimetre we can put between us and the fumes makes a difference but at least by insisting on it I feel I'm being a good parent. The world faces me with huge threats I can't control and the only response I can think of is making us walk in the shelter of the wall. Sky is still so young ... I have to get things right until she's independent and then, perhaps, I can sink down into her shadow.

But today I'm slowing down for another reason.

"I'm calling here."

Puzzled, Sky waits for me at the corner and I take her hand as I turn down the broken path of the African lady's house. She's distracted, playing hopscotch on the coloured tiles – is it my imagination or do they show up brighter today? But the bell that worked when we asked about Ten Pence makes no sound this time. Then the knocker slips out of my gloved fingers more heavily than I meant it to, rapping like a dawn raid. I look round. No other adults and children are in the street yet. Just five minutes change to a schedule and the familiar daily scene looks very different.

"Knock again." Sky's voice is breathless from hopscotch. She has an afterthought: "Why are we here, anyway?"

"Do you want to do it?"

I can't redirect her thoughts as easily now she's nearly eight, but this time it works and she reaches up. Because she's only just tall enough to catch the knocker, her rap's less strong than mine. We hear a child's voice inside shouting in their language and the mother answers. This time no face peeps out from the yellow curtain.

"They're not coming," says Sky.

"They have to come soon, it's school." Yet for all I know they don't have to. They may have a doctor's appointment. They may just not be ready.

"They might not want to come with us."

"Why wouldn't they?"

"We're not friends. She doesn't speak English."

"Yes, she does – remember?" Memory dawns on Sky's round face.

But she's right, we can't hang around on their doorstep if we're not wanted. We dawdle away and turn into the main road. I use a trick from the Regency romances I used to read, and drop a tissue to slow us down but Sky picks it up immediately. At least she's well trained to pick up litter, but as for my good deed, I don't think I'll get the chance to perform it today.

SAFIYA

I stop Xoriyo just in time from putting her head between the curtains and the window. If we're not expecting anyone, I don't want her face showing. The Indian man was right on Friday: "Don't let them see where you live!" Although, why *you*? Why not *we*? Maybe those ignorant thugs were aiming at his turban as much as my headscarf? But somehow, I think not. Turbans have been around this part of London for longer, and that kind doesn't take on men as much as women.

I'm up and down. Saturday in the park was an innocent, lovely time, a time for healthy play among the falling leaves of the golden English autumn. Today, the first day of Muharram, the image reminds me only of the tree on the boundary of earth and paradise. Whose name will the angel write on a dropping leaf this year? In the past I've found our traditional New Year story beautiful and reassuring – because we have no control over death, we have no choice but to accept the will of Allah. Alongside my western education and despite my medical studies, I continue to believe that but today I find it dismal. I do not want to hear the wails of O Hussein! O Hussein! for ten more days. I am glad for that reason to be away from the Somalis and yet there is a paradox. If I were in their company I would feel less sad as the New Year begins.

The man who threw the stone has won, if I dread even a daylight knock so much that I won't open the door.

In any case Xoriyo has already disobeyed me. She's now peeping from behind the thicker curtain through the right-hand pane of the bay.

"It was Sky and her mum, from school."

"Sky?"

"The one who lost her rabbit."

She doesn't say, the one whose mother picked you up when you fell. When you were downed by the sting of a cowardly stone and a vicious shock. There are things it is safer not to discuss, she's learnt that from a young age. I move to the window myself and Xoriyo ducks towards the pane again. She pulls the net across her face giving her a strange scarred appearance but she soon untwists herself, coughing.

"These curtains smell," she says.

There is nothing nice about those curtains, the colour, the silly flounce at the bottom. Now they smell, too. If I could change them I would. But if I could change everything I don't like in this flat, I'd be nearly rich enough to buy my own. What was I thinking, telling Xoriyo we'd smarten it up?

"You're not supposed to wrap your face in them," I say. "Come, get your things."

The knocker raps a third time, and this time I don't jump. The knocks are getting gentler, and I'm more ready. Xoriyo has already darted back to the window but whoever knocked is standing too close to the door for her to see. At the gate, still in the street, are the turbaned gentleman and the smaller of the boys she played football with. I don't remember their names.

"It's Mandeep!" shouts Xoriyo. And then, turning to me, she hisses: "Remember, I don't speak English!"

How long is she going to keep this mask on? Given that Sky knows it's fake already... As we walk together to the school, the grandmother who knocked is coughing and grinning but she says nothing. Perhaps, like me, she can't remember our names. The children skip and dribble an imaginary ball and don't say a word to each other, and the grandfather goes on ahead, stiff and dignified like a general who prefers not to acknowledge his motley troops. After we've left the children in the playground, we walk back together and they leave me at my gate with a nod. I wish they could escort me to work, to the shops, and along all the other more complicated paths I have to follow. The world feels a bleak place today when they've returned to their smart house with the shining cars and the shrubs and the lights that come on in the dark when anyone approaches.

I have no work today. To feel less alone I switch on the radio. "Coming up in an hour..." it's the voice, deeper than usual for an English woman, that tells you about Woman's Hour. Fawzia told me to listen to this programme when I can because it will unlock many English secrets, unknown to me even though I was born here. She says if I choose to distance myself from my own community I must have the tools to enter another, and I wonder as I always do how she can straddle both so easily. The deep voice intones: "What happens when an apparently contented husband suddenly turns violent? We speak to women whose lives were turned upside down when ..." I'm not properly listening, there's nothing new about *that* subject, but the presenter catches my attention again. She always says *and!* a quick, sharp syllable to signal a contrast, more interesting, less serious, less common, more quirky. Today it sounds as though it's just going to be more boring: "We continue our series of handy household tips our mothers knew. Did you know, for instance, that if you wash net curtains by hand and hang them up wet, they'll dry without creases?"

Ah! I didn't know ... if I do this now, the windows will be bare for no time at all. I stand on a chair to slip the curtains off their sagging wire, and almost overbalance as my eyes meet those of the rabbit lady coming down the road. She waves but I jump down and dash to submerge the curtains in the soapy water I'm running into the bath, hoping she won't knock, wishing she would. Disgusting grey seeps from the curtains. I wonder if they've ever been washed before and just as I assume she isn't going to knock, the sound raps through my head. She knows I'm here.

Shameful yellow curtains oozing dirt in the snot coloured bath! I let the grey water out and quickly start running in fresh with more soap for a second wash, before going down to answer. She's standing with her back to the door as though she knows she isn't welcome, already preparing to walk away. Her shoulders are rounded and her clothes emphasize a clumsy shape that would be better hidden. The latch clicks when I open the door and she turns at the sound, but not completely, as though she expects me to dismiss her.

"I just thought I'd see if you were all right. After Friday... We called for you to keep you company walking to school but you must have gone already."

I'm grateful for her fib that gives me an excuse for not having answered, and ashamed that I didn't. But also I feel manipulated into a role: I'm the victim, she's a local allowing me onto her territory. My instinct is not to like this woman, although the only contact I've had with her has shown her to be kind and thoughtful. Is it because Xoriyo said her daughter is bossy and noisy? Is it because she herself is awkward?

"It's ok."

I should say more. I'm being very rude.

"Thank you. But really, we're fine."

"Your little girl...?"

"Xoriyo's fine."

"That's good. Well, if you ever need anything, I'm at the top of the road. Number 20. Downstairs flat. Not like you, I see you've got the top floor…"

She's talking for the sake of it and I block the front door with my body, willing my hips wider so she can't see in. I smile but I say nothing. I am not sure why I am being so cold. I don't like it that this woman has seen me so vulnerable.

"Well, goodbye, then…"

As she turns she stops. It seems I have another visitor. The Indian lady from the rich house must have gone home and come almost straight back here. Colliding with the rabbit lady, she just avoids dropping a plate covered with silver foil.

"Sorry I can't shut gate, innit! Hands full here! I bring you pakoras and sweets. Very nice, innit!"

She grins at the rabbit lady. "You friend, too? Nice!"

Suddenly I remember the running bath and with a quick "Excuse me!" I run upstairs and turn it off just in time. The yellow curtains billow on the surface in hideous nylon swirls, glassy beads of water caught in the mesh. When I come out onto the landing the Indian lady is standing on the square of dirty carpet inside the door and the rabbit lady is just behind her, both their heads craned round like periscopes to look up my stairs. I stand at the top, no idea what to do. I have nothing in the house to offer but tea and fruit. I intended to fast today, for the first day of Muharram.

"You come get these or I bring up? You give back plate when you finish, innit. You and little girl."

She starts up the stairs and her foot gets caught. With no free hands she'd fall forward if the rabbit lady didn't catch her from behind. The food she is so kindly offering would be spoilt on the carpet and all because I am too ungracious to invite her in. To invite them both in.

"Please…" I gesture them up into our living room. I see it through their eyes and want to disappear with embarrassment.

"Nice shawl," says the Indian lady. "OK I sit on it?"

The rabbit lady crosses to the bare window. "Great view you've got here. You can keep tabs on everyone coming in and out of the close."

"Yes, if you're quick you can see the bus coming in time to catch it."

My small talk slips out, surprising me. The Indian lady is balancing the plate on her lap and breathing heavily after the stairs. Only Fawzia has been in this room since we moved here. I must remember my manners to an older lady, to two guests not from my family. I offer tea.

In the kitchen I wonder what they're saying about me, what they're thinking about the landlord's room. But when I get back they're together on the sofa looking through the magic carpet book. "Beautiful pictures, innit?" says the Indian lady. I can't ask her name again.

"A magic carpet's such a brilliant idea." The rabbit lady looks dreamy and I feel more sympathy. "No petrol, no engine noise…"

"No walls, ugh! You fall off!"

"Is this your daughter's story for the project? It's much better than mine."

"We have good story, I'm giant woman ironing, then I dance like little girl!"

"We've got a story about mice, I don't even like mice. No humans at all, Sky's very disappointed."

"But you not tell nothing about story, Mandeep say secret!"

Together they're so busy talking about their stories they don't realise I haven't answered. It's good she said the boy's name and the woman reminded me her daughter was Sky – which is a pretty name. Now it's just theirs I need to learn. The pakoras are delicious and light. I'll have to fast tomorrow instead … The Indian lady takes none for herself. She wheezes and her chesty cough rumbles from deep inside her. The hot tea must be a comfort and I refill the cup without her asking.

"You lady who lost rabbit, innit? What you called?"

"Teresa. And you?"

"You just call me Auntie. That's what we say, in Punjabi, to older lady. Respectful, innit!" and she bursts out laughing which turns into a stream of coughing. Teresa pats her on the back and leaves her hand there rubbing gently and it's a kind gesture but I do not know if this lady welcomes it. To distract Teresa I pour her more tea. It's as though the three of us are engaged in a dance, each marking out elements to assert ourselves and cause no offence.

"Thanks – great tea, but I already need the toilet."

And suddenly this Teresa person has got up and is off looking round, so familiar, and she'll see the bath full of terrible curtains!

I have almost never had an English person inside my house and I don't know if the way she's behaving is the way any English person would behave, or if it is just her.

"Auntie" grins. "You shock, innit! She ask straight away for toilet. You pretend you don't need, if it you, innit?"

When Teresa returns she's all cheerful and practical again. "I'm not surprised your curtains needed a wash! My nan lived in this close before me and she remembers the people that lived here getting them. She liked them – latest fashion then!"

"When?"

"Oh, I would have been tiny. We used to walk round the close admiring the way people did their houses. She was as nosy as I am." At least she is honest. "There were flouncy curtains and lacy ones and orange ones with big holes." I must look puzzled because she adds, "They were meant to have holes. It was a fashion. Yours are the only ones left now. When they sold the house to your landlord he must have saved money by keeping them. What number are you again?" she asks Auntie without stopping. "Is it you have those lovely plantation shutters?"

I'm not sure if Auntie hears everything, because she sits apparently oblivious to the question, taking big slurps of tea. Teresa turns to me. "I can give you a hand hanging them up again, if you get them rinsed."

I cannot ask a guest to do that! But Auntie must be a mind reader, and more awake than she looks as she agrees. "Hard job innit, by yourself! And she offer, why you not say yes?"

My morning's already out of my control. I relax into honesty. I'm safe again, with company and friendly help. I squeeze the water out as much as I can and before I know it Teresa's in the bathroom too, her strong forearms pulling wetness from the fabric as though I'd barely touched them. "Don't want them to drip," she says. We take chairs to each side of the bay and thread the curtains onto the wire, too close to notice what Auntie sees straight away from her place on the sofa.

"You shrink, innit!"

It's a disaster. They may be cleaner but they look even more ridiculous than before, waving pointlessly half a metre above the sill. I'll have to buy material and make more, and sewing has never been my strong point while spare cash and spare time certainly aren't. Oh how embarrassing in front of these two strangers, too, whose homes are better and richer than mine and who would never make an error like this. I expect they've never washed anything in the bath in their lives – well, Auntie may have done, back in India when she was young. But Auntie is rocking backwards and forwards on the sofa with laughter, wrinkling my shawl under her and even picking up a corner to wipe her eyes. "You not worry, I have old curtain at home, white, nicer than this anyway innit, window same size too. Houses all built same on this close, before people add bits. You come back to my house, I find for you. My daughter in law Suki, she buy new every year. Then you throw these away innit, out of fashion – when you say Teresa? – thirty years ago?"

Teresa nods harder than I ever saw someone nod – I almost think her head will drop off. I'm infected with laughter and for the first time since Fawzia was here and Xoriyo made faces about the nappy smell, I relax completely and enjoy the joke.

TUESDAY 4TH OCTOBER 2016

TERESA

ast week the reminder in yesterday's newsletter
would have got on my nerves. We'd lost the rabbit, we'd bickered endlessly, we'd got nowhere with
our story. *Who do the school think we are, don't they think
we have anything better to do?* the parents whinged in
the playground and I was in a mood to agree. With
all the school sends out, it's easy to think the teachers are getting at you, even if like me you did child
development at college. Most parents just blunder
along; there isn't a manual.

But what a difference a week makes! Our story
hasn't exactly moved on but the ingredients are
in place. Sky's more cheerful and Mr Chan asked
if Nathan could start straight away on Thursday so
they can work on both stories together. Nathan's so
funny, commandeering items in my house – Sky gave
me a list after they'd gone. He can think again about
taking down my curtains, but I will put my mind to
other yellow and gold things they can use. Sky can
work on her town mouse story herself. If something
comes of it all well and good, and if not we'll still
have cooperated on Nathan's. I get the impression

his dad's good at helping with techie stuff but baffled by anything more creative. Although, he seems able to magic up money.

And then, unexpectedly – well, I manoeuvred myself into it – I started getting to know the two foreign ladies. (Unless Mrs Ahmed – Safiya? – was born here?) Hopefully having tea together cheered her up after Friday. Come to think of it, *her* terrible curtains would make a costume for Nathan's story.

Mr Chan approving of me, and having a laugh with Safiya and Auntie…that's three positive encounters in three days! Every time I meet a new person and see myself through their eyes, it's like Tony loses a bit more power over me. Better still, these are people he wouldn't expect me to know. People who'll get to know me in my own right, not just as his wife; who can take me in new directions and open up new worlds. People who don't think of me as a smoker – and yesterday I wasn't! Not once!

Although it would be nice to meet someone I could share a bottle of wine with. That ain't gonna happen with these three. Well, possibly Mr Chan if he drinks, but he'd take some chilling first.

I wonder what happened to Xoriyo's father?

THURSDAY 6TH OCTOBER 2016

Mr Chan

That was impulsive! But it was not a disaster.

The TV programme said it's unlikely the initial meetings will produce a final result. They're more like a chance to practise your pitch and identify what you really require. This first date wasn't a bad encounter, a touch embarrassing, but I have dipped my toe in the water. I must make appointments for times when we can reasonably drink alcohol, I think, to loosen things up. Yes.

I find it extraordinary, the number of ladies who respond to my profile. So many beautiful, calm, cool looking women, younger than I, in good careers it seems. The problem will lie in how to filter out the most suitable – I couldn't meet this many women even if Teresa had Nathan every day of the week! Even if there were no Nathan, but that doesn't bear thinking of.

I haven't stated my Hong Kong Chinese origin. I should have thought it obvious from the photograph. Perhaps if I put more emphasis on it I should attract fewer responses? It's not an experiment I wish to try.

I must put a stricter filter on my requirements. London is too full of childless professional women aged 25–35. I didn't add a religion or skin colour for fear of appearing racist, but perhaps I will narrow it down by postal district or salary. Perhaps I shall specify: only dark hair. Also too many of them say they are "bubbly". Bubbles are best kept for champagne, I think. I want a serious person to help me take good care of Nathan. And I will be firm – no animals. No cats or dogs, fur and excrement to complicate our routines and our eventual home. A glance through the website tells me rejecting bubbles and cats will eliminate a fair percentage.

But it was not uninteresting, to meet this ... Selina. She resembled her photograph, attractive, smart. It was a pleasant appointment with a presentable young woman in a hotel coffee shop for a reason other than business – though in the event I found I command only business talk, unless I introduce the subject of Nathan too early. I never remember the Netflix films I doze through late at night, I have no interest in popular music or reality TV and I do not work out. These did not strike me as gaps in my skill set until this afternoon. This Selina worked in IT but she had no understanding of programming or gadgetry at a level I should find interesting. We talked of the weather and property prices, then she apologised because she had to go. Well, only another fifteen minutes and I should have had to go too, to pick up Nathan.

I must consider what my interests are, for the profile. I appreciate I've hardly been precise about myself. It is difficult, to sum myself up in thirty words, without cliché, false modesty, or risking my anonymity. I need to stand back and observe myself as others may see me. *Quiet, calm, intelligent. In the range solvent to prosperous. Not flashy but I appreciate good quality and innovation. A businessman with a warm heart and one son. Wltm...* That left only one word to describe the lady I wltm so I put, *lady*. No wonder there were so many replies.

The programme said it's best not to dwell on what the other person may think of you. But I'm amused to think we must have had similar opinions of each other. Attractive. Smart. Clean. Nothing in common but courtesy and perhaps a void at the centre of things. Yet, I took pleasure in buying coffee in a hotel for a young lady and giving the waiting staff the impression we were friends. I shall do so again.

"They've had a whale of a time!"

Behind Teresa the two children bounce breathless into the narrow dark hall, swathed in something dingy and yellow. Nathan has a foil crown on his head and he's clutching a large golden spoon.

"Watch out Daddy or I'll turn you into gold!" he shouts in the high-pitched voice that signals he's excited and over tired. He runs towards me and throws his arms around my waist as the spoon clatters to the floor.

I'm embarrassed and extricate myself and he stands back, considering me more gravely with his head on one side.

"No, still grey," he says.

He manages to disencumber himself from the yellow stuff – a nasty kind of netting that reminds me of something but I cannot think what – and Teresa smoothes his hair and clothes (I'm surprised and a little put out by how easily she touches him, anticipating his needs as well as I could myself).

"Goodbye! Thank you!"

"See you tomorrow, Natty!"

There's no need to wonder if the arrangement is a success. Children transfer allegiance so easily; I experience a small stab of hurt. They have even given him a terrible pet name and he seems to like it. Well, I do not own him. And maybe I shall soon make new friends too.

Between Teresa's flat and ours, there's a garden with tasteless gnomes that fascinated Nathan when he first saw them. We had to gaze at them a long time while he told me imaginary stories about them, fishing and hammering and goodness knows what. I don't want to go through all that again so instead I ask him something that's been bothering me.

"How would you describe me, Nathan? If you had to tell somebody else what I was like?"

"Quiet. A bit strict. Old. A bit boring...sometimes." He sneaks a look at me as he says this, not sure if it will be allowed.

"When am I boring?"

"When you go on and on about homework, which isn't fair because you know I'll do it."

This will not do for a seductive thumbnail portrait.

"Ah. Do you have any tonight?"

"Only a story to read and talk about with you. But I've read it already. It's about a prince who's looking for a wife, but she has to pass some silly tests first. Like, she has to sleep on lots of mattresses with a pea underneath and if she can feel the pea it'll mean she's a true princess but if she can't it won't. Why would something like that tell you she's a true princess?"

I'm a bit bewildered myself, but I do my best.

"I suppose it would mean she was very sensitive and could feel her way through things and recognise what lay underneath."

"But if she could get bruised by a *pea* through nineteen mattresses – the story said *nineteen*, Dad! – she'd be really delicate wouldn't she? All her bones would break if the prince even touched her and what use would that be?"

"It does seem rather ridiculous, yes."

"I think it would be a pain. She wouldn't be able to dance with the prince or play with her children."

A ridiculous thought intrudes: *Young lady aristo-crat, sensitive, doesn't like peas, wltm handsome prince.* Stop it, think about your son.

"Would you prefer somebody rough?"

"No-oo, but someone who could make me better if I was hurt would be good. This one sounds like she'd need looking after all the time so she wouldn't be able to care for anyone else. Teresa said something…I can't remember…funny words…" His face screws up in his effort to recall.

"You've talked about the story with Teresa?"

"Oh yes, and Sky…that's it: Teresa said she would be 'high maintenance'. What does that mean, Dad?"

"She would cost the prince a lot of money, wanting special attention and entertainment all the time. Those wishes are not cheap to satisfy, you know. And she would probably keep changing her mind and getting tired of things and asking for new ones."

Nathan is thoughtful. He kicks a pebble off the kerb and watches it roll along and disappear down a drain.

"So why would the prince want her?"

"Perhaps she would be very beautiful and good company for him."

"Would you like a beautiful woman to be good company for you?"

"Why should I need company? I have you."

He punches the number on the entry phone pad and I hurry away from my falsehood.

"I think we have done your homework as we walk along. You may play on the tablet while I get supper."

Friday 7th October 2016

SAFIYA

"Mrs Ahmed, I wonder if you can spare me five minutes, please? I'm Mrs Saltley, we met when you came in to print some photos the other day."

We were leaving, straggling along behind the main crowd. I was surprised to find myself disappointed when no-one we knew waved or came running over. Of course, on Fridays, people are in a hurry to start their weekend.

"Has Xoriyo been naughty?"

I look at her, and she shakes her head emphatically. Not that, then. Xoriyo's own teacher doesn't seem to be around.

Mrs Saltley leads us to a classroom in a part of the school I haven't seen before. Everything here is brightly coloured. Children's photographs and self-portraits are mounted on the wings of butterfly-shaped cut-outs, with uneven writing on the other wing: "*I am Aadem. I am 5. I speak English and Urdu. I like cars and Power Rangers.*" The furniture is tiny and there's a large carpeted area with a big box of bricks and a doll's house. Xoriyo's delighted! A smaller child sits cross-legged, placing careful bricks one on top of the other to make a tower. The child's headscarf is tighter than Xoriyo's and well fastened so that only the oval of her face is showing; she has a long navy skirt and she greets Xoriyo in Somali.

The teacher gestures to the table furthest from the children and now I understand. A Somali woman in a dark grey abaya, I would say younger than I am, sits bewildered at the table and another teacher is there … Of course the other teacher isn't guarding the Somali lady, but that's how it appears. They are silent with each other and both teachers look embarrassed.

"We can't get an interpreter and we need urgently to ask this lady some questions," says Mrs Saltley. "I'm sorry to have to ask you, but we couldn't think of anyone else. I don't know if you know Mrs Osman."

I wasn't aware there were other Somali families in this school, so no, I don't know her. It is only polite to greet her now I'm here, but I wish the school had asked me first if I was willing to get involved.

"Mrs Osman has asked permission to take her daughter on holiday for six weeks, from November 20th, and to return her to school in January after Christmas."

I nod. I see where this is leading and I want even less to do with it.

"Please would you first of all thank her for letting us know her plans. Then explain to her that we do not authorise absences of that length, and if her daughter is away for that period of time we cannot guarantee there will still be a place for her in this school when she returns."

"Please, I am Faduma," says the Somali lady. She looks respectful, frightened, annoyed and puzzled all at the same time. When I explain about the possible loss of a school place she shrugs.

"We have to go for so long because my grandfather is sick."

I'm caught between my wish not to become involved and my doubt whether the grandfather's illness is the real reason for the trip. I look sideways at the happy little girl on the carpet, standing up now. Xoriyo has helped her make the tower so tall it reaches her shoulders and she's jumping with excitement. Any minute it will topple over. The butterfly children stare at us from the walls. A smaller notice board by the only adult-sized chair has staff information: _Assembly times have been changed to 10.15; Epipens are for named individual emergency use only! Staff training: Oct 5th: Phonics. Oct 12th: Safeguarding. Oct 19th: Exploring British Values._ What on earth are British Values?

Mrs Saltley coughs for my attention and repeats:

"In that case please ask her, is it possible for her to go and leave Leylo with relations in the UK? It is not good for a child to miss so much school, and as I say, she may even lose her place here."

I think we all know that's not what we're really talking about. Sure enough, Mrs Saltley takes a deep breath, glances at her hands with their modest engagement and wedding rings, juts out her chin and says directly to Faduma: "I am sorry to have to ask this, but we need to know if you are taking Leylo overseas to be cut?"

I could refuse to have anything to do with this. They should be using a professional interpreter, someone who will not run into Faduma and her daughter in the playground, someone who has been through training on how to ask these questions, someone who can, perhaps, make a real difference to the outcome for this child. The tower falls and the two girls scream with pleasure and mock fear. I don't want them to hear this conversation and I tell Mrs Saltley so.

"Girls, go into the computer room and play *Education City*," she says. But the little one, Leylo, runs to bury her face in Faduma's abaya. The mother's face looks down on her fondly. Quick Xoriyo saves the situation:

"Come, look, we can do this with the bricks now," she points out, setting out a row of bricks to start a house off. "We can make the doll's house some neighbours."

I lower my voice and ask the question.

Faduma looks straight back at me with a reproving expression that could be there for many reasons.

"No. My grandfather is very sick and if we don't travel soon we may not be able to see him again in this world."

It is insensitive to ask why they need to be away for so long, but Mrs Saltley asks me to do so.

"It's what my husband's arranged. He's bought the tickets already. We won't get a refund if we change them."

"But you may lose your child's school place!"

"Yes, I am sorry. We didn't know."

Did they know?

Mrs Saltley sighs. The interview is going round in circles. After saying goodbye to Faduma, who shows no wish to speak any further to me, she asks me to stay behind.

"I'm sorry to have involved you, but there are procedures ... if we think there is any danger of the child being cut, we have to ask and make a report within two days."

Xoriyo is fidgeting at my elbow, waiting to go home. I want her magic carpet to sweep us up and swish swiftly away with us. I want us never to have encountered the ugly issue in the bright classroom.

"I do not actually wish to be involved with this," I tell the teacher. "I don't wish my daughter to over-hear the conversation, for one thing, and I don't wish to interfere in the business of local Somali people I do not know."

Xoriyo looks at me, and then at Mrs Saltley, big-eyed.

The teacher apologises again.

"You understand, though. It's a child protection issue, and there are no interpreters available." As though making a decision she stops, then looks me straight in the eye. "Have you … would you do this to your daughter?"

"No."

This teacher can be absolutely sure of that, whether I help her in this case or not. I know she is only doing her job, though she's not doing it the right way by involving me. I realise too that women like Mrs Saltley are one of the keys to protecting Xoriyo's generation from what happened to mine and to so many before us and so I *should* help her. But I don't want to. I want to shut my eyes, close my memory, pretend there is no issue, pretend nothing ever happened to me and I have never had pain or inconvenience or midwives looking at me with pity in their gleaming eyes.

"And, in your opinion, do you think that's what they're going to do? Such a long trip abroad, with a girl of that age, from your background: three factors that we've been told to look out for … Although it isn't the usual time of year, is it?"

I say nothing.

"Perhaps I was wrong to ask you, if it's something you believe in yourself. And why should I have thought you didn't?"

"I do not agree with it."

"Agree with what, Mum? What are you talking about?"

Mrs Saltley looks surprised by Xoriyo's sudden switch into good English. But she smiles, becomes authoritative again, warm and reassuring.

"Nothing, my dear. Don't worry – I tell you what, would you like to play with this new game while I talk with your mum?"

No, she would not. I am taking her home. The school has been clumsy. There will be too much explaining to do, now, too soon. Xoriyo is too clever not to have spotted something, so it's the beginning of her worming the truth out of me sooner or later. Every true word will take away more of her innocence; every scrap of information will lead to a new piece of fearful knowledge and another step down into the mire of what generations of women have done to each other in the name of virtue and good marriage prospects and because men told them it was right. This is why I cannot think of Somaliland as home in the way my parents did, this cruel practice remains too integral to it. For this reason alone I'd have to think of the imperfect UK as home, as well as because I grew up here.

I wonder, sometimes, whether English people think every day about whether the UK is their home, whether the subject waits to ambush whatever random thing they may be doing. And if so, how many generations does it take for a family to lose the obsession? Or is it an individual thing? Fawzia seems to feel at home anywhere. Clumsy English Teresa, I suspect, doesn't.

Good people like Mrs Saltley are trying finally to stop what happened to me twenty years ago happening to today's little girls. And do I help? No. I don't want to make enemies among the local Somalis, and whatever my personal views, I cannot class my own parents as child abusers. They fed, clothed and housed me; they gave me a faith to live by; they saved me from a war-torn country and supported my university education. They loved me. What they did was wrong, but it was done to my mother and to hers, and she believed it was right to do it to me: is that abusing a child? Now they have passed, is there even any point thinking about it? I don't want these issues in my mind any more than they already are every time I burn as I pass water or clog with hard menstrual blood, any more than I had to in the days of stinging penetration and the bitterness of giving birth for the first and last time. I can protect Xoriyo but for that I have already needed the strength to divorce my husband and move away from my wider family. I cannot now also take on the ills of others – so I must hope the charmed face of the little girl as the tower fell around her will not haunt my dreams. I cannot even assume Faduma wasn't telling the truth. Maybe her grandfather *is* sick, or maybe he is sick as well. Let them take their flight, and let me drift with Xoriyo on a magic carpet above the violent world. The unmarked women of the west must fight the dirty thorns and slicing knives with their laws and their protocols. I have already suffered my fair share of pain.

ALKA

Mummy's on the phone. Again. Nani and Nana brought us in from school and I *must* show her my party invitation because Janki said her mum needs to know how many people are coming. She said they might have garba music so I could wear my chaniya choli. I sit outside my old bedroom on the soft carpet with my back against the door, ready for when Mummy's off the phone. Nana's watching cricket on Sky and Nani is busy with Sunil. It's Friday so they're fasting but Nani's given him a biscuit to keep him quiet. Now he's broken it in half and I can hear him trying to make them eat it too. I think we're making them very tired. Last night I heard Nani go up to bed only just after me.

Mum's voice on the phone is not like when she's trying to explain things to me and Sunil. Then she thinks and she's slow, as though she's threading beads slowly on a string, thinking which word goes best with the next one and not using up too many. Now the sound is fast, high, low, excited or angry or suddenly stopping. But I think the person she's talking to isn't saying much, it's more as though Mum stops because she's dropped all the beads and has to find one – any will do – before she can go on.

"I can't bear to leave the house! I'm so ashamed to let people see me! My face is still bruised and ugly, grey one day, yellow the next, then just when I think it's clearing up I wake up and it's grey again. My eyes are sore… I never went out without make up, you understand? Never! Now, okay, I understand why not on my eyes, I see it's important they don't get infected, but… make up would take attention from the bruises… I know people notice them… Huh…? Yes, I could walk with my head down, but then if the teachers speak to me, or Alka's friends' parents… what will they think? I know it's not my fault. People keep telling me that, saying I've nothing to be ashamed of but you don't understand. Walking around in public showing everyone I couldn't even stop my husband laying his hands on me. I mean pushing me, he pushed me, it wasn't his fault I fell… What? Walk into a door? Oh yes, who's going to believe that? Half the street must have seen the police here… Next door, she looked after Alka, she knows… it's so shameful. To have all those people in the school playground looking at me… Dark glasses? In October? They'll think I'm mad! Everyone knows what dark glasses mean. That's as bad as telling them straight out."

Poor Mummy. Does her face look so awful? I'm used to it now. She shouldn't worry what people think. She shouldn't be weeping. Anyway, I heard her tell Avni it was an accident. So how could it be her fault?

I twist the knob and go in to put my arms round her but she's sitting on the bed turned away from me. In the time it takes to cross the room, I change my mind. The idea of seeing tears on her face frightens me too much. Grownups shouldn't cry ... maybe if I go downstairs and come back later she'll be like Mummy again, and I can ask about the party. I creep away backwards and close the door behind me and it doesn't even click.

If I go in the garden the fresh air may help me breathe quietly again. They said at school, if you're feeling sad, fresh air will help, go somewhere safe and run around or just walk and look at the trees and flowers and feel the wind on your cheeks. The leaves are falling faster now, there are more on the ground than on the trees and you can't see the squashy wet grass between them. The wind has blown newspaper onto the garden; it looks untidy and sad and I want to make the poor garden feel better again. Also, if I help with things, maybe people will help me. The side gate is open and the boxes and bins are at the front because the bin men come on Fridays and I go through to throw the newspaper away. There's the close stretching out in front of me and now I'm by myself it looks wider than when we set out together for school, me between Nani and Nana or with Sky and Teresa. I tiptoe to the edge of our drive, where Dad puts the front wheels of his car because Mum's takes up so much space ... Mum hasn't had her car out for a long time. I think last time was when she used to drive us to school and we watched other children walking and sometimes it took so long to park they got there the same time we did. But Mummy said she had to have the car because she was going straight to the gym after, or straight to coffee, or straight to have her nails done and then in the evening she would show us the nails on the steering wheel each with a long line of light gleaming down the centre that moved across as she turned every corner.

When I look back, no one has come out. I could walk along slowly for a look at the other houses. If I go just three along, I can see into Mandeep's where they have a golden picture on the wall that I like, and if I go a bit further I can just see the main road and the buses and lorries… It seems different. My own road that I've lived in since I was a baby is mine to explore by myself for the first time, but the light is greying and I can hear my breath. Each normal size step feels it's putting a huge distance between me and our house, so I take smaller steps. There are more papers blowing near Mandeep's house, I'll go just that far and pick them up to be helpful and then I must run back because I'm not really a naughty child and anyway Mummy must have stopped crying by now. I step past next door's drive and the low wall on the house after that. I used to walk along it but I'm not going to make people notice me. Anyway they have a prickly plant with red berries that's grown up close to the bit I walked on so my feet might not fit any more – when did that happen? Haven't I walked on that wall for a while? Doesn't Sunil walk on it either?

I'm tiptoeing forwards. I only have my slippers on and I'm trying not to touch the pavement much because the wet will come through and Mummy will know I went outside in them. Now I'm at Mandeep's house but although the curtains are open the light isn't on and I can't see the picture. I'll be in trouble soon – just to those papers to tidy them up then I'll go back and no one will know. It's only my road, I'm quite safe. But I'm not old enough, I'm not supposed to be out here by myself until I'm ten, Daddy said. But Daddy won't be home for a long time.

Bad men might come like the policeman at school said, or a big dog … there could be someone behind me, creeping silently along and ready to snatch me away like the little girl in the newspaper or take me to the forest and leave me there like Snow White or Hansel and Gretel, but I have no Hansel to help me find my way home with pebbles and hard crumbs of white bread … I grab the paper and twist round before I'm so scared I wouldn't dare move ever again and I run as fast as I can slipping sideways on leaves so my foot shoots out and I only just stop myself falling. I get to my house and the side gate is still open and in through the back door where my wet slippers leave grey smears on the kitchen floor. The paper is still in my hand but I'm not going out there again to put it in the recycling box and now it's me who's crying because I'm frightened to death as they say, yes, I've frightened myself to death and I need my Mum and I run in and she's still sitting on the bed but there are no tears on *her* face and she says "Why Alka what on earth …?" and I throw myself at her arms and I notice she shivers a tiny bit but at last she goes from still to moving her arms round me and that must be the first time for ever so long.

"... I tell you she came in with it, in her hand, just a bit of wet crumpled litter but something made me look. Yes, tomorrow, they're gathering at the park gates and marching along the main road ... so now I have to face violent men outside and in, there's no getting away ... police? What can they do? They allow this march, they say it's freedom of speech and as long as there's no violence ... Yes, of course, they're still violent men, their thoughts are violent, what they want to do to us is violent. This is the last thing I need right now. Alka will have to miss her party, that's all, I'm not letting my mother and father take her ... no, no cars allowed, the road will be closed ... I've hardly been out yet as it is and if you think anyone, anyone from this house-hold is going out while those people are in the neighbour-hood ... I didn't know because they didn't tell me ... I don't watch the news. I suppose they didn't want to upset me. Alka didn't tell me about the party until today either ... that is what Hitesh has done. When he struck me – when I got pushed – it's separated me from the rest of the family, I don't know what's going on ..."

When I was so upset we cuddled and she soothed me and let me lie down next to her on my own bed and we talked about school and my homework and at last she let me tell her the Rapunzel story. She listened so, so carefully. All the time she was asking, "But can't the princess escape this way? Can't she escape that way?" and each time I had to explain, no, it wasn't possible, the tower was too tall, there was only one window, the witch's magic was too strong, the prince hadn't arrived yet, then when he did arrive he didn't know what to do and her hair wasn't long enough so they waited for it to grow and then they thought it wasn't strong enough but at last ... Mummy sounded so happy when the princess was finally out of the terrible tower, riding away on the bouncing back of the beautiful horse with her arms around the prince's waist and the witch trapped behind her own high garden walls. They had snapped her wicked broomstick in two so she could never fly to hurt them again.

"Ah," Mummy breathed softly, "you see, all was well in the end because the prince was so brave and clever."

"It was Rapunzel who thought what to do," I said. "She was the clever one and the one who put up with a man climbing up her hair. That would have really hurt!"

Mummy seemed surprised.

"Well, ok, I'll agree with you Alka. What a lucky prince he was, when he had the task of freeing a prisoner, to come across such a clever and beautiful one."

"And she had wonderful hair too!"

Mummy pulled her own plait over her shoulder and stroked it, and then she ran her hand down my loose hair.

"But I don't think Rapunzel's was like yours, my own little princess." It was lovely to hear her call me that again. "Because the prince would have slipped, on the oil. So I'm not sure you can act her yourself, because she must have had yellow hair."

"There's no oil on my hair now. Nani hasn't put any and neither have you, for ages."

"That explains the knots and tangles then. We must do it tonight."

But she didn't move, so I thought maybe I *would* be able to act Rapunzel. She paused, thinking which bead to slip on our string of talk next. I hoped she would choose a nicer one this time.

"And so how will you tell the story, at school?" she asked, and I told her, we are all supposed to do it together, the whole family.

She said that sounded wrong, to her. "You've told me so well by yourself, you don't want the silly grownups taking all the credit. And anyway, we have no handsome prince. Although there's every chance I'll still look like an ugly witch by then…"

There were two things I wanted, to go to Janki's party and to have help with my story. The party is tomorrow, so it was more urgent to ask about that. First I said what I knew she wanted me to say even though it's not quite true: "You *don't* look like an ugly witch!" Then I told her about Janki's party invitation. Three o'clock tomorrow. They need to know straight away.

"Of course you must go, princess," said this new kind Mummy. "Go and find the invitation so I can check you've got the time right. Unless it's that bit of paper you've been holding all this time?"

I was still clutching the leaflet I'd picked up outside Mandeep's house. I gave it to her and ran downstairs to find the invitation from all those days ago when Janki handed them out. I ran back upstairs breathless but the door was shut again. While I was rooting through my bag, she'd started another phone call. Now here I am outside on the soft carpet once more, back against the door, legs sticking out waiting as though we never had our cuddle, we never had our story together. I'm listening to my mother's up and down phone voice shrieking at her friend about bad men stopping me going to the party. So there *were* bad men out there tonight... This time I don't cry, I don't think of going in to ask her to make it better.

I think: I must just be brave like a clever princess and if I cause no trouble maybe an answer will come, like when you wake from a dream.

SATURDAY 8TH OCTOBER 2016

Mr Chan

Unfortunately our Friday night treat, from a different source to our usual one which is closed, I believe for a family bereavement, backfired on us and we have both been up in the night with upset stomachs. Nathan was very distressed because he has had few such complaints in his short life and was worried when his pyjamas were soiled I would be angry with him. Some children, I understand, are forever puking and messing themselves but fortunately once babyhood was over this has not been a problem for us and so I suppose he was unfamiliar with the sensations – and indeed the effect. Feeling none too happy myself, I changed sheets and washed and made up a sugar salt solution which of course he thought was revolting. Perhaps he also thought it was part of some punishment for losing control… I tried to reassure him. I was just reflecting, this is when a child needs his mother, this is when I am not adequate when – goodness me! – I was caught short myself and had to run from his room! When I returned he was asleep and this morning he was almost his usual happy self again, although I noticed he only nibbled the piece of dry toast I gave him for breakfast and did not ask why there was none of his usual fruit and cereal.

Children's health is so dramatic! One moment they're ill, and the next everything is fine. The same is true of their moods. Off they go to bed in a temper (to be fair this is rare with Nathan), then wake up serene. Not like an adult. For us once our aches and pains come to the fore they drag dully on in the background and our moods, positive or poor, may be sustained for days, even months. We should live in the moment, as children do.

Anyway neither of us is feeling one hundred percent, as I explained to Teresa when she phoned to ask us round this afternoon. We have seen such a lot of this lady and her daughter and it is of course a success, but I was at first surprised she wanted still more of our company this weekend. (It's a shame she didn't suggest tomorrow, when I might have been able to leave Nathan there while I had a date in town – an enticing possibility has arisen that I should like to capitalise on.) I understood Teresa's kind thought better, once I had been downstairs to fetch the wet wipes we keep in the car and seen the appalling leaflet lying in the foyer among the usual mailshots and free newspapers. This march will go straight past our living room window and it will be difficult to keep Nathan from noticing it, whereas tucked away at Teresa's end of the close he needn't even have known it was happening.

SAFIYA

"Shall I do the bedroom if you do the living room?"

Xoriyo hands me my duster and bustles away. I hear her humming as she wipes everything within reach.

I'm rooted to the spot, the duster clenched in my fist on the mantelpiece. Thoughts circle in my head, thoughts that come too often, thoughts that impede me continuing with my day.

Teresa was so keen yesterday – clamouring, I'd almost say: "Please, yes do, do come over tomorrow afternoon. You're not doing anything are you, you and Xoriyo?"

I'd hesitated. Xoriyo timed her pace to mine, kept hold of my hand. She didn't increase the pressure, gave no sign of how she felt.

"By 1.30pm, no later, and stay until 4pm. That would be great!"

I didn't understand why the timing was so precise, but despite living here from the age of two, save that one trip back, punctuality is an English obsession I have never understood. What's a few minutes here and there? I fit in with it for work or I would lose my job, and for Xoriyo's school as part of the give and take between school and families, but for a social visit it's a bit, well, anal.

I wipe the duster slowly over the carved wooden box my mother gave me and replace it on the shelf. There is everything to like. Teresa lives in the same road, she's also a single parent, our daughters are in the same class, she has been kind. But there's some-thing … too insistent. She is needy. It makes her unattractive. I ought to be truthful. Her neediness reflects my own, but I recoil from viewing myself as lonely or at risk.

She walked home with me most mornings and evenings this week. Twice she wasn't there. I think she said her daughter had started the after-school club. One day Auntie was just ahead. Auntie loves to talk but she and I don't quite know which words to choose. She didn't turn round. Was it because Teresa was already chatting away at my side, or because her husband was with her and even though he's kind, a male presence changes things for us all?

Teresa would have helped the words go back and forth, Mr Auntie or no Mr Auntie. Uncle? How silly.

I know had I been at school with Teresa, she wouldn't have associated with me. And I and my friends would have kept away from her, initially from hurt feelings, then from dislike. How could we like white people who hated us …? Although, the UK signed up to the Geneva Convention. In what they call "the war" they took in Jewish refugees … later they took my own family in as refugees, and although the process my father told me about was neither assured nor warm, it was speedier than it would be now. In a nation that proclaims such values, surely not all the individuals can hate us. Yet I have few friends who are not Somali. Even during my pharmacy studies I lived at home with my mother and did not mix with other cultures except to explore the properties of drugs and interventions, the legal requirements, the structures of corporations, and to take exams, each in our private silence.

Even if most parents told children of Teresa's age not to play with us, some of them must have changed over time: there have been so many initiatives and support groups and well-meaning events, during my education and now during Xoriyo's. Teresa wouldn't have mixed with me in childhood, but hopefully by now she – and I – have been educated out of our prejudices. There is nothing, nothing at all in Teresa's behaviour to me that suggests she objects to the colour of my skin or my mother tongue or my culture, or even my religion, loathed and divisive though the national media now appear to find it.

And yet...I sense...that not only is she needy, she also hangs around me because she's intrigued? Now she's grown out of fearing me, or being disgusted, she's free to find me exotic and fascinating and she wants to earn Brownie points for associating with me? Brownies! Where do I get that expression from? I was never in the Brownies!

My ill will is disproportionate.

Her curiosity gives me a welcome opportunity to spread Somali culture, show off, impress! Or would that be boasting, any more pleasant in me than the voyeurism I sense in her?

It's always possible that she's motivated by simple friendliness, making my doubts even more unjust.

My circling thoughts always return to the same thing: my family could not have gone back. My daughter was born here. London is the nearest to anywhere we can call home. We must make of it what we can.

At Xoriyo's age, it's less subtle. White children are still being told not to play with black by their parents, and often by other white children. They'll follow the crowd regardless of what the teachers say. At school, Teresa's daughter may exclude Xoriyo from her group of friends. I cannot inflict that on her at weekends as well as in the classroom.

I thought it was what I'd been aiming for, the bittersweet isolation of this flat so many tube stops from the clan that was my own and the sub-clans that were not. I thought I wanted to integrate. Now others are trying to integrate with me, and I'm holding back.

"You're going really slow! Come and look, I've done the whole bedroom and the hall!"

The paintwork here is too shabby ever to gleam, but she's done a good job and she bounces with satisfaction. I'll go over the furry dust higher up later, not to hurt her feelings.

"Well done, my angel! Now, shall we make a bas-bosa cake for Teresa and Sky this afternoon? Run and check we have all we need!"

I can make basbosa cake with my eyes shut, and over the years I've taught Xoriyo so well I now hardly have to do anything. When she was tiny she only ran her finger round the bowl to lick out the mixture: now she takes charge, batting me impatiently with a tea towel to criticise my slowness, pouring half the hot sugar syrup and then standing back to check she's covering the surface evenly. The cake emerges from the oven golden and fragrant; the flat smells of comfort and we share a warm square straight from the tin.

"Look, two big-chinned greedies covered in crumbs."

Our selfie, which I thought would celebrate tall mother and smaller daughter gazing at each other proudly, eyes glowing as we cook good food together, is ridiculous, but Teresa and Sky will surely enjoy our gift.

The letterbox clunks as we're going downstairs with our box of cake and Xoriyo scoops up some leaflets. How many new windows, pizzas and carpet cleaning services do people think we need, in our small flat with my small income? How many invitations to have our property valued, join a gym, or meet the god of the smart-suited Jehovah's Witnesses who ring the doorbell every weekend? I bend to put all such offers straight in the recycling box but as I straighten up, Xoriyo already running away from me into the close, one catches my eye and the pleasure glow from our cooking cuts out like a fused light.

It shouldn't be a surprise. Since June I've read more often of women's headscarves torn away, of restaurant staff threatened (after the abusers have scoffed a good meal), of stones like the one thrown last week. Yet each time is like the first time I heard of such things when I was younger than Xoriyo. I shiver in fear of violence and counter-violence, in shock that the cosy domestic morning can be so rapidly punctured, in cold anger that such stupidity exists. Today, the anger is uppermost.

On Teresa's doorstep I'm sharp.

"I'll leave Xoriyo here, if I may, I have things to do."

"Oh! I hoped you'd both stay. Now my little party's really spoilt – Nathan and his father are both ill and can't come either…"

"All the more cake for you, then."

I push Xoriyo to offer the box of cake and, taken off balance, she thrusts it into Teresa's hands like a weapon. They both look at me in surprise.

"Come in just for a minute, anyway, please."

Teresa holds the door so wide and so firmly that to leave I'd have to make a complete turn to get away from her offer and her daughter who stands behind her, waiting to see what will happen.

She tells Sky to take Xoriyo in the living room and through an open door I see toys and cushions spread out invitingly. She leads me through into a kitchen at the back; I do not want to follow, no. But an invisible thread of unwilling politeness pulls me. She makes no move to put a kettle on, but stares at me.

"You invited us so we wouldn't have to see this!"

I brandish the disgusting leaflet at her, my hands shaking.

"It seemed a good idea. At this end of the close we may not even hear them, whereas it's in front of your living room window."

"That's my problem, not yours!"

"I wanted to get your daughter out the way. She doesn't need—"

"She'll have to grow up with it."

"But she doesn't have to start yet."

We're both silent. Teresa's right, why impose this on Xoriyo while she's still so young? And yet, what does Teresa know about how to face up to such people? What gives her the right to keep barging into my business, this overweight smoker who loses her daughter's pets and who I know is on a pretty high dose of Citalopram from the prescription I filled when I was doing relief cover down the road. Let her sort out her own problems, whatever they are, before taking decisions on *my* behalf, about the welfare of *my* daughter! In the back of my angry mind I know it's not Teresa I'm so furious with, but it's Teresa who's here now, an unmissable target, slumped against her kitchen counter with her untidy hair and her freckly flesh but also with a quality I didn't expect. More than courtesy: dignity.

She swallows and her calm voice stings me.

"You still have time for a cup of tea, if you want one? With this delicious looking cake you've brought? Before you take your daughter – Xoriyo, did I say it right? – away again?"

I do not often lose control. I realise I'm close to it now, and I too lean against the counter to steady myself. I look down, breathe deeply and consider. I can hardly ask her to look after Xoriyo while I storm off in a huff.

My words come out as a stupid mumble.

"I must go and show I have a right to stand there, and witness, and tell them what I think. Otherwise they've won."

"I'd offer to come with you, but I'm not taking my daughter into a situation like that."

Unspoken: *and neither should you.* She sets out two mugs and plates and switches on the kettle, reaching behind me with an apology. Perhaps it's the apology that finishes me.

"The point is – I'd rather come here because we were friends than because you pity me as a poor Muslim woman who has a fascist march going past her front window. And if you're going to knock on my door, protect me with your company walking home, even help me wash my fucking curtains, I'd rather it wasn't because you were showing me how fair and anti-racist and, like, condescending *welcome to my country* you are, but just because we get on, as friends, like any parents of children in the same class!"

"And who do you think my friends *are*, then?" she counters, voice a bit higher, eyes now more angry than hurt. "Who do you think there is, nowadays, to be friends with round here?"

"Well don't do it just because I'm all you can get!"

"You *are* just about all I can get, actually! I didn't grow up here, I told you, my Nan did. We came here a year ago after she left me the flat. Lucky us, to have it, since I'd just split with my husband. But I don't know anyone, or not many people, any more than you do. Everyone in this street's more settled here than I am, even if they do come from all corners of the globe! Everyone – well, nearly everyone – has some cosy happy family life, they're not interested in me and Sky and our problems. You don't have a monopoly on being lonely, you know, just because you're a fucking Muslim woman living for god knows what reason on your own without a man!"

The girls are standing in the kitchen door, big-eyed and absolutely still. Xoriyo dives a sudden swoop at me, throwing her arms round my hips, head down hard on my chest and Teresa reaches her own arm protectively round Sky.

We're united in shock that our daughters need to comfort us for our behaviour.

I stroke Xoriyo's hair. It's hard to apologise to a child. For the moment I can't do so directly.

"Teresa's put our cake out, look." I make my voice as steady as I can. "And you're invited to stay and play with Sky while I go out. What were you doing in the living room?"

Xoriyo's head comes away from my chest. She checks me over with a careful look and takes her cue. How I love my responsive child! She's always known how to find the path that will skirt around the damage.

"We were playing with Lego. I helped Mummy make the cake. I can show you how, if you like …? When we've finished making the castle in the other room …?" She looks at me and I nod. But who am I to bestow approval after the scene I've just caused?

Teresa takes the baton.

"That'd be lovely, I can tell I'm going to love your cake."

She puts a piece in her mouth and I watch her struggling it past the tension in her throat. Her silence gives the space I need.

"The thing is," I say directly to Teresa, pretending not to care what the girls think, "they want us to hate each other. It suits their purpose."

"All the more reason not to. Girls: your mums had a silly row but it's fine now. Pretend you didn't hear it, we said bad words and nasty things but now it's over."

She looks at me over Sky's head: it *is* over. We're friends, of a sort, of what sort remains to be seen. It takes a little time, not surprisingly, to settle the girls back with their castle and their juice and cake, for Xoriyo to relax about staying in this house of storms without me. Then Teresa clears her throat.

"Well, if you *are* going down there, it's due to start in fifteen minutes."

More quietly, in the hall: "You know your daughter is safe here with us."

As she opens the door we see her neighbours on their front drive: the little Indian girl with the lady who must be her grandmother. The child is beautifully dressed in vivid mirrored satins and sparkly slippers, but her face is sulky and her hair a tangled mess. "Bird's nest", my mother used to call the long unbrushed hair of such careless girls and women.

"Hey Alka."

Teresa has so many voices! This is a gentle tone I haven't heard before. "How are you? You're looking very smart today!"

The grandmother, tired and worried. "She dressed herself up to go to her friend's party, but her mother won't let her go."

I'm curious, and Teresa's having a think. "Well, that's a shame, Alka, but I tell you what. Why don't you come in and have tea with us? Sky has another friend round, and we've got cake … I think I know why Mummy doesn't want you out this afternoon, you know, and she's right. It's better to stay indoors, but we can have fun together."

Grandmother and I hold our breath. Now Sky and an excited Xoriyo come running out: "Yes, Alka, come and play! Sky's got a brilliant castle!"

Alka jumps. "You speak English?" and Sky laughs.

"Yes, isn't she clever, she made everyone believe all that time she couldn't!"

"Wow!"

Alka is so surprised she forgets her sulk. I'm pleased her presence will change the atmosphere, after such a row. The children run inside and we three adults smile, spontaneously now. I don't touch people easily, apart from Xoriyo. But I hold Teresa's hand in a gesture of shaking it longer than I'd ever have thought I would. Then I turn to go.

Mrs Kaur

So funny, these men. They get an idea, they don't wait, they want the thing straight away. My husband took the car yesterday and then I found him on the drive, struggling to get his arms around two big boxes to lift them from the boot. He couldn't see over the top and I had to tell him where to lift his feet for the doorstep.

I played the game of not asking what was inside.

"You want a snack?"

I brought chai and warm atta biscuits from the oven. I was baking while he was out getting boxes.

"You want to watch cricket? You want me to massage your feet? Your shoulders?"

He nodded. He was playing the game too. I waited in the sunny chair. I ate my biscuits and made enjoyment noises dunking them in chai. I gazed at the Harmandir Sahib photograph on the wall. I am never tired of looking at this. My husband looked at the cricket on TV and perhaps he was seeing it. We shall never be too old to practise patience, my husband being patient about telling me, me being patient about learning what he has done. I went to the kitchen to wash up before the school run, and the boxes were in the hall. I pretended not to notice but when we went to bed there they were in the middle of the carpet in our room. "My days you want me to fall over those things?" I said in my joking voice and he smiled his lazy smile and he still did not tell me.

Today is Saturday, with sunshine again and a clear sky. It would be a nice afternoon for the autumn colours in the park but Aman and my husband both say no. It's only half past two and Mandeep and Gurdeep have been kicking round the house all day already. They are good boys but today they are tired of their tablets, their play station and all the electronic things, new ones more expensive every year. Only one I understand is TV.

"You should do your homework, Gurdeep," my husband tells him. "It's a chance to get it done and leave you free tomorrow."

But Gurdeep has the laptop open to talk to his friends on his Facebook thing. He tells us they're not going out either. Every time Gurdeep looks up from Facebook and starts to tell more of what his friends are saying, Aman's big eyebrows frown at him so he stops. Then he groans because Aman takes the laptop away.

"Everyone come to the big table," Aman says.

We eat at the polished table in the back half of the living room at special times like Diwali or on birthdays. Otherwise we don't use this part of the room much. It's a quiet place for the boys' homework

or I used to protect the table top and then cut material there, but I buy my salwar kameez now and I
have enough saris for many years to come. I haven't
done sewing for a long time, but I think maybe I will
sew something soon because it's a calm stretched
out thing to do, not hot and quick like cooking and
there is pleasure in making something that lasts, is
not gobbled down the moment it's finished.

The doors in the middle of the house are usually
open to light both ends of the living room. From
the front bay you can see right down the close to the
main road. In this close the bigger smarter houses
like ours are furthest from the traffic. One big
house has been made into flats where Teresa lives
but others mostly have families like ourselves and
the Gujarati family where the police came.

From the bay window you can see who is coming
up the close, or who is leaving their house. You see
the bus go past at the end and you know if there is a
traffic jam. I like to watch, thinking of the journeys
people make. Some journeys take a long time, you
start with the noisy main road and the motorway to
the airport, then you take a plane to India, America,
all over the world. You see the family you haven't
seen for years, the new baby, the wedding with jew-
els and gold, with luck you catch the old people in
time to get their blessing and say goodbye, then you
stay in the country to look around. You see all the
changes and new buildings and what is better or
worse since your last visit... Or there are the little
journeys people make, to the corner shop for milk,

to post letters in the box for a journey of their own, to the gudwara for more cooking in the langar and to pray...All the big and little journeys are mixed up together on the main road with lorries and cars and silly cyclists coming inside the lorries so some days one of them gets killed.

"You are like the little old lady on the TV series," my husband teases. "You watch what happens in the close and at the junction to the main road and if a murder happens you will be able to tell the police everything."

"Do not joke about murder even for a story," I reply, but I do like that programme.

Today I take a quick look and I'm surprised because there's no traffic on the main road, it's all quiet. Usually there are so many cars and lorries and buses, so many rumbling engines and screeching brakes and fumes.

Today Aman shuts the middle doors.

He puts his finger on his lips. "No questions."

Ah, now we'll find out what the big boxes are, placed waiting on the shining table. Gurdeep comes in slow; he's nearly a teenager now, he has to look like he doesn't care. But Mandeep hops up quick on a chair and goes bang tap bang tap all excited. The boxes are so big if you sit on a chair one side you can't see the person opposite.

Aman and my husband stand by a box each and use their keys to slit the cardboard. Whoosh it goes opening suddenly like a zip. Aman wins, you have to be strong against thick cardboard but for a moment he and my husband were like two planes taking off next to each other from the tarmac, what do they call it? Synchronised! Then Aman zoomed away younger and stronger. They look at each other very pleased when the flaps are open. Then they are unpacking corrugated card and many shreddings, maybe from important documents. Mandeep starts throwing paper everywhere.

"No no, Mandeep, we must be careful. Go slowly, not to damage what's inside."

My husband lifts a waterproof bag from his box, puts his big palm under to support whatever is inside and places it gently on the table. Mandeep is more and more excited! He takes the corrugated card, puts it on his head and wags his ears about. Then my husband unzips the bag, and lifts out a beautiful new Kacchi dhol with drumsticks and a strap.

"Ah … aaah …" We make a similar sound as one.

"Now, who is going to try this?"

My husband has a smile I learnt a lovely word for in the English class and never forgot: *beam*. My husband is *beaming*. Mandeep is jumping up down up down.

"No, these dhols are expensive and you will break them if you're silly. So Gurdeep first."

He fastens the strap on the dhol and hangs it round Gurdeep's neck. The strap fits diagonally across his chest and under his armpit, tickling probably. Gurdeep is not sure, I think, if he likes it or not, and he tries tapping the skins of the dhol both sides with different fingers like he's seen at weddings.

"No," says my husband, "for this one you have sticks. This one is called *tili*," and he shows a thin cane stick, "this one *dagga*." The dagga is a thicker, crooked wooden stick and my husband shows Gurdeep which end to hold. "For you it will be best with the dagga on the left side and the tili on the right. The dagga keeps the beat and the tili makes higher sounds."

He takes the sticks and beats a rhythm on the ends to show. The first rhythm my husband beats echoes strong against the wooden floor and the table and echoes strong too in my head. It repeats, repeats and keeps repeating and I think back to the dancers who came to my wedding, then back further to the servants who taught me their style of dancing when I was a little girl and I think why didn't we have drums when Aman was small? Many other families did. Well, now we are going to change all that!

Mandeep is sensible now, standing still hardly breathing so he'll be given something from the next box. Aman lifts out another, smaller, drum, both ends the same size this time and no sticks.

"This one's called a *dholak*. Now, are you going to be careful? Ok, sit cross-legged on the floor."

My husband starts to push the table across the carpet to make more space and Aman stops to give him a hand because lifting it is better for the legs. When they turn back Mandeep is sitting like a natural on the floor with the dholak. Already he's trying it, tap tap tap putting out long fingers, arched fingers, trying different places on the skin, hard, softer, harder. Gurdeep watches and begins to get the rhythm too. He goes tap tap tap tap with the tili and bangs hard with the dagga but my husband says *no no, just a bit lighter please.* I'm laughing and then tears come suddenly too and I slip back to the front room to fetch the tissues from the coffee table. I just stop there one minute because I think I hear more drumming and banging from the road, but they are not like the gentle sounds my grandsons are experimenting with. My husband comes. He takes my hand firm and strong.

"You come back and we will play you a concert."

In the back part of the lounge with the middle doors closed we can't hear the banging from the front anymore. I forget it quickly because Aman and my husband make me sit one side of the table between the boys. We are the audience now. My husband hangs the Kacchi dhol round his neck; he has to change the strap because Gurdeep is not yet quite his height. Aman sits cross-legged on the floor with the dholak, he is so quick and graceful, with his back to the glass doors and light shining in on him like a hero in a fairy story. He nods to his father to let him start and my husband begins with a light tap tap tap, then a little bit more and Aman has his ear on one side to listen and the boys are holding their breath. Aman chooses a good moment to come in, he begins with his fingers and palms so little and light, then faster, brighter. He must have been practising to get so good! Mandeep slips off the chair and finds space to slap down his feet, dancing with his whole body now. Gurdeep is too embarrassed for that but he leans forward with his elbows on his knees, head nodding, nodding. I clap to the beat and my feet begin too, tiny slap slaps on the floor where the men can't see. Then sitting on the dining room chair my arms stretch out, stretch out and my wrists are moving, twisting to make tiny signs, discreet inside my sleeves so no one knows I'm dancing except me. My husband does one beat, I do one movement, he does the next beat, I do the next movement and Mandeep looks and copies me, just our dance we're doing together, Mandeep on display and me in secret. Everyone's heads are nodding bang tap bang tap … Gurdeep finds a bhangra track and my husband and Aman play with that behind the drumbeats and Mandeep is still dancing, Gurdeep is still tapping on the table to join in.

I peep in the box because there is one last parcel they forgot but my husband spots me and grins and takes two beats out to wag his finger at me. Another secret! But they are off again, tap, pat, pat, tap … When the bhangra stops they look at each other so satisfied, the loving father and son and grandsons, all happy together.

Now there's no more noise, only the memory of them playing in my head. Mandeep dances off through to the front of the house and this time no one stops him, Aman opens the middle doors, the sun shines on the Harmandir Sahib and all is quiet and sunny in the street. Maybe I imagined the ugly noise before, the only music was us, a happy Punjabi family playing music together.

When I look in the box again the last parcel has gone.

SAFIYA

Walking away from Teresa's, I hear shouting from the main road. From here, it's just noise. I can't tell who I'd be waiting with.

Fifteen minutes. That's longer than you'd think. But I can't pop home, since the last thing I want is to give away my address when a marcher spots me locking my front door. And I can hardly go back to Teresa's.

Between here and the main road is no man's land. I've left the dressing room; I'm not yet on stage, where I will ... what? Make a gesture, shout a slogan, just stand, visible, or perhaps, be booed away.

I walk, self-consciously slow, along this quieter part of the pavement I never used before taking Xoriyo to Teresa just now. Perhaps I look out of place, but it's quiet, there's no one outside washing their cars like I see from my back window most weekends, no one chatting to their neighbours in the easy-looking conversations I've envied. This part of the close is more prosperous, more private than my rented patch. Most front gardens are paved for parking, but they must once have been pretty, and one still has grass. Not only grass: Xoriyo stopped on our way up to point out the stone gnomes and the wishing well, the toadstools and the wooden tubs of flowers. I inspect them now: chipped and faded, they must have been put there years ago with love and for fun. Their owner's grandchildren enjoy them now, perhaps. A face glances from the down-stairs window. I can't tell if the woman knows I was only passing time looking at her gnomes. She didn't smile; she showed no visible malice either.

Nonetheless I move on.

At the bottom of the close, instead of turn-ing onto our path, I stroll through the pedestrian entrance of the flats opposite, past the "Private: Access for Residents Only" sign. The landscaped borders bulge with healthy shrubs and the gravel lies obedient on the paths. Some ground floor flats have private patios with tables and parasols and there's no clutter of bikes and clothes horses on the upper balconies, as we had in the flats we've just left. The blocks look on to an oval courtyard. I walk as slowly as I dare around the inside of the oval, feeling I'm being watched, but I see and hear no one inside this development. Noise swells from the main road, on the far side of the blocks that shelter me. Harsh shouting, one group dominating, another taking over: there's obviously a code of behaviour but now the slogans blur in a cacophony of different voices and I don't follow. Whistles blow and whoops and hoots ... If I close my eyes it could be just a football match playing too loud on someone's TV.

Things are kicking off, then.

I've been sensible and have very little money on me, but I keep my phone to hand. I pause for a quick prayer and three deep breaths. I walk purposefully past the big white stones placed on the verges against unwelcome parking and away from the shelter of the flats.

I'm on the main road. The pavements on both sides are lined with people.

Nobody notices me at first; they have their backs to me as I pass along behind. Where can I stand? I want to be seen, I'm here to defy these brutes by my visible presence, a headscarf-wearing Muslim woman here, a flesh and blood banner proclaiming I'M NOT AFRAID OF YOU! But there are no gaps in the crowd where I can show myself at the kerb. Now among the shouts there's music, brass instruments and drums. It's cheerful, I detect good humour, a burst of laughter at a slogan shouted through a megaphone. There are more police than I'd expected, and another surprise is how relaxed they seem, joking with the onlookers. I'd steeled myself for something more threatening. I thought I was being brave, but this feels more like the carnival Xoriyo and I went to last summer in Mile End.

A tall young man turns and grins. He's so thin you wouldn't see him if he stood sideways. "Want me to make room? You won't see much – there's only going to be about thirty of them," are the words I hear but I don't at first realise he's talking to me because, well, because apart from when I was at

university, young white men usually don't. I hesi-
tate ... He misunderstands.

"It's ok – if they look like they're going to throw
anything, we'll shield you. They won't dare though –
look how many of us there are!"

He looks so insubstantial I can't see how anyone
could find his bravado a threat but I'm beginning to
understand – this is a counter demonstration and
what it lacks in muscle it certainly makes up for in
number.

"Here, Mum, move over," he tells an older woman
next to him. Another surprise! It's Mrs Saltley from
the school. She greets me as though it was just an
ordinary day in the playground, and sighs.

"I wish we didn't have to be here, but since we
do, isn't it brilliant there are so many people and the
police are so relaxed? I've not been to one of these
things for years, but Rob told me to come and it's
true, the opposition's more impressive if it isn't just
young students."

She pauses. "But you, you shouldn't make yourself vulnerable. You haven't brought ...?"

I shake my head. It occurs to me if I had put
Xoriyo in potential danger by bringing her here,
the friendly, reassuring teacher might be inves-
tigating my parenting just as she had Faduma's. I
walk such a narrow line between being trusted by
those in authority, and being typecast even by the
more thoughtful, well-meaning of them. As for the
police, she's right, they are relaxed. But I've seen
too many Somali men and boys on the wrong end

of rough policing to feel much confidence in their presence.

"Is anyone else from the school here?"

"Not many staff, no. They'll say they have too much marking and…many of them are just not political, you know. They put their heads in the sand and don't want to see the connections between things."

The music's louder; the shouting intensifies. The policemen – and some women – are still smiley and joking but they've adopted positions of stiff readiness. Although it's all easier than I'd expected, and I'm reassured to be standing with people I slightly know, I remember the stone that was thrown, the cousin who had her headscarf ripped off, the boy who had an epileptic fit in a police cell and the one who was chased home and stabbed in a stairwell. What am I doing here, away from Xoriyo? I'm a selfish, stupid, bad parent and supposing I do get hurt, I haven't even told Teresa who to contact!

Now the shouting's nastier, the humour's gone. Mrs Saltley too stiffens and sighs she hopes it won't turn ugly. She doesn't shout, herself, just stands, arms folded, contempt on her usually kind face.

"I taught some of these," she tells me. "Sad little bullies then and sad big bullies now. We did our best, but look how they've turned out."

There are probably not even the thirty marchers Rob predicted. A pathetic little posse of tee-shirted pot bellies, their placards barely visible inside the double line of police who surround them as they

march. Anything they shout is drowned by the counter slogans of the crowd and in a strange tinge of
sympathy I realise how frightened they must be,
inside their police cordon. Somebody throws something and it catches one of them in the face and
everybody on both sides flinches until we hear it was
only an egg. Police move swiftly to arrest the egg
thrower amid derisive yells to let him off. Probably
too late, I consider my escape route – dodging back
inside the flats might be best though I couldn't get
inside the actual building. Looking up I see the
Chinese dad of a boy in Xoriyo's class leaning out
of a window filming events on his phone, his son
beside him. Mrs Saltley follows my glance and waves:
"That's Nathan. I taught him last year. Nice little
boy." If it does turn nasty perhaps the Chinese man
would let me in. If he recognised our connection.
But probably to him I'd be just another Muslim
woman in a headscarf.

In the time it took to think *and to me he's just
another Chinese man*, it's over. The motley bunch of
Britain Firsters, hardly an advert for their nation, is
jeered on down the road protected by their unsmil-
ing escort.

Now the crowd stands around smugly, some jiggling to the gentler music, others beginning to move
away. The remaining police stand easy, firm and in
control. I look around and though I don't see any
other Muslim women, there are a few young Hindu
and Sikh men, and several Afro-Caribbean men and
women. I hear what I think is Polish behind me, and

male voices speaking Urdu. They all look pleased with themselves in the sunshine, and now come the incongruous chimes of an ice cream van. The politics of hate provides good business for this opportunist, but I'm so relieved it's over I don't mind. I have just enough money on me to buy for all of us as an additional peace offering when I pick up Xoriyo. I join the long queue of my neighbours and those who have come further to support us.

Mrs Saltley is next to me, equally relieved matters have passed off smoothly, I can tell. Unprompted she begins to tell me about people she's worked with over more than thirty years in teaching.

"It's not just because my son asked me. I also think teachers should make a stand on these issues. If we don't, how can we assure you your children are safe with us? But it can so easily go wrong. I remember a teacher, a young man called Blair Peach, who died at an anti-racism demo the year I started university. There was a mass outpouring of grief and resentment over that, and the police *have* cleaned up how they manage demos since then. Even so I always worry, and I'd stopped coming on them – a mixture of getting older, thinking they don't change anything, and fear. But since the referendum, everything's so much nastier, I thought Rob was right telling me to stand up and be counted. There's a famous saying – do you know the one? – about good men not saying anything."

I know the one. How often have I heard it recently, since June 23rd?

"All it takes for bad men to do evil is for good men to say nothing."

"Something like that, yes. However, we're women, perhaps it doesn't involve us?"

She's laughing but I wonder if it's a dig at me for not helping her more with the business of Faduma's daughter. When you talk as an equal to someone you only know through their professional role, you both have to tread carefully. She takes the first step.

"Let's talk about something pleasanter. How's your little girl getting on?"

I tell her how much Xoriyo's enjoyed making her fairy story book.

"I wish we had time to do more on fairy stories, as we used to. They're incredibly powerful for helping people make sense of their lives. But sometimes too powerful, and we need to teach how to unravel the magic from reality."

In the sunshine the queue has barely moved. She looks along it to judge how long we have.

"I'll tell you a story of my own. When I started teaching it was in secondary schools, in Yorkshire. We had lots of pupils newly arrived from Pakistan, with no more English than your daughter."

We both let that pass.

"We took a group of them on an outing in the minibus to some caves in the Peak District, called the Blue John caverns after a semi-precious stone that's found there. They mine the stone in winter, and in summer guides take groups underground. Two of our new pupils were very beautiful young girls, maybe thirteen years old although a lot of the passports were pretty vague then … These two hadn't understood our instructions for an outdoor trip and they'd turned up in their best outfits. One of them, Amina, had a silky pale pink shalwar kameez and dupatta, and sparkly pointy sandals and she looked so lovely… It was hardly suitable for exploring underground but anyway we went ahead. Before the entrance to one particular cavern the guide warned us he was going to switch all the lighting off and lead us by torchlight, because the rock formations cast spectacular shadows in all sorts of shapes. If we were lucky we might see the shape of a witch riding a broomstick! And there she was, pointy hat and chin – everyone oohed and aahed. It was dark, hard to see what was going on, but as we emerged into the next cavern, the children were all telling me to check these two new girls, Amina and Tasreen. They were terrified, crying and shaking. To them the witch was quite real – I suppose they'd had such huge changes from rural Pakistan to urban Sheffield, and the folk telling traditions were so much stronger there … the guide got a helper who brought the three of us out more quickly because there was no way those two were going to cope with being underground any longer. They were hysterical. It took me ages to calm them down and by that time the others were all out too. I was young and inexperienced and their fear shook me; my whole mindset was so far from understanding how anyone couldn't see it was just a shadow on the wall. Nowadays of course you'd have a risk assessment, but I don't know if that could cater for a witch!

"Anyway, we were just gathering back at the minibus when Tasreen looked at Amina's back and started screaming—"

My phone rings. Automatically I stop listening to Mrs Saltley and answer Fawzia's call. She's seen the march on Facebook and she's checking we're ok since she recognised the route past our house.

"Come on ladies, make your minds up."

I'm muddled, caught between Mrs Saltley's story, Fawzia's call and the need to make choices. You'd think the ice cream man would be pleased to do such good business but he's surly. Quickly I order five cones, fumble with my phone and my money and realise I need at least two more sets of hands.

"Dozy Muslamic cow, get a move on."

The ice cream van man looms over his counter. I probably do look dozy, and certainly shocked but there's a derisive shout from behind: "Muslamic? Go back to school mate and learn the proper words!" and to my own surprise I'm giggling.

"Just go, full stop!"

Mrs Saltley takes three of the cones for me. "And I don't want anything and she's not paying you either, after you spoke to her like that! I remember you, Brett Turner, and when you were in my class you knew better than to talk to anyone that way! Don't you even know why we all came here today?"

Most of the queue turns away in disapproval. The ice cream man slams down his shutter and takes sulking refuge inside. There are a few desultory shouts and someone suggests rocking the van.

"No!" calls Mrs Saltley firmly and at the side of my mind I register better natured laughter at the primary teacher's continuing authority. But I'm in no fit state to return straight to Xoriyo. Mrs Saltley and her son walk me away from the van and sit me down on a low wall. It happens to be outside my flat, but I'm not giving away my address.

"Silly young man. He sounds worse than he is – he's from a nice family you know. His mum only lives up there, the house with the gnomes. She wouldn't be too pleased to hear him talking that way."

Ah, the house with the wishing well... The ice cream drips and I try to laugh, balancing sticky hands and despair.

"You have them..."

Mrs Saltley's son takes the two cones from me and makes a joke of licking them alternately before the drips fall. His dumb show gives me time to calm down.

"Please – finish your story. It'll take my mind off him."

"You sure? Wait..." She throws her cones into what she doesn't know is my bin and produces a packet of wet wipes. "Rob, can you go away a bit, I just want to talk to Mrs Ahmed?"

When he's obligingly moved away, still licking – this boy's tact has a lot in common with Xoriyo's – she goes on.

"So, yes, Tasreen was looking at Amina's back and screaming. All over the back and hem of her lovely clothes there were reddish brown stains. The poor girl had started her period. Tasreen was gabbling at her in Urdu and they clearly had no idea what menstruation was. No one had told them what to expect and it must have been her first time. There were no public toilets and I had nothing with me – honestly I was green! I've never been on a school trip since without pads and tissues and plastic bags but you live and learn ..."

Ruefully I indicate the wet wipe she's passed me for my hands and she nods.

"The other teacher was a man. Neither of us spoke Urdu so I thought it would be more discreet at least not to tell him. But I couldn't think how to reassure the poor girl. So I'm afraid I just got everyone sat down in the minibus as fast as I could, and we dropped her home first and I somehow managed to walk behind her so no-one could see the bloodstains ... when her mum answered the door I just sort of turned her round to show her ruined best clothes and her mum looked very shocked ... It haunts me to this day that those poor girls must have thought the witch in the cave did bad magic that made blood come from – you know. I hope her mum dealt with it sensitively, but god knows what *she* made of schoolteachers taking her daughter to see witches and then that starting."

Not as bad as what happened to me, but we're not competing here. It must have been pretty traumatic.

"Amina was away the next day. When she came back we didn't say anything about it. In fact her English improved quickly and she did well, better than her friend. But it showed me as a teacher to be more aware of girls' needs. Life can be hard enough for any young girl without adding superstition into the mix."

She looks embarrassed. "I wasn't – you know, criticising you for—"

I cut her off. "Poor girl, what bad luck. I'm a pharmacist, you know. I sometimes end up having to talk about sensitive things with people and we don't speak each other's language. It *is* difficult."

"Are you now? But – you'll have to excuse me – was your daughter not born here? There seems to be a bit of mystery around her English—"

"She's very strong willed, Xoriyo."

"You mean she's just not speaking until she's ready? I've taught a few like that, in my time. You can't push them or it gets worse. But it's best not to let it get ingrained, if possible."

"You wait and see. She has some surprises in store for when she does her fairy story. If someone could just help her a bit with the presentation."

Her son's approaching, drips of ice cream hardening on his tee shirt, and out come the wet wipes again. The mess he's got himself into makes us both smile.

"It'll be our pleasure. Well, it's been good to chat to you. You'll be all right now?"

I'll be all right. Two steps forward, one step back. Maybe a hundred steps round the close to Teresa's to find out how the mix has gelled there. And who needs ice cream anyway, when you have basbosa cake?

ALKA

All that time sitting on the special table doing easy work, and Xoriyo can joke and sing and play skipping games in English just like any of us! She taught us one she remembers from her old school. We played it in Sky's garden, on the patch in the middle where the grass is dry.

"Pet…er, Pet…er, pump…kin eat…er…ha d … a … wife … and … could … n't … keep … her," she shouted breathlessly between skips. Then she jumped out and whisked the rope out of Sky's hand and kept it turning as Sky ran in:

"Put…her…in…a…pump…kin…shell…an d…there…he…kept…her…ve…ry…well!"

I was happy to hold the end of the rope because I'm not good at skipping and anyway this *chaniya* is still a bit long for me. I watched Xoriyo and Sky take turns. Sky's stronger and when she jumps she comes down thump and all her body shakes, but Xoriyo's quick, running between the rope at exactly the right time however fast we turn it to try and catch her out. We tried a few more rhymes before going back inside to the castle.

Xoriyo's right, it's great. There's a drawbridge, turrets, winding staircases and even a clever green dragon with plastic flames coming from its mouth. You can put the tiny princess dolls with their pointy hats in different places to hide from each other or make the dragon catch them and then bring a knight with a sword to rescue them.

"Let's make the dragon eat the knight so the princesses rule the castle by themselves."

We make eating noises, Sky's the loudest because it was her idea.

When Sky finally stops munching Xoriyo brings the knight back to life again.

"Otherwise they won't be able to have babies," she explains and Sky makes him kiss the princesses and we fall about laughing. Gross!

Xoriyo calms down first and turns to me. "You're dressed like a princess too, but what happened to your hair?"

"She got caught by a dragon and kept in his cave and he ate her hairbrush ..." Sky is rocking with excitement on her knees, pink cheeked and hot.

Xoriyo looks serious. "If *you've* got a hairbrush we can make it nice again."

She sits on the sofa with me in front of her on Teresa's fat cushions. Gently Xoriyo pulls Sky's brush through my long hair with pauses and tuts, easing matted clumps apart and unknitting the tangled strands with careful fingers. When she has one side finished, Sky brings a hand mirror to show me the glossy waves falling nearly to my waist, and then she begins to make a plait. She's breathing hard into my ear with concentration and she's slower than Mummy – but she's being kind to me! – and the finished plait is even, not too tight or too loose and when she moves round to begin the other side I feel so calm and soothed. Like in a dream, her fingers move across my head, pulling just enough for me to know they're there, not so much it hurts. Now Xoriyo's watching, head on one side, thinking.

"*Mirror, mirror on the wall…*"

"It isn't on the wall," complains Sky and I wish she hadn't interrupted because I was feeling like they had me under a spell, there on the soft cushions with the smooth hairbrush and the quiet words and Xoriyo's huge dark eyes… eyes that shine and think and begin again:

"*Mirror mirror in my hand, Who is the fairest in the land?*"

"Her hair isn't fair, it's black."

The dark eyes do some more thinking. "I think fair means beautiful in the story."

"Hey, your English *is* good, isn't it? What if I tell them, on Monday, you can speak it this well? Make rhymes and everything? Then you'd have to do harder work, like the rest of us."

Now Sky really has broken the spell. Xoriyo doesn't say anything. It's like we were back at school.

"Alka? Do you think it's fair she doesn't have to do hard work?"

Sky always wants people to take sides. It's not what I want us to talk about. I think Xoriyo's been clever to fool the teachers. If that's what she wants to do, it's her business. Perhaps she just likes having Mrs Carmel, the special helping teacher, always nearby, warm and encouraging. I wouldn't have done what she's doing, because I like sitting on the clever table getting praise for the best work, but I still admire the trick she's played. Anyway since everything happened I don't care so much. It's Sky's problem if the work's too hard for her, perhaps she should stop talking when Miss Patel's explaining it to us.

The mirror makes me think of Mummy, always checking her face to see if it's back to how it was before. She used to spend ages on her makeup and now she can't wear it she's got time on her hands, but I don't know what she does with it. In our house everything's the opposite to how it was, Nani doing the work, the bedrooms all changed, Mummy not rushing off in her car to her appointments, Dad not speaking. It's Navratri but no-one's said we'll go to a garba. I know it's very late on a school night, but you'd think just once … or tonight at least because it's Saturday. I'm surprised Nani didn't say we'd go. She must be too tired.

It's like I'm in a story I don't recognise, where I'm only allowed to hear part of what's happening, or there are difficult words like clues in a treasure hunt and you have to work them out to find the answer. Well, that's like at school, only at school they call it comprehension, and I'm good at that. I overheard Mummy again on the phone last night

"... *because he's of previous good character*..." She was talking about Dad. "Previous" means before and she's right, he was good before, like a good character in a story. He isn't home a lot and when he is he doesn't talk, but *I* think – I hope – he's still good, because he's trying to be kind in other ways. I keep finding presents in my school bag, sweeties and bangles. I think they're from him. Then Mum said, "*I'm withdrawing my statement.*" When you withdraw something you take it away and a statement is something you say. So she means she's not saying something any more. It's true, she doesn't say much now, except on the phone. That's why I listen, to hear her voice more.

She talked about *evidence* too: a word I know from school because last year when we did Guy Fawkes they caught him when the barrels of gunpowder were *evidence* he was planning to kill the king. Evidence is proof someone's trying to hurt someone else.

"Alka!"

Sky pulls, not hard, enough to show me she wants an answer.

I want the comforting glow back. "Can't we just carry on playing hairdressers and not talk about school?"

"There is one school thing you do have to think about though, Little Miss Princess." Sky's crossness has come from nowhere. "Natty wants you in his story and time's running out. If you don't say yes soon he's going to use me instead, but I've decided I don't want to."

That might be nice. Nathan's kind and gentle, almost not like a boy at all. He knows I've been sad and sometimes across the table I can feel him trying to make things better.

"He's going to be a king and he wants you for his daughter. All you have to do is look beautiful and then you get turned into gold, and you can't speak any more and he's sorry. But you didn't speak much before, anyway."

Xoriyo watches us, dark eyes still thinking. "Why didn't she speak?"

"Because she was a princess and they don't have to. All they have to do is look beautiful and Alka's better at that than acting. The only thing she has to do is turn into gold. We practised on me last week."

Sky's rummaging in a toy box. She pulls out a long piece of yellow cloth, it looks longer and longer the more she pulls. Xoriyo starts to say something but stops. Together they make me stand up. I'm sad, I can't hold on any longer to the soothing dream when they were doing my hair. We get in a muddle while they're wrapping the material round me. Maybe they didn't mean it to be this tight. Xoriyo fastens it a bit like a sari and when I try to step forward I trip, so she tucks it in the waist of my *chaniya*. They've covered me head to foot, and where my eyes can see through the material everything's gone yellow. I'm surprised how hot it is. When I open my mouth to tell them the sound comes out muffled, and Sky's words are hard to hear too.

"Don't speak, you've turned to gold. Anyway, remember what I said about princesses. That's why I decided not to do it. It's boring if you can't speak."

"Not for me," says Xoriyo.

That's different. Xoriyo chooses not to speak, but they're making me stay quiet. I don't like how it feels, wrapped in hot material so I can't move or talk. Also I'm confused because it doesn't seem like Nathan to want to make someone uncomfortable.

"Now you've got to pretend I'm Natty – he's your dad in the story – and I'm giving you a hug but I'm sad because you can't hug me back."

It's true, I can't. My arms are inside the material. There's a tickling smell like washing powder and my nose itches. I thought it would be good coming in here, not as good as Janki's party but better than staying home with Mummy one minute being kind and the next minute going back to cross again, and Nani all tired and the men not speaking to each other. I've been trapped inside the bad secrets in our house ever since the bad night, and now I've got out but these girls have trapped me another way. Sky spins from friendly to spiteful in seconds and Xoriyo is strange … Even Nathan who I thought was my friend, it's for him they've played this trick on me. Sky's changed the name she calls him, so maybe he's changed too. The washing powder smell creeps up my nostrils and when my sneeze explodes I can't help tripping over onto the floor. Do the girls know when I copy the sound of them laughing I'm only pretending, because I'm desperate not to let them know I'm so lonely inside my brilliant colours and my yellow veil?

TERESA

The girls fuss tenderly over Alka.

"Oh, are you missing Janki's party? Never mind, we can play games here! In the garden, in the fresh air! Who needs a silly party!"

Maybe the kind feeling they get from soothing her wipes away the tension from the grown-up row; anyway, they're getting along pleasantly enough for me to give myself a few quiet minutes in the kitchen.

Even when I sit down my breath still thumps, my stomach's swollen, my fingers fidget. The row shook me, and the effort of putting things back to normal for the kids. Slowly, deliberately, as the counsellor taught me, I set my mind on one thing at a time. Stand up, fetch a cup, refill the kettle. I don't want more tea, I want hot milk with cinnamon sprinkled on top and a spoonful of honey – my mother's remedy for shocks and, sometimes, grief. I use a mug Sky "gave" me at Christmas – with my money of course – but she chose it so I like it. You can be kind to yourself even in small things like choosing a favourite mug for your drink.

Hot milk and cinnamon, to take away the cold feeling. Xoriyo's mother acted like she hated me. Bitch! But… maybe it wasn't me she was reacting to. Maybe it was all the white people who've treated her like shit in the past. All the being kind to yourself in the world wouldn't make up for that. You'd still be a victim. And you'd find it hard to be kind to others—

PING! My hand flies to my mouth and the other one grabs the counter in shock. Between the first and second ping I recognise the sound, but it's too loud, too insistent. I rush to silence it before the third ping. My stress levels must be higher than I thought, lurking beneath the thinnest surface so even a predictable signal from the microwave can make me jump out of my skin.

The children have found calm in being kind to another child. Now I must prioritise being kind to myself. The problems of other adults are out of my league, at least until I've learned how to do that. I wish I could afford to try private therapists until I find someone right. Or until time solves my problems, or I do myself. That free NHS counsellor the GP referred me to was so gorgeous! I had no faith he'd understand my needs, with his blonde hair and flat stomach, his broad shoulders and his confidence. He looked at his watch too often and spoke so calmly it felt like the words came from a machine. When he went on about mindfulness, I got distracted and stopped listening. After two sessions I dreaded any more, and cancelled them. But

something must have stuck because I have been feeling better.

The GP and the NHS counsellor had questionnaires about whether I'd thought of ending my life,
but you can't, when you're single with a young child.
I'm not that far gone, I'd just like some easy adult
company at times. For now I take my milk to the sofa
and watch the children. Maybe I can lose myself in
their safer, kinder world.

They're busy trying to put together as much as
they can for Nathan's story. I heard Sky refuse to
let anyone be in hers, and Xoriyo's is a secret – "It's
about my own family," she whispers mysteriously –
but including Alka in Nathan's is making the poor
child feel wanted. It soothes me to watch them.

Although they do seem to have her rather
trussed up. I loosen the material before the poor
girl suffocates.

Perhaps their play isn't so innocent after all.
People spot a victim so fast! Alka's like me, she needs
to develop a thicker skin. Children are so vulnerable, have to work out so many problems every day,
big ones and tiny ones that matter so much to them.
And adults are no different … It's awful Mrs A and
I rowed in front of Sky and Xoriyo, but I hope at
least we demonstrated how to resolve things. Her
nastiness was the stress speaking, not her. I'd back
her in a fight against anyone. She and her daughter
seem better survivors than Alka and her mum, for
all their lovely home and posh cars and grandparents helping out.

"Girls – why don't you play something else now?"

"OK! Let's play families. I'll be the mummy!"

Sky leaps in, bossy and jostling for position as always. Well, I can't protect the others all the time. Let's see what happens.

"I'll be the baby." Alka makes herself a nest on the cushions, thumb in her mouth, waiting to be cared for.

"I'll be dada!" Xoriyo's gruff voice has us in stitches. "Hang on, Alka, I've got to marry Sky before we can have a baby!"

Alka scuttles over to sit next to me until she can exist again. Sky and Xoriyo get sidetracked into devising an elaborate ceremony so Alka invents her own wedding play with Sky's dolls, which are all female. Simultaneous bridegroom-free weddings take place in my living room. I'm amused and point it out.

"So what? Brides are more exciting than men anyway."

It's hard to argue with Sky on that one.

"Or maybe they're…" I cough really loud and Sky does me the favour of not carrying on.

When their role play begins again, I see Xoriyo's idea of a man's role in the household is as hazy as Sky's. But when they ask Alka for information she just says you don't need one really.

When Sky was smaller and her friends came to play, I had to intervene every few minutes to pat better hurt feelings and bodies. This seems more stable; I tuck my legs under me on the sofa and I become absorbed, a spectator in their imaginary world, taking real pleasure in their pretend successes.

When Mrs A comes to pick Xoriyo up I'll try and make another arrangement, so she knows my invitation wasn't just about keeping them away from the march. I do hope she's ok out there.

MR CHAN

The half-closed blinds make a slatted pattern on the walls in the bright sunshine. The flat is airy and quiet. The cleaner came yesterday and I'm pleased to see no swimming specks of dust. I like the quiet hum of the tumble dryer as it restores the disorder of our disastrous night. Crises over. This should be a weekend of quiet recovery for both of us.

"So I'm better now, why can't I go to Sky's?"

Nathan's disappointment has caused him to mope.

"It's always better to wait a while, after a stomach upset. We'll have some clear soup with noodles later, and if you keep that down we'll go out somewhere tomorrow to make up. Shall I work on your story with you instead, for now?"

My organised flat has fewer potential props than Sky's so we are only discussing, not rehearsing, the method he and Sky have devised to transform her into gold. Then a glance outside tells me the demonstration will have a good number of onlookers. Fortunately our double glazing is so thick it's hard to hear what they're saying.

But my son cannot live in a bubble. This march is unpleasant, but it provides an opportunity for a history lesson.

"Come to the window. Something's happening I want to explain to you."

"Wow, Dad, it's like when they had carnival. Look, balloons! The ice cream van might come. Can I have one?"

"I don't think an ice cream would be a good idea right now. But yes, they do look cheerful. It's not what I'd have expected."

"Open the window so we hear the band!"

I can't see it would do any harm, as things are now.

It is hard to work out how to phrase my explanation of the march in children's terms. I don't want to alarm Nathan, but I want him to arrive independently at the correct response to the demonstrators. I want him to link Christian teaching on loving our neighbours with an understanding that when people get on with each other it makes a world where we can do business.

"There's Mrs Saltley!"

Ah, yes. I am not sure teachers should attend demonstrations, but there she is, easy to spot with her wide hips and the usual bright flowery skirt shifting in the breeze, standing next to a tall young woman in a headscarf. Now with the window open the angry shouts do penetrate. Instinctively I put the phone down and place my arm around Nathan as he watches in fascination. I'll close the window again if it gets too nasty.

"What stupid looking people."

"Stupid is not a word you should use, Nathan. It's not nice."

"Well, they are, Dad. You said yourself, they want to chase anyone foreign out, that's stupid. Everyone you work with is foreign. Half my teachers are foreign. That food we ate last night was foreign, wish they'd eaten that, that'd stop them marching." He grins up at me. "And we're foreign ..."

"Well, no, we are British citizens."

"You know what I mean. Anyway, look, they've almost gone. There were more people watching than marching."

Yes, in the end, it's all a storm in a teacup. Let us hope for a world in which all such demonstrations are as insignificant as this one. Had I known how small it would be, I would not even have pointed it out to my innocent son. Though he seems to understand the issues well enough anyway: perhaps they have discussed such things at school. I remember a lot on the subject in their various policies, all of which I had to read and sign when he was first enrolled. Policies on behaviour, on racial discrimination, on equal opportunity and a new one this year, called "Diversity". To my mind schools should stick to the three Rs, though Nathan seems to have come to no harm.

I showed him the demonstration to make him think. And think he does, my goodness me! The next question to pop from my bright son's brain almost floors me:

"If we're foreign here, even though we're British citizens like you say, will we be more foreign or the same sort of foreign when we go to Spain in the summer?"

"More foreign, I suppose, since we don't speak Spanish. Although for the time being we hold the same European passport."

"And when we go to see Gung Gung and Pau Pau in Hong Kong? Would we be more or less foreign then? Since we do speak Cantonese?"

He is relentless. Surely, at seven, he can't have predicted the flaw in my argument. Yes, we do speak the same language, but our passports are different. He should soon be told the history of Hong Kong, how his grandparents are now Chinese citizens despite their UK passports, how if I go to mainland China I'd be treated as a Chinese citizen too because I was born in Hong Kong, but he would not. He will need to know the technicalities and implications of this, if when he is an adult he still wishes to visit a Hong Kong that may, when the fifty-year rule ends, be a very different society. Although so far things have gone more smoothly than any of us anticipated.

"At school they said we're all world citizens. But if they're right, how can anyone be foreign, anywhere?"

He is so clever, my son. And I must remember, he's only seven. A different part of my brain thinks something must be wrong with the ice cream as the queue has dispersed and people are waiting for the police to reopen the main road.

"They *are* right, at your school. I shouldn't worry about it anymore if I were you. Shall we go back to Ancient Greece now?"

WEDNESDAY 12TH OCTOBER 2016

Mrs Kaur

We hope to see as many of you as possible at the festival on **_Friday 14th October_** *between 10am and 2.30pm. Please fill out the reply slip below and return it to your child's teacher tomorrow!*

I/We would love to come to the Fairy Tale Festival on Friday 14th *October.*
It would be best for us to present our story in the morning / in the afternoon (delete as appropriate).
We would like 1 2 3 4 tickets (circle as appropriate).
Child's name_____ Class _____

"Look Bibi, there's Gurdeep!"

Mandeep runs ahead to join his brother, but Gurdeep tries not to see us. He's with his grammar school friends, blazers slung over their shoulders and their ties as short as they can make them; he doesn't want to walk with an old woman and a little boy. Mandeep makes himself tall with a straight back to try and blend in. I drop back to

Teresa and her daughter and Gurdeep pretends to take no notice but I see he is keeping an eye on his little brother.

"No husband today?" asks Teresa.

"No, he is watching TV, about elections in America. Every day something new. I tell him 'leave it, not worth wasting time on' but my husband cannot stop watching."

Sure enough, almost as soon as we are through the door, even before Gurdeep can rip off the blazer and tie he hates so much, my husband is shaking his head, wagging his finger at us.

"There will be big changes for the world if the yellow haired chump gets in."

Gurdeep falls about laughing. "Chump! What's this word?"

"Trump, chump, you made another rhyme! We did rhymes at school today and we had Nathan on our team so we got the most and Sky's team lost. Lump, jump, chump!" Mandeep is trying to impress his brother.

On TV there are people shouting, someone is holding up a picture of a *terrible two* – I heard these words in English class: they mean a child two years old when he screams to get what he wants. The picture is funny because the child looks like Trump, but my husband is not laughing. Then the camera moves to a meeting inside a big room and a man comes down the passage in the middle wearing a funny suit with a brick pattern. Now my husband does chortle, he cannot help himself. But straight away he looks serious again. He explains to the boys the man is demonstrating against a wall the yellow haired Chump wants to build to stop people coming into America from Mexico.

"He's not a chump, he's a spaz."

Gurdeep's voice is disgusted and Mandeep leap-frogs round and round on the carpet shouting "He's a spaz, he's a spaz!". My husband clicks off the TV remote with a look of thunder. He does not often look so severe.

"I can't watch with all this noise. And what is this 'spaz' you say? Does this word come from what I think? You think *my* words are old fashioned, Gurdeep, but *your* words are very nasty. You are old enough to know better."

The family is not so happy today. I go to the kitchen; sometimes if you offer sweets it makes people sweet again too. This Chump in the living room is spoiling everything. Gurdeep comes to find me, bless him! "Don't worry, Bibi. In a few weeks it'll all be over and we won't hear about him anymore. And hey, guess what? We were reading Shakespeare in school today and there was, like, a man dressed as a wall in that, too! Two men dressed as walls in one day, how about that?"

When we go back to the living room my husband has gone elsewhere for his peace and quiet. Mandeep puts the TV back on to choose a game before his brother can have a say.

"You two play together, nice, like when you were little?"

"Not that one, that's so gay. I'm going to get my homework done."

So Mandeep plays the game alone. There is something wrong but it's hard to say what to do to put it right. I think more than sweet food is needed.

My husband calls from our room. His face is grave.

"You were maybe little bit harsh with Gurdeep?" I venture. "He is only using words he hears at school. Now we are all unhappy…"

"But such words … such words make differences between people. The boys must understand, first you call people something bad, then you begin to think they *are* bad. Gurdeep chose a nasty way to describe people who have been born with a condition they cannot help. We must not insult people purely because of a medical condition. And they are often such sweet people. But you are right, I must explain better to the boys. There is no point telling them off if they do not understand what they have done."

He clears his throat and smiles at me.

"Now, I have something to show you."

From his desk he brings out the last, smaller package that disappeared from the big box on the day we gave the boys the drums.

"Shake it – gently!" he says and his tired eyes are amused. "Now open…"

"It does not matter what is inside, I shall appreciate your thoughts in buying it," I say, holding my hands out for his before I show greed by rushing to open his gift.

"It does matter, because this is something you have been really, really wanting for a long time, and you have been so patient. Whereas for me, I am *im*patient, I really, really want you to hurry and open this parcel before I burst out the secret!"

My old husband looks the same age as Mandeep, he is so excited to see what I will do.

I know from the sound what is inside, but he is enjoying the surprise so I pretend I do not. When we first came to the UK, these precious things were stolen from our baggage, in an inauspicious start. Now I accept we made the right decision to come, but at the time the loss of my fine silver ghungroos, chosen by my mother when we married, seemed an omen of greater troubles to follow. I wore them as a young bride. They jingled happily with every flex of my ankles, decorating the start of my life with my husband, and when they were stolen I worried that he too would be taken from me in this cold country. We reported the loss to the police, but they had no idea even what ghungroos were; my husband said he wrote down the word for them many times but they never remembered it the same way.

"You will put them on for me?"

"I am old ... old women do not wear ghungroos."

These are brass, but I am sure my husband has chosen well and they will make a sweet sound. I am so happy to have some again, and when I pass I shall leave them for Suki; I remember she did not have any when she married Aman.

"To me you are not old."

I say I will put on the ghungroos later, maybe just for my husband, and when I do I will tell him the same sweet, kind lie he has just told me.

THURSDAY 13TH OCTOBER 2016

SAFIYA

This morning on the walk to school we fell in naturally with Teresa and Sky. Teresa greeted me gently but Sky cut straight to the chase: "Where was Xoriyo yesterday?"

"We stayed home to fast. It's important. Even if you don't fast the other days of the first month of New Year, you should do the tenth day."

"How can it be New Year? We haven't had Christmas yet!"

"Ssh, Sky. I think they have a different calendar to us."

Teresa is trying so hard. I must cut her some slack, she is listening, thinking, doing her best to walk in our shoes.

"Actually we use both. But the Islamic year depends on the moon. It's shorter, so our special times fall on different dates each year."

"It was good this year, we told the story of the angel and the tree but Mummy always makes it nice, not sad, and we didn't have O Hussein. And we have yummy pudding, we started it last night." Xoriyo smacks her lips and quickly I invite them round after school to taste some. But Sky will be at the after-school club, and Teresa must pick the boy Nathan up too. Perhaps we could go to them later?

So now Xoriyo and I have a couple of hours at home before we're going to be off out again. She crouches on the carpet with crayons and the back of a cereal packet and busies herself making little cards with pictures. Dull autumn light falls on her rounded back through Auntie's new-old white nets.

"What are those, sweetheart?"

"You know the boy on my table, Zachary?"

I don't, but if she says he's on her table, so it must be.

"He doesn't talk. So he has this special teacher I told you about, Mrs Carmel, and she makes pictures like I'm making, and when he wants something he points to the card with the right picture. Like toilet, Lego, water…"

"And when it is she who wants him to do something?"

"She has a card for it. Do your writing, change for PE, you know. But today he did a show for us. He was shy to do his story to the whole school so he just did it for our class, holding up cards. It was really good, we clapped him a lot."

"And that is what you're doing now?"

"Yes, a story of my own to give him tomorrow. He was really pleased when we clapped, I mean he doesn't smile but he jumped up and down a lot so that's how we knew. Mrs Carmel said he's never told a whole story before."

She colours red so hard on her picture the pencil point goes flat and scratches the paper.

"Guess what story he did?"

I shake my head and take the pencil from her to sharpen over a saucer.

"It was about someone called George who killed a dragon and saved some princesses – all without words but we could understand every bit."

I murmur surprise and admiration.

"Wasn't that clever? He was so proud, it made us happy because he was, and Mrs Carmel was proud of him, and Miss Patel was happy…"

Yes, it's heart-warming that the class care so much about this boy. Such children were called "special" when I was at school and I don't remember noticing the work they did. Even so, as I pack our remaining pudding to bring to Teresa's, I realise I am not sure I want my bright Xoriyo sitting next to him all year.

Taking refuge in her kitchen as Sky, Xoriyo, the Chinese boy and the beautiful Indian child from next door play in the living room, Teresa and I enjoy the special taste. It helps cancel memories of the basbosa cake sticking in our throats when we were fighting. I explain the recipe my mother handed down to me from her diplomat neighbours in Hargeisa. The yearly ritual when Xoriyo and I mix the grains and pulses, the fresh and dried fruit, the salt, honey and milk with water to bind it. Then how we enjoy decorating it with patterns of orange and lemon peel, and jewel-red pomegranate seeds! Sometimes when you open a pomegranate it's dry and black and you cannot know how long it has sat in a crate on its travels, but the chopping board could not contain this one: juice stained the table and floor crimson and Xoriyo laughed and smeared her fingernails clumsy red.

When I tell Teresa this dish is made in Turkey where the "Noah's Pudding" name comes from, she recognises the name. I think Noah and the Ark is more like a fairy story than a religious one to the British, with their toy arks in every nursery. Otherwise, I think I know more about her so-called religion than she does. I had to remind her who Moses was.

"Didn't you sing hymns and learn Bible stories at school?"

"No, my mother did, but we didn't by the time I went. Why, did you?"

"I went for a while to a Church of England primary school, so yes, we heard these stories every day. And I was frightened, when they showed me pictures of Jesus on the cross. I thought it was so cruel, images everywhere of him suffering with the nails through his hands and toes."

"I thought you were brought up in – where is it? – Somalia?"

"No, we left when I was two. I went to Sudan for a visit, when I was younger than Xoriyo, but I've lived here all the time."

She picks pomegranate pips from her mouth. "Somalia – Sudan – what's the other one? – Ethiopia…Aren't they very poor? Would it be easy to get the ingredients for something as rich as this?"

"My mother's neighbours were Egyptian. This was more their tradition than ours, and I think it came from Turkey anyway. But at the time, her family could easily have afforded this sort of thing for special occasions. They lived in an important city, Hargeisa, which is now the capital of Somaliland, and her father had a government job. They left because of war, not poverty."

I have told so many English people this, about my mother's status and prosperity, but it never seems to sink in, that in Somaliland – yes, even in Somalia – there are distinctions of wealth and poverty, rank and insignificance, as there are anywhere.

"At the time? And now?"

"I think there may be almost nothing left of her home or the town she lived in, as she knew it, although much has been rebuilt in recent years."

"Like the pictures we see of Syria on the news?"

"Well, no, like I say, it's been rebuilt. Much of Hargeisa is brand new, with all the facilities you'd expect in an important city. It's growing all the time – you can see online, videos of it when they were celebrating the 25th anniversary of Somaliland in May this year."

I wonder if she'd understand about all the people going back, entrepreneurs investing energy, money and goodwill in a new young country to replace the one Barre destroyed. I'm not sure I understand them myself, returning to the scene of the holocaust their parents ran from.

Let's hear about *your* problems, I want to say, let's see what misfortunes and injustices *your* family has suffered. In this kitchen that was your grandmother's, I bet someone once drank away the housekeeping or couldn't pay the loan for the fitted units. Your kettle must have boiled to comfort grief or sterilise foul sheets; at this table someone must have checked bank statements with a pencil and despaired. Why don't you tell me about that? The physical ball of rage that overtook me last time I was here is rolling in from my heart, and I must swallow it, for Teresa is trying so palpably hard.

"Mum! MUM! Come in here and see our play!"

Sky ushers us to front row seats on Teresa's soft sofa. The four children parade past, and we try not to laugh at their ridiculous costumes in the domestic clutter. The Chinese boy is in the lead with a cardboard crown, guiding the beautiful, lost-looking girl-next-door. They both seem to be wearing my old net curtain; so *that's* why Teresa wanted it. Behind them marches Xoriyo, stiff and as tall as she can make herself, with a plastic sword and shield and a plastic helmet showing through the scraps of yellow paper glued all over it. Then Sky, on all fours and dressed in brown, lolloping along with yellow ribbon wrapped around what must be meant as her forelegs.

Nathan! That's his name. He announces the title of their play. He moves cleverly around the room selecting yellows, brasses and anything that could be gold, touching them in turn and making it seem he is transforming them. The scene makes more sense as he highlights each focal point, but his play is not only clever. I'm moved when he tries cuddling his "daughter" and she remains a cold statue, and amused when his dog (or is Sky a cat?) jumps quickly out of the way before any more limbs can be solidified. Now Xoriyo steps forward. She swaps her soldier's props for a homemade wand. There's some dialogue, but I'm hardly aware of it because I'm laughing so hard at Sky's antics and as Xoriyo's wand works strategic magic, the "gold" falls off and the characters return to their normal state. "King" Nathan and the Indian girl (what *is* her name?) embrace, perhaps rather longer and harder than two children of the opposite sex should? At any rate I am glad it isn't Xoriyo in the role. Teresa and I make a show of clapping long and hard enough for a much bigger audience, until we're interrupted by the doorbell. The Indian child's mother, very glamorous and shiny, has come to get her – a shame she didn't arrive for the show – so it's time I took my daughter home too.

"Stay longer!" shouts Sky, but Xoriyo is happy to leave now the story has been rehearsed, and perhaps we should not outstay our welcome.

Yet again we take two steps forward, one step back, seeing Teresa. Our relationship mirrors my wider relationship with what I have heard called "the host society". Here since babyhood, educated here, working professionally here in a caring role, paying my taxes and bringing up a child who will also be an asset to these "hosts", I cannot see anything positive about the term. The counterpart to host is guest but until the UK welcomes all equally, from the most genealogically documented aristocrat to the last refugee arrival strapped under a lorry, how can we "guests" relax? Teresa is hardly shouting "Get out!" But when she invites me in and makes careful conversation (*"Somalia – Sudan… Aren't they very poor?"*) I sense she's measuring the minutes, the input she must make to show she's offered houseroom and is not a local barbarian. Afterwards I expect she congratulates herself, pours alcohol and settles down for a comfortable chat with someone more familiar, until she feels it's time to have another go.

I'm almost certainly being unfair.

Xoriyo is crunching happily on a biscuit Teresa gave her to bring home.

"Do you get on okay with Sky?"

"Yes, now she knows I can be useful. You know, in her games and plays. We make a good team."

"Does she bully you?"

"Not in her house. She wouldn't dare, and anyway Teresa would sort it out. Why don't you like Teresa?"

She takes such a huge bite her mouth is too full to repeat her question when I avoid answering it.

"What about at school?"

"At school we sit on different tables. She's got – different friends."

"Who are your friends?"

"My friends? There's people I play chase with, in the playground. But in class, we don't talk to each other, because they think I don't speak English."

Sky knows you do, I think. And that other little girl and boy. You can't keep this apartness up much longer.

"At Sky's house, it's different." Xoriyo takes the last bite of biscuit and wipes crumbs from her mouth. "We're all acting someone else."

Xoriyo runs her bath. I look at the news on my phone. A clinic Fawzia once used will close when its funding ends. Another cut! More cuts mean fewer prescriptions, fewer prescriptions mean fewer chemists, fewer chemists mean less work for me.

This country, with the wit and humanity to create an NHS that was the envy of the world, is mutilating what it nurtured! This clinic sums up everything – attitudes, practicality, expertise – our host government could justly be praised for! What do they do? Cut it.

I considered referring myself there, after I married – another good idea, that you could self-refer to a clinic the other side of London. No need to involve family, community, neighbours, gossip, censure, attack. I wasn't brave enough in the end. You still need courage, even with special facilities, safe clinical procedures, privacy and comfortable chairs. You still have to find spaces in your schedule that explain an absence; spaces in your nights when you won't dream of what they'll do. Energy and courage to display your body, permit the alteration of your most intimate parts, already interfered with, bruised and wounded, torn and stitched, and to tell the whole story to the counsellors before, during and after the "procedures". After we came back from Sudan, my mother told me the best thing was to leave the scars to heal and not talk about it. However trained the counsellors are, the lessons of hundreds of years of history die hard: there's a lot to be said for saying nothing. The British take pride in their stiff upper lips, but they have nothing on the silence and fortitude of millions of African and Asian women who suffer, impose the same suffering on their daughters and granddaughters and have kept the whole thing so secret down the generations that it's only been recently Westerners even knew such pain and cruelty existed.

I glimpse Xoriyo, through the open bathroom door, squeezing the sponge and watching the drops trickle down her arm, trying a harder squeeze and a gentler one to make them faster or slower. "Don't forget to wash before the water goes cold!" I call. She has such fun in the bath!

It stung most when I used the toilet and hurt when I bled. Later I learnt possibilities for palliative care. But my studies also taught me to fear marriage and motherhood. I thought I was in love because Abdi said I was beautiful. I thought I'd bear the inevitable pain because I'd been bearing a version of it since I was seven and my mother, aunts, and grandmother had all borne it. But the first time with Abdi I went into shock and after that I could never let him near me without dosing myself with Z drugs so that after washing I could fall asleep. Then the pain would be less in the morning and if he began again I could usually fend him off. Our love didn't last: how could it? I was frightened of him; I self-medicated to ease my fear, but with that came another fear, of losing my job and my registration if I was found with medication intended for customers. By midday at work, the pain would recede and I could think straight. If Abdi's frustration led him to khat, if he got into trouble with the law: anything along those lines would give me an excuse to leave him. The UK host makes it easy for a Somali guest to follow such paths – you might almost say beckons him along them – and I'd have felt compassion for him if I had not been silently even more sorry for myself.

So many of us bring up our children alone; so many prefer to do so. If our hosts notice, nobody asks us why.

"Mum, which is the clean towel?"

I find the biggest one we have and wrap her firmly as I did when she was a baby. She rests against my body and allows me to hold her and this holding is a moment we can both enjoy.

I had a consultant for the delivery; they don't leave women like me to the midwives. You do not have to go to the specialist clinic that is closing if you have a baby: the NHS will suggest a caesarean and they'll repair you as best they can while you're under. But you don't get the counselling, the discretion or the soft furnishings that way either, and on behalf of those women who do use the clinic, as Xoriyo cleans her teeth, I find and sign a petition.

I could do more. Being asked to interpret last week reminded me of that, as does this news of the clinic. I imagine sharing my story, breaking my silence and sharing it with Teresa.

In this chapter, I would tell her, Abdi has left me and we came here and at present Xoriyo and I are safe. Our home is adequate; we're making it more comfortable: if we had to move again it might strain Xoriyo's adaptability beyond repair. The head pharmacist hinted last week at a permanent post that would fit school hours. Perhaps there'll come a time when the locals' thoughts do not automatically class us alongside Syrian refugees. Poor people: only a generation ago if wheels had turned as slowly as they do now, it could have been my own parents freezing in a tent on a beach near Calais, awaiting a welcome from the UK that never comes.

I remember a burnt-out car, outside our flats on the estate, and then a spate of them. The police who came said if you park a car with some visible damage – a broken wing mirror, say, or a couple of small dents – it will be vandalised within a week and others nearby, but an identical car left in good condition in the same place will not be touched. Those Syrian refugees are the damaged car: at the mercy of any barbarian whose entertainment lies in smashing them further, until they're written off. Whereas Xoriyo and I are sleek and healthy, housed, fed, schooled and employed. If we can keep up appearances we may come to no harm. My way of coping comes from my mother's advice. Leave well alone, and the scars will heal as best they can. No, I do not want to tell my story for the entertainment of others, not even yet for Teresa, but I will make sure Xoriyo has a story she can tell proudly.

And Xoriyo will be safe.

TERESA

"Let's put our feet up, Mum!"

Sky's on one end of the sofa with the iPad, I've got a final cup of tea and I lean back in relief. My favourite photo of the two of us last summer grins from the mantelpiece like it's congratulating me. Hard work today! But I think the elements came together. Even prickly Safiya pleasant and forthcoming, the children together happily creating stories, Alka more cheerful, Nathan bursting with achievements to tell his dad. So much acting: the children in their parts, Safiya acting the polite guest, and me acting appreciative.

"What did you think of that pudding, Sky?"

She makes a face.

"Well done for being polite, then."

I don't think Safiya noticed what a job I was having to swallow it. Beans and wheat –not my idea of a dessert, and the pomegranate looked prettier than it tasted. The tradition is, apparently, to give – what's it called? "Noah pudding" – to your neighbours. But if every neighbour gives it to every other neighbour, how would they ever finish it? Like that story of the poor woman who had the magic pot that only made porridge. I always thought that sounded disgusting.

I'm being flippant. If you came from a place where there'd been food shortages – no, let's be honest, famines, whatever she may say about them leaving because of war – you'd probably think that pudding was delicious. Safiya said it's supposed be a mix of whatever food Noah had left when they'd finishing building the ark, so it must have been welcome after such hard work. Fattening, though, with other effects Sky's already enjoyed teasing me about. My friend who's a practice nurse in Canning Town tells me you can't educate Africans against over eating; they have such a culture of associating fatness with prosperity that they don't easily take on board messages about dieting or BMI. Not that that's a problem for Safiya or Xoriyo. If my daughter and I were as slim as they are, I'd never worry about calories again.

Anyway, what was this war they were escaping? I'm so ignorant about any wars other than the London Blitz my grandparents talked about whenever they got the chance. I wrestle the iPad from Sky and she yelps in irritation.

"Let's find where they come from on a map of the world."

"Why?"

"I think we should... her mum and dad obviously knew where Britain was, or they wouldn't have come here." (Or did they just end up here, like all those refugees after you see them being pulled out of the sea in Greece?) "But here *we* are and we know nothing about them."

"Whatever ..."

Sky finds it first. Now I know what it looks like, one of those countries with an easy to remember shape. Italy's a boot, India's a diamond and Somalia's like an elbow.

"No," Sky argues. "It's more like someone holding their arm up to show you how strong their muscles are."

She's right. The whole of Somalia is a hooked coastal strip. Perhaps the people there were all sailors and nobody went far inland. If they did, they'd be in Ethiopia where a vague memory tells me there *was* a famine and tiny stick-like babies and Bob Geldof who wrote the song you hear every Christmas. But Safiya said her parents were well off, fleeing war not famine and anyway now, the city her parents came from has been rebuilt.

Hargeisa's here, on the bit of the map that goes from the wrist (no, hand) nearly to the elbow. It's in a part called Somaliland. The biggest problem now, for Somalilanders, is they're independent but Western governments don't recognise them as a separate state. According to this site, anyway. But they do recognise the south which is in complete chaos, and that's where Mogadishu the capital of Somalia is.

Why would our government not recognise a country which apparently has an embassy in London? In the Mile End Road, though, not Kensington like most of them...I'm Googling Hargeisa, which they can't even decide how to spell. Sometimes it's Hargeysa. Anyway, both spellings return images of green roofs and modern buildings, off-white under a piercing blue sky, with greenery and calm streets of beige stone, modern cars and every now and then a more important landmark, a school or a hospital, a factory, a company HQ. The photos include lots of proud people wearing green, red and white which must be the national colours, and there's a symbol that keeps coming up with two hands clasping each other in friendship. I don't understand why the hands are white, but that's by no means the only thing I don't understand. It doesn't look a bad place, now, if you can stand the heat. Cleaner than here, though I suppose any official government photos would make a place look good. There's an airport, and you can fly via Rome or Addis Ababa – another amazing place name. But if a country doesn't technically exist, how could you plan a future there? I discover from Wikipedia, though I never know how reliable that is, that there's a private zoo and some amazing cave paintings, but no postal service or alcohol and you shouldn't wear trousers if you're a woman or go at all if you're gay. I scroll past that pretty quickly as I'm not in the mood for talking about it to Sky. I scroll past horrific pictures of skeletal children, too: it's unclear whether they're in Somaliland or Somalia and I've never been able to look directly at such images. I'll make a donation next time I'm in Oxfam.

Well, we've learnt some geography if not much else. Sky is muttering "a boot, a diamond, an elbow" like a mantra so she'll never forget that. As for me, whenever I learn a few small things, I shudder: they just show up the wider ignorance around them. My knowledge of Safiya's background is still hazy, and I know nothing of Nathan's, or little Alka's or Auntie's except they're from somewhere on the Indian diamond. The same place, a different one? I wouldn't know, but there's clearly nothing to stop us finding out. The counsellor did say I should broaden my horizons!

"Well done, babe!"

"Well done what?"

"Well done to find the countries and those photos for me. See, we can go all round the world from our own living room. But let's stop now; you need an early night before your star performance tomorrow. Shall we put some polish on those paws of yours?"

Sky pushes the iPad off my lap, throws her arms around me and gives me a big kiss.

"Thank you for having everyone round and helping us with our stories. And not arguing with Xoriyo's mum. I hated it when you did that, but now it's all lovely again and tomorrow you're going to be *so* proud of me, you just wait and see!"

I hold her tight, tight, tight until she squeals. Yes, it has been a successful day.

ALKA

So I will be in the performance tomorrow. I'll be Nathan's daughter. It's not what he calls "a speaking part", so I'll be silent in gold and then silent not in gold. I'm glad I'm not his wife, but being his daughter feels good. He'll protect me; after his big mistake with the gold he'll be wise for ever. You learn from your mistakes, like Nani said after I put too much oil on my hair.

I would have liked to tell my own story too, though.

There was a police car parked outside our house while I was playing at Sky's but I didn't notice when it went. Maybe it was when we were doing the play for Teresa and Xoriyo's mum. They clapped and clapped, so much we didn't hear the doorbell at first.

"Oh, Mummy, you look beautiful!"

When Mummy came to get me her face was perfect like it used to be, with make up on. Her eyes were perfect almonds and her mouth was glossy pink and her cheeks were bright on her smooth skin. Once Nani joked she could boil a four-minute egg twice in the time it takes Mum to do her lips: I wonder if it took her that long today. She showed me once, with a base coat of moisturiser and three different pencils. You do the outline first, then go sideways for shading. Then you put gloss on top, and do the outline again in skin colour in case you've gone over the edges. Between each bit you blot your lips on a cotton pad. You have to keep stretching your mouth as wide as it'll go, to make sure you've covered the whole of it. You make like the opposite of a kissing face at yourself in the mirror.

And that's just the lips. You do them last, after the skin and the eyes. You can make yourself almost into a different person, but it takes time and you have to learn how.

When I'm eight I might choose a makeover party for my birthday. When she stopped being cross at me for not coming, Janki told me the party games they had at hers were boring and she wishes she'd had just a few girls for a makeover instead.

Mum didn't stay long on the doorstep; Teresa told her she looked wonderful, wanted her to have tea, coffee, juice, cake, anything – but Teresa tries too hard. The other mums don't always want to be with her. I can see that with Xoriyo's mum, even though they were eating cake together. I think Teresa goes too close to people. She wants to know too much and she's waiting for the other person to swap and ask questions about her, but the other person doesn't.

There was no chance Mummy would stay.

So now we're in our house and it feels different. Nani's put out treat plates of pretzels and Pringles and Mum went to meet Dad when he came in instead of staying upstairs in my room. The Pringles aren't even finished and nobody explains anything to me or Sunil but they say *come and eat together round the table.* Like we used to. Mum is talking loud and sometimes she speaks at the same time as Dad, then they both stop and say, no you go first. The first time it's funny, but it happens a bit often and then Nani takes Sunil for his bath. I look from Mum to Dad and back again. They're putting food in their mouths too fast and they look like they're acting, like Teresa was with that cake thing Xoriyo's mum brought.

"Can I tell you about our play?"

Nana clears his throat.

"I will take you for a walk before bed, Alka, and you can tell *me* about your play. The clocks will change soon – on the same day as Diwali, this year – and we won't have many more chances."

Through the window the blue sky is turning pink, and I think, it will be nice to watch the sunset with Nana.

But when we're out in the close there doesn't seem much to tell. My role is simple. I walk on stage behind Nathan, stand still to get wrapped in the yellow cloth, and stand still some more. Then I have it taken off, show I can move again, and curtsey when the audience claps. When I asked Nathan how he knew they would clap he said, because Sky will do something that makes them clap. Or maybe that other girl will – she's quite clever that way.

"Xoriyo?"

"Is that her name?"

I said to Nana, how could Nathan have someone in his class for all term, even use her in his play, and not know what her name is?

"Maybe she is not important to him."

"And I am?"

"He is clearly a very wise little boy." Nana squeezes my hand. "He knows who is the most beautiful girl in the class."

I skip by his side with a warm bump in my heart. We're passing the garden with the gnomes. Once when I was little he stopped and made up a conversation for the one with the fishing rod and the one on the toadstool, and I always hope he'll do it again. But his eyes have gone far away.

"Yes, you are beautiful. But you know, Alka, if you think beauty is the most important thing, you are making a similar mistake to the ruler in your story who wanted everything to be gold. I sometimes wonder if your mother understands that."

I have the still, cold feeling that comes when an adult is going to tell you something important. I tug Nana's sleeve and point up, to stop him. Tonight the sky glows, darker pink under the blue, and stripes of orange and red make a pattern under the shining clouds.

"Yes," says Nana. "Even in dirty London the sky can tell a beautiful story."

"I thought you said beauty wasn't the most important thing?"

"Perhaps for nature, it is. If nature forgets to put on a display like this sunset from time to time, or if the birds don't sing and the flowers don't bloom, human beings will forget what nature is worth and destroy it even faster than they are doing already. But for humans, it is more important to be kind and intelligent."

"Mummy *is* kind and intelligent." It's true, usually.

"Of course … but she did some silly things, and they cost your father a lot of money. And all because she thought she could build a business around beauty."

The sun is a half circle now, sinking as though Ganesh thinks we've had enough.

"Is that why he hit her? Whatever she did, he shouldn't have hit her. That's what they say at school, anyway."

"Oh, my little wise one. I didn't realise you knew … you're so young."

Nana's voice is sad and his footsteps slow. The gnomes are several houses behind us now; the even spaces of his words measure the pavement the same way as Mummy's beads on a necklace. Now he speeds up, like he's decided what to tell me.

"Anyway, since you do know, the police are not pressing charges and your parents have decided to put the whole thing behind them. And so after your show at school Nani and I are going home – until Diwali, at least, we'll be back for Diwali – so they can work things out without having us in the way. But you are a sensible girl, Alka, as well as a beautiful one, and I want you to promise me one thing."

I realise we've stopped. We're at the entrance to the close where the traffic noise is louder and the exhaust pipe fumes go up my nose. The red sun winks farewell on the horizon and although my chest is tight I'm happy because the police are not *pressing charges* – I don't know what that means but it must be good or Nani and Nana wouldn't think they can go home – and I'm filled with pride. Nana is going to trust me with something important. He thinks I'm more sensible than Mummy, and although that's weird, it kind of makes up for the way she's ignored me since … Daddy *did* hit her! Any chance I'd been wrong about that vanished when Nana called me wise. It proves I've understood right.

Daddy *did* hit her. Will he hit her again? Would he ever hit me, or Sunil?

"Will you promise me that one thing?"

There are promises in so many of our fairy stories, but this story is true, and I don't know what comes next. Should I snuggle up to him or squirm away? I'm beginning to need the toilet.

"You haven't said what it is."

The sun has gone now and the deep dark blue is turning grey.

"As I said, you are too young for this. But now that you know, you cannot go back to *not* knowing. So I am asking you, if ever, if *ever* your Daddy hits Mummy again, please will you tell me and we will come back and make things right."

"And if he hits me or Sunil?"

"Oh! I doubt he will do that. No, no, you don't have to worry about that at all."

"And if you're away?"

Nani and Nana go to India sometimes, on big trips to see the places their parents grew up in, and they go to Canada to see our cousins. I want instructions. If they're going to give me responsibilities, they must tell me clearly how to carry them out. Like being a monitor or on the school council.

"You see, I said you were sensible. You have thought of everything. If we are away, text us or Skype us, and if you cannot get us, maybe tell your teacher. Or tell that lady next door if it isn't a school day. Or even phone 999. You know how to do that, don't you?"

"If I tell people they'll think we're a horrible family. They already whisper about me, at school, since ..."

He sighs and pulls me into a hug I don't want. The dark sky presses down and his words make everything worse.

"I know, I know. And if I were a younger man, and where I was born in Kenya, or in India, we would deal with this differently. Your mother would be living with Daddy's family, and might never tell me what had happened. Or if she did, our families would sort it out between us, and nobody else would ever know."

Does he mean, if Daddy hit Mummy in India, it would be ok?

Or wherever they were, if no-one knew about it, it would be ok?

"What did Mummy do?"

"Never mind what she did. I do not want you to know any more than you know already. Some might say, it was your mother's fault and she deserved it, but… to hit your wife is against the law in this country, so whatever we think we must abide by that. Otherwise once you start getting into trouble with the law there is no end to it."

"But you told me to ring 999."

Nana stands up much straighter.

"Yes. But actually, no. I am sure we can keep things in the family, and I am sure it will not happen again. Let us look on the bright side. Mummy and Daddy are friends again and that is all that matters. I am sure if we all behave sensibly it will never happen again."

He smiles down at me and the wrinkles round his eyes go deep inside his skin. "You will see. You will all live happily ever after, I'm sure."

Poor Nana, Mummy is his daughter and he loves her. Like Daddy loves me. I'm sure he's right: if we're all sensible – I can make sure Sunil behaves, and I can help Mummy not to only think about being beautiful – and if Daddy keeps his temper, everything will be ok. I'm cold, out here under the black sky with Nana's hug finished. His body stands straight but his head looks down at the cracked pavement: he says nothing more.

I *am* sure he's right, but I wish I dared ask, and I wish he would answer.

Does he mean it's ok for adults to hit each other even though children mustn't? So did he ever hit Nani?

Does he really mean I must help Mummy to behave herself because I'm wiser?

But still Nana says nothing more and we are both shivering when we turn back towards home.

I wonder if, after the prince rode away with Rapunzel, he hit her.

FRIDAY 14TH OCTOBER 2016

SAFIYA

On the dark stage darker shapes shuffle towards the middle. When the lights come up there's a family, both parents and two children, all dressed in brown, one clutching a teddy bear. The mother fills bowls from a cardboard box cooker, they touch them and leap backwards sucking their burnt fingers. Off for their walk they go, pacing back and forth at the rear of the stage, as a third child enters and tries the food. The family is still pacing as she sits on the chairs and lies on the quilts they've placed on the floor, all the time singing: "*When Goldilocks came to the house of bears, oh what did her blue eyes see?*" I don't know this song but many of the children in the audience join in when the dad from the stage encourages them, clapping his hands and conducting. It's cheerful, tuneful and we're all involved straight away.

How will Xoriyo follow this, all by herself?

I wonder even more when the stage is cleared for the next story. Three children appear, one with a crutch, one dressed in bright red and yellow strips of fabric sewn onto a drawstring cloak. I could make that, I think, out of a remnant. I should have offered to make something like that for Xoriyo.

The children hold up black shapes cut from cardboard, the shapes of huge rats with black string stuck on for tails. In the stage lighting the effect is sinister. From a bag they pull more "rats" and throw them across the stage. The child who is not in costume reads from a large scroll-like paper, clearly and fluently, and yet he must be only the same age as Xoriyo.

> *"Hamelin Town's in Brunswick,*
> *By famous Hanover city;*
> *The river Weser, deep and wide,*
> *Washes its wall on the southern side;*
> *A pleasanter spot you never spied..."*

He shakes out a large sheet of blue material. It must be silk as it waves with a soft shimmer. Such a clever way to represent a river! My mind drifts, watching the rats, until one word hits me like a stone:

> *"... To see the townsfolk suffer so*
> *From* vermin, *was a pity."*

I heard the word "vermin" somewhere else recently. In my ear it has the strength – no, more – of the worst swear word; aggressive, taunting, ugly. But suddenly the child in red and yellow is blowing on a recorder, wavery, discordant notes irritating my already disturbed ear. They must irritate the rats too, as some hidden helper pulls the tails from the side of the stage and the rats disappear under the blue silk water. It's ingenious. The audience gasps and a few clap.

Now the recorder player is asking for money. The child with the scroll puts a big gold chain round his neck – it's a medal like the ones they gave Xoriyo at her last school for running the best in the class. He's digging in his bag for coins, but it seems he isn't giving the recorder player enough. It's a PE bag turned inside out so the school logo doesn't show and the coins are the chocolate money you get at Christmas. I always wondered who started their Christmas shopping in October.

Where *did* I hear that word?

The recorder player begins again. This time it's a simple tune I remember from a concert at Xoriyo's old school. Schools all use the same ideas, it seems! This must be a tune all children learn if they do recorder. Maybe I could ask about her learning here, although she's never shown an interest.

The entire front row of children from the audience walk on to the stage and follow the recorder player off into the darkness at the side. Only the child with the crutch is left, alone, too slow to follow. He turns to the audience, leaning on his crutch, and speaks in a sad voice:

> *"The music stopped and I stood still,*
> *And found myself outside the hill,*
> *Left alone against my will."*

Now I remember where else this story cropped up – it was when Sky recognised the word "vermin" the day someone threw stones at me! My limbs go taut: this is a disgusting story. We're in a primary school for goodness sake; are we not welcome here either? Is the child on stage not welcome with his friends because his body isn't perfect? No-one should make children act stories like this! But a laugh goes up and my attention is forced back to the stage. From a gap in the curtains a huge cardboard hand is reaching out ... stretching, stretching for the disconsolate lame boy. No, it can't get to him ... it manages, and taps him on the shoulder. He turns, takes the hand and is pulled gently back through the curtains to join his friends.

So, a relatively happy ending has been achieved. But what of the bereft parents and the unpunished dishonest mayor? And we still don't know if the child will recover and throw away his crutch.

Fawzia pats me on the arm.

"It's just a story. What's upsetting you? Look, Xoriyo's next."

Now there's a chair in the middle of the space, with a light shining on it. An electronic screen comes on at the back of the stage and a teacher wheels on a trolley with a box-shaped machine like the projectors they used when I was at school. The teacher sits on a second chair next to the machine and I don't know ... I'd hoped Xoriyo would be telling her own story. Surely she hasn't made them believe she's *that* far behind, with her silly play of not speaking

English! I'm feeling sick on her behalf and Fawzia leans into me again.

"Don't be nervous ... it's a good school."

Xoriyo enters stage left, very thin and tiny. Her white headscarf bobs along until she reaches the chair, and the white covers of the book she's made show up at her side, but otherwise her navy uniform makes her almost invisible until she sits and the light shines on her. Her legs dangle, swinging back and forth. Next to me a lady is talking to her neighbour.

"Ssh!"

I get a dirty look and a cluck.

"Take no notice," whispers Fawzia. "Concentrate on your daughter."

The teacher passes Xoriyo a microphone. That's a good idea.

"The story of Momotaro the Peach Boy," says Xoriyo. Her voice is small but clear. "Words and pictures by Xoriyo Ahmed."

She's about to go straight on but the teacher places a hand on her arm to pause her and there's a small warning buzz from the audience. "Oh, I forgot," she mutters, just audible through the microphone, and my heart is in my mouth. She walks over and places the book on the machine and I understand. Her little book is magnified now, on the white screen above the stage. The whole audience can see her beautiful handwriting and the lovely cover. She's written the title in the middle, and where the letter "o"s should be she's drawn peaches, carefully coloured in shades of pink and apricot with not an outline crossed, decorated with leaves and bendy stalks. She's made a border of more peaches, all exactly the same as though she's done them on a computer. Maybe she has, at school, and how would she print them if not at school? It seems I'm not the only one with secrets.

Xoriyo's calm spreads over the audience. She tells her story slowly, gravely, giving us time to admire each page, with a shy smile when she turns one over. Sometimes the teacher helps her reposition the book on the machine, and occasionally tells her to pause, but mostly this is Xoriyo on her own, confident and easy, trusting us all to understand her work is good and her future will be rosy.

She's illustrated each page with a drawing or photographs, and where I would simply have stuck them down, she has added details with a thin pen, or chopped elements out and restuck them in another photo. When she comes to the page with an enormous peach and the cut-out baby boy inside with his tiny nappy and his big round grin, there is a gentle chuckle from the audience.

At the end, when the first claps sound I see even in this short time on stage my clever daughter has learned something. She holds the audience still by putting up the palm of her hand and the teacher, watching her, copies so everyone understands they may not speak yet. She puts one hand in her pocket and brings out a real peach. Placed on the machine it grows, huge, round and pink looming over the hall and the audience. "It's James and the Giant Peach!"

whispers a child below me in excitement, but Xoriyo hasn't finished. She slithers down from the chair and steps to the edge of the stage.

"I wanted to do this story because the pictures in the Momotaro book looked good enough to eat; I wanted a peach like that. And my Mum did a kind thing, she bought me peaches and then my cousin brought me a baby and they've all come to hear the story today! Come up on stage Mum and Fawzia and baby Mahdi because it's your story too."

The teacher is waiting and smiling; the children all looking round to see where we are. I don't want to go on stage, to stand there lit up in front of everybody but Xoriyo's shading her eyes with her hand looking out across the hall for us and I can't let her down. As for Fawzia, she's already half way there, baby Mahdi's eyes big over her shoulder as they pass. At the side there are steps to climb and I nearly stumble because I'm so overwhelmed and I'm reminded of the same thing happening when I went on stage to receive my degree on my graduation day. When we're all safely there the teacher steps forward, speaking without taking all the importance like the head teacher would.

"That wonderful story was by Xoriyo Ahmed who only joined us in September. Let's all give a warm welcome to the Ahmed family!" and everyone is clapping and cheering and Xoriyo is hugging against me with the biggest of big smiles on her little face, and Fawzia is holding her son above her head like a sports champion with a trophy and there we stand, being applauded by this big crowd in the new place we live in. And it's truer, more solid, stronger than being on our magic carpet and I think, yes, here she will be safe.

MR CHAN

"Didn't the little African girl do well? Nathan told me she spoke no English when she came in September."

Teresa grins. "I think there's more to her than meets the eye. I reckon all children, if you give them the chance, can show you things you wouldn't have believed they could do. Have you met the mother? They live opposite your flats."

I shake my head. I am constantly amazed by the network Teresa seems to be a part of, spanning parents and children of all backgrounds. I suppose if you can stay to chat in the playground when you've dropped your children off, and you feel easy having other children to play in your house, you become part of a daytime group. She even says hallo to the many grandparents. Of course for women it's easier to make those links, other women trust you and chat more comfortably and I suppose also for many of the mothers here, their religion wouldn't allow them to speak to me ... And yet Teresa told me she doesn't have much of a social life. She must mean in the evenings. She has a daytime life and then when the curtains are drawn and the couples are together, she's alone. I do know this feeling, but I can fill the time with work.

The African mother is striking. She has intelligent eyes like her child, and her long straight skirt and plain top and scarf accentuate her slender limbs, though I imagine that is not her intention. She must be as tall as I am. How much I'm noticing about the women around me, these days!

Such thoughts are not ones I wish to be having right now so I concentrate on responding to Teresa. "I haven't met her, no – where are they from?"

"They speak Somali but also excellent English and the daughter was born here. Mum's a pharmacist, part time. They've just moved from further in."

I bow slightly. "I am constantly humbled by your knowledge of other lives, Teresa."

She laughs but can't answer as it's time for the next act. I must say the school has been admirably efficient in the way they've staged this: only the gaps between acts give away the ad hoc nature of the event. So much planning we take for granted! Now, like all parents watching their children, Teresa's face goes round and tense with pride, eyes fixed, breath held, willing her daughter to do well.

"Ssh! It's Sky."

Teresa needn't worry. My goodness, how right Nathan was, this child can hold an audience! Sky strides jauntily onto the stage, a basket of props over one arm. She's wearing something grey with long sleeves and grey leggings that show every bulge.

From the off she has us all laughing as she turns, wiggling her bottom, wagging the big white pom-pom tail. She has rabbit ears fixed to one of those plastic hair bands girls wear. Nathan pointed them out to me once, he said he'd like one because you could put all sorts of details on them to show different characters, and I dissuaded him but only by pointing out they looked hard and uncomfortable. Otherwise he didn't see anything intrinsically wrong with a boy wearing such items.

Sky plays with the spotlight, bounding in and out of its range, but when she lets it settle on her I see painted whiskers on her cheeks and how she holds her teeth over her lower lip and how her nose wrinkles high in the air. She's dumpy and clumsy, and what she's presenting is quite ridiculous: even so, she has self-belief, and she carries us with her through her story.

"The town rabbit," she announces in a portentous tone, retrieving a top hat from her basket. Of course when she tries to place it over the rabbit ears it won't stay, and her repeated futile attempts produce more audience laughter. Instead, from the basket she draws a larger than life gold fob watch, a bow tie, and a small blue jacket which she struggles into. She prances loftily around the stage. "It's the White Rabbit!" shouts a small voice and she bows. Back to the teacher with the machine she skips, to present her in a lordly manner with a photograph. It's beamed down to the hall: a rabbit in a hutch with straw, china feeding bowls and a cramped chicken wire run with scanty grass. I'm reminded of the tiny house I sold last week in Hackney, a million pounds with a dark, pigeon-stained rear yard like a hen coop.

With ceremony she replaces her costume items with a cloth cap and greets the audience in a rolling West Country accent. She takes a large bite from a carrot and for some time can only munch loudly, staring out at the audience which reacts in delight. It was brave to use a real carrot – Sky's mouth really is full and this will take time. As she crunches, the screen shows a rabbit running about a lettuce patch in delighted freedom.

Yes, she's a clever girl, Sky. She uses one side of the stage to represent the town rabbit as her story unfolds, and the other for the country cousin. She's helped by the precision of whoever's doing the lighting; each time she waits for the spotlight to centre before announcing the next stage of the story. Her comic lines and gestures are worthy of a child who's been professionally trained. Next to me Teresa has relaxed, knowing it will be all right, proud, laughing, beaming with achievement. The applause at the end is a sudden thunderclap and the rabbit becomes a child again, enjoying her success for perhaps an instant too long. The teacher has to call her off the stage.

Teresa's busy receiving congratulations from all around, as a small child pushes towards us through the crowd from his place on the assembly hall floor. He's stuck between grown up knees and stomachs

and for a moment no one notices him. But I'm looking down, trying to become invisible while so many
eyes are on Teresa next to me, so my eyes meet the
child's, and oh dear how disconsolate he looks. He's
at that suspended point before tears when an understanding adult may be able to head them off, and it
seems the adult in question must be me.

"Oh dear, oh dear…" My encouraging smile
to the child doesn't succeed, or maybe frightens
him. His face clouds completely, eyes welling, forehead scrunched. A teacher's arm reaches expertly
through the bodies and pulls him through, passing
him to a motherly looking lady who I remember was
an indefatigable helper when Nathan was in the
nursery. She scoops the mite onto her lap. "He was
told his mum would be here because his sister's in
the next part of the show." She mouths this explanation to enquiring faces and their necks move sideways in sympathy.

How could a parent not come to something
as important as this? For I do see, now, how much
this means to all the children. My own son wasn't
exaggerating.

Never mind. The next story is his. I mustn't
drift, today, I must take note of everything, and not
via my phone or a video but myself, present in the
moment. My help with the project has been at best
half-hearted, and now I see the efforts some families
have made I'm ashamed of my inadequacy.

The yellow net curtain and cardboard crown,
with the benefit of stage lighting and an audience of

uncritical enthusiasts, does not look nearly so paltry a costume as I'd feared. I'd assumed Nathan would be embarrassed by his home-made props and by how much had to be left to the audience's imagination. I find it doesn't matter: the overflow of goodwill in the hall fills any gaps easily.

But why has Nathan got himself three girls to act with? Is he ever going to have a good male chum?

The three are very different. He's right, Alka's appearance is almost perfect. Her small face is quite symmetrical, her dark eyes huge. There's another appearance for Sky, a lolloping animal again, catching every laugh and almost all the limelight. The African girl commands a different kind of attention. Am I witnessing a small rivalry here? Sky's every gesture is wider, more blatant, but the smaller girl has a quietness about her that pulls your gaze. Her velvety voice speaks the words clearly and both girls extract maximum value from whatever small thing Nathan's asked them to do. As for him, he struts around in his kingly role, leading Alka who is certainly beautiful but also rather wooden, by the hand. She tends to pull back to the shadows at the rear of the stage, and each time he has to bring her forward more insistently to show her off again. I'm not sure if their hug is quite in good taste, and look round to see if I can identify her parents to see their reaction. But Teresa catches my eye and shakes her head silently, pointing to the small boy still snivelling on the helper's lap.

One must always be honest: I think probably my son's strengths lie more in directing than in acting.

And silent, graceful Alka's perhaps in modelling. But still, he has done well. The narrative is clearer than I expected and he's deployed his characters and props with ingenuity. It will certainly give me something to talk about on my next date! I do now understand why the school devoted so many home-work slots to this project. Teresa has of course been a great help, and I think we must buy her some flow-ers or perhaps a bottle of wine. No, flowers, from Nathan; wine might appear to come from me and she might think I wanted to drink it with her. She's a kind woman, but she lacks the style and grace I am searching for.

Teresa nudges me; it's annoying but she's right to stop me missing the rest of my son's show as my thoughts – of her! – take me wandering away. Now the children magic gold things back to nor-mal – cleverly, a gold pot is turned around and the other side is brown; gold drapes unravel from the unspecified mammal played so energetically by Sky; the child princess is unswaddled from her yellow net to reveal a stunning Indian costume beneath. The mammal makes a bound of joy and curls itself rubbing against the child's legs: the African girl turns to the audience. I am sure she's winking. She holds up a placard with uneven capitals: "LAUGH". The audience becomes an additional character, and laughs as directed. I notice a young woman, with a Mediterranean face. Her beautiful high cheekbones are framed by dark curls that tickle the child on her lap; she's whispering to him quietly, pointing things out. He looks a few years younger than Nathan so perhaps he needs the explanations. Teresa leans towards me:

"That's Maria, she's a classroom assistant here, and her son's in Reception. I bet she's especially into this one as she's Greek herself. Her little boy was born on one of those islands where people go on holiday. Well, I don't, but in my dreams…"

The Greek king's stage celebrations are continuing rather shapelessly – a touch of editing was needed here, I think – when Alka's sullen face lights with a charming smile. Turning with her gaze, I see a stunning woman arrive at the hall door with an elderly couple in tow. She has sleek flowing hair to her waist, a heart shaped face with almond eyes, features so even a geometrician must have plotted them. Her slim figure is emphasised by skinny jeans and what I believe is called a tunic, expertly cut to conceal and suggest at the same time. As if at a slow-motion tennis rally, the audience glance from the child on stage to the young woman and back again and, like a tiny ball boy, the whimpering child escapes from the helper's lap and ricochets across to her.

But her daughter's part of the show is over. The king, the princess, the versatile African girl who manipulated all the other roles so deftly, and Sky's indeterminate mammal line up on stage. The African child hands out more placards. The actors bounce their signs high; even Alka has risen on her toes the better to display hers: "CLAP!" it shouts in bright red, and the three others: "CLAP!" "CLAP!" "CLAP!"

How we do clap! It's a stroke of genius. My clever, clever son.

The audience chatters between acts, but the head teacher has only to stand, a warning finger on her lips, for us to fall obediently silent. A family takes the stage in height order, parents, two boys who walk exactly as their father does, two girls who move like younger versions of their mother. They all wear blindfolds, so we can't see if their faces are equally alike. Each has two hands on the shoulders of the one in front, with another adult, not so visibly related and with no blindfold, leading them. The head teacher's finger stays on her lips. A huge grey elephant looms from the screen at the back of the stage. The unknown adult stares at us with a big question on her face. One by one the family approach the elephant, feel whichever part they can reach, return and describe with their hands what they've found. No sound. The adult's questioning hands become more and more urgent, the gestures from each of the others increasingly fraught. It's a passionate argument conducted in silence, and becoming ill-humoured ... they can't see each other and neither can they hear each other's signs. There'll soon be chaos! The leader lines them up, one by one and turns them to face the elephant. She stamps her foot hard on the floor – we all feel the vibration. They whip off their blindfolds, stare at the elephant – and begin to laugh, clutching their sides, mimicking and deriding the gestures they'd been making: the father who'd outlined a trunk, the mother who'd smoothed two tusks to points, the tall boy who made his hands flap like paper ears, the smaller one whose palms described the flanks like a brick wall, the girl who pulled the tail and the small-est one who had felt the hard toenails and leathery feet anchored splat on the ground.

All without a sound. With speech and hearing missing, this family has shown what happens when sight is lost too. How we admire and applaud!

Expectations run high now and those of us who can read the round clock on the wall know we're heading for the finale. The projector is removed from the stage and the screen explodes with silent fireworks. The audience is near fever pitch!

Who is this? An elderly turbaned gentleman, with a drum, tap tapping as quietly as he can, with just the tips of his wrinkled fingers, to quieten us too. It's clear he has the patience to continue as long as necessary, and there are many hushes and shushes before we settle.

Now, on the screen behind him arrive a younger man on the left and a teenage boy on the right. Ah, so another family has participated fully and this is how they've engineered the presence of three gen-erations with the father at work and the older boy at his own school. All three must be good players, for the old man keeps in time with his filmed relations. The pace increases, the movements become more intricate.

An elderly lady and a smaller child, Nathan's age, appear on the stage to rapturous applause: the child is obviously popular. He has his own drum and he joins the others, but the elderly lady looks fed up. She leans on a stick, grumbling.

"Eh?" shouts the boy. "Speak up!"

I don't understand her. Clearly some of the audience and her family do, but she isn't speaking English. The boy ignores her, and she repeats her phrase, several times. Eventually she turns to the audience and invites them with a universal gesture, to repeat her words to the boy. By now we all know them, and the boy and the others stop their drumming and listen when we come together as one to make our point. I wonder what language we are speaking.

"Oh, we have no foo-oo-oood?" he says in English, drawing out the word and turning to the audience.

"Hungry, hungry," she agrees, with a sob.

"Aah …" soothe the audience.

"And we have no MUNey?" The same stretched intonation and surprise.

"Poor, poor. No money. Sell the cow."

Sky's universal animal takes a cameo on stage, without her rabbit ears or her cat mask this time so as not to confuse us. She gets a laugh but attention quickly returns to the boy and his grandmother.

We move through the story: the boy meets an old man; he exchanges the cow for beans; the old woman is furious. It's clever: nothing is translated from the old woman's speech, but the boy responds in ways that make it clear what's meant. Of course, the story is familiar and many people can pick up nuances unavailable to me because they *do* understand her language. All the time, the drums accompany, slow, sad, fast, excited, cheerful, disappointed. The old man's face remains impassive whatever the mood of his fingers. The characters on the screens adopt a listening pose, reacting with their drums. They have dovetailed each element with great precision.

Perhaps they shot some of the film in their garden since now the boy on stage mimes climbing a sunflower on the screen. I've never liked sunflowers, gross clumsy things, so this is a good idea: they work far better as stand-ins for a beanstalk than unusually floppy in a small vase as in the Van Gogh posters I noticed on the school walls. When the boy reaches the top, the show returns to the front of the stage. A teacher brings on an ironing board, the old woman grumbles her way through shirt after shirt while she answers the boy's questions about her husband the giant. Soon we hear him coming: the old drummer incites the audience to join in:

"*Fee-ee, fi-i-i, foh, FUM!*"

The boy hides at the side of the stage, and on the screen there's a montage – goodness, this is sophisticated! – I am impressed and surprised at the same time. It's like those Disney films that have a message for the adults viewing alongside their kiddies: hidden humour, usually. To my mind I consider this subversive for a primary school, but no one stops it. The montage starts with small figures in the distance walking towards the audience, swelling gradually into one huge close up face. Among the figures morphing into each other I spot a number of past ogres, Stalin, Mao, Amin, and here come more recent ones, bigger and sweatier as they approach: Mugabe, Kim Jong-un, and finally the huge red glistening face and yellow crown of Trump the would-be POTUS (a mistake including him in this political category, I think. Anyway, he'll never win).

The *fee-fi-fo-fum* whips up louder; the drumming is fiercer; the old lady irons more and more frantically and the boy peeps out in fear and fascination... The Trump face chosen for their angry ogre is cheerful and triumphant which I should think is terrifying for many of the adults in the room, but a relief for the children, some of whom whimper and turn for reassurance.

How does the rhyme continue? I remember now... yes, in these circumstances they are right to have omitted "I smell the blood of an Englishman!" Still, they're sailing close to the wind for a fairy story presentation in a school for young children. Yet the staff have made no objection so far. I know many people do believe such stories to be allegories of real events.

Quickly, while the giant is busy boasting and demanding his dinner, the boy escapes down the beanstalk with a golden harp made of shiny paper and card. It's good to see Nathan's props get a second outing! Later the story repeats and this time the booty is a golden hen fashioned from a soft toy. If I know my son he'll be kicking himself he hadn't found such an item.

Finally the boy clambers down the sunflower for the last time with a handful of gold coins, and – what is this? The old lady has thrown aside her ironing board! She too descends the sunflower, surprisingly nimble with graceful gestures before she shimmies offstage. A pause to allow audience anticipation – and she returns, now rich, adorned with a gold shawl and bracelets around her wrists and ankles that ring bells as she glides across the stage to a chair grandly covered with shiny cloth. The boy mimes chopping down the sunflower – they haven't bothered to make a prop for the axe, perhaps they ran out of time – and the video runs in reverse, Trump's huge face dwindling through a smaller Amin and a diminished Mao to a tiny Stalin, now just a dot in the memory as the ogre or ogres are vanquished never to be seen again.

The drumming continues, though the old man looks to be tiring. The boy points to various children in the audience: up they come, among them Nathan and beautiful, smiling Alka. The old lady beckons Alka to her chair and slips bracelets of bells over her wrists and ankles, and Alka takes an unexpected lead, twisting, stretching, head on one side, graceful arms and hands outstretched to the beat of the drum and the music now playing in the background. Her brown eyes shine and the sparkles of her vivid costume light up the stage as she invites other children to join in and the adults to clap along. Then, on some signal that may be spontaneous or may be pre-arranged – the blend is so skilful it's hard to tell – the drumming gently diminishes and the music quietens, so we are calm and ready to listen again. From the corner of my eye I notice Alka's mother, her eyes transfixed on the performers. At the centre of the stage the old lady and her grandson speak together, quiet, deliberate, very clear, the old accented voice and the boy's high treble, first in their own language and then in English:

"Mandeep and his family and everybody else lived happily ever after."

The drumming stops, the family bows, and the audience erupt with joyful applause. Their story included all of us.

SAFIYA

We don't want to leave. We celebrate in knots, reliving our triumphs of the afternoon. At last we have begun to tell each other our stories! The gracious head teacher announced pupils in the show could be taken straight home, earlier than usual. The school would like us gone, so the cross-legged audience may burst from captivity on the floor into a playground uncrowded by parents and buggies. But it's hard to retrieve our own children.

"The stage was our magic carpet!" shouts Xoriyo and off she runs, arms outstretched, spread-eagling into the wind with her friends wheeling round her like squawking birds.

Outside the gates the local Pied Piper arrives. His engine rumbles to a halt; his chimes ring out and the children flock towards the wire fences where the teachers struggle to pair them with a parent before they escape to the pavement. I can't say I like the look of this Pied Piper, any more than I liked the one in the performance or the one whose mother keeps gnomes in her garden. When I see Mrs Saltley push through the crowd I wonder if she's going to send him away, refuse him the chance to earn his dubious coins. But when she speaks to him he grins, and she trots back to take her place in the playground, watching the remaining children play until their own parents arrive for them.

We queue. We queue a long time, but most of us are fine with that. We have lots to talk about and the sun is shining this autumn as I don't remember it before. I'm with Teresa who's claimed Mahdi for a cuddle; she also introduces me to Mr Chan, the Chinese man from the flats. If we needed it, he might give us shelter now, for he'd know who we are. Today I am optimistic we won't need it.

As we queue, Auntie and her husband come through, a couple of the bigger boys helping them with their drums and ironing board. The queue stands sideways applauding them again along a spontaneous imaginary red carpet. Auntie grins, wheezes, looks exhausted. I'm glad to see a car draw up into the disabled space for them: she looks as though she has no strength even to walk the short distance to the close. The car rolls smoothly away and Auntie manages to lean forward from the back seat to give us a last wave, the bell covered bracelets just visible on her wrist.

"Like the Queen," remarks Teresa. The queue smiles.

Our attention turns back to the ice cream van. We're getting nearer now. The children are checking the pictures, ready to choose. The man is taking longer than his colleague at the demonstration, but this time people are laughing as they turn from his window.

We choose, and Mr Chan offers to treat Teresa, myself and our children. He bows to the beautiful Indian girl and her family. "I cannot leave you out, for adding so much beauty to our lives," he says, and the mother preens herself. She's less striking close to – marred, I think, by the thick make up she's applied to every feature. The little girl's sudden ravishing smile puts her mother right in the shade. But they all seem happy, which is the main thing. I shouldn't spoil everything with my dashes of criticism!

Now we find out why the ice cream man is taking so long. As he passes over each purchase, he adds an extra flourish. Mr Chan turns to pay him: he looks at Nathan and when Nathan thanks him he says, with great care, a word that sounds like it would be spelt: *mhsai*. Alka gazes wide eyed when he speaks to her. For me he tries Arabic, with a pretty good stab at an accent. Poor Teresa is quite disappointed only to hear "You're welcome". But he says it with great kindness and his eyes shine on hers longer than on anyone else.

"How do you know them all?" asks Sky. I haven't seen her so impressed before.

"I was in Mrs Saltley's class, years ago," says the ice cream man. "She taught us to greet people, say 'thank you' and 'you're welcome' in the languages children in the class spoke at the time. I've always remembered and I try to get the right one for the right person." His eyes settle briefly on me, and I confirm with a smile that his Arabic was a fair shot. "I love seeing the pleasure it gives people, and it's good business – my customers usually come back!"

We can't hold up his queue any longer. Perhaps we could eat our ices in the park while the October sun holds? The children will play on the bright green grass while our mixed group enjoy the autumn sunshine. We can sit on the swings or spin on the roundabout as we try to understand each other, starting in a small way like the ice cream man, and continuing all our lives even when the roundabout slows for the winter and we go our separate ways.

Is it enough? It is all we can do.

ACKNOWLEDGEMENTS

T hank you to all the children, parents, carers and colleagues I knew, as a pupil, teacher, parent, governor and advisor. All human life was there, the richer for having originated from all over the world.

One of the best parts of parenting and teaching was using stories. Recent governments haven't helped greatly with supporting creativity in the school curriculum. Undaunted, imaginative colleagues and authors continue to provide food for thought. Thank you to all of them for their ideas, whether we know each other personally or not.

When you leave teaching, after an hour, a day, a term, or several decades, your head is buzzing with all the people you've met and the stories you've heard. The summer holiday I retired, I spent a week at Dartington Hall in Devon, taking a writing course with Dame Professor Marina Warner. Her inspirational knowledge of fairy stories, myths and legends, and the connections she made between past and present preoccupations, provided an unexpected framework for my undigested experiences of creativity, performance, childhood, education and society and started me off with this book.

Thanks too for help with many specific questions to Nisha Kansagra, Lisa Hardy, Kashmir Sandhu, Kuljit Parmar, Joy Ellis, Carolyn Baker and Maurice Cheng; and for editorial work to Karl Drinkwater. Jennie Rawlings at www.serifim.com came up with the fantastic cover design for this edition.

My ever patient and supportive agent Bill Goodall at The Bill Goodall Literary Agency worked as hard as ever throughout to help make this a publishable novel.

NOTE FROM THE AUTHOR

Thank you for reading The Magic Carpet. I hope you enjoyed it. Please consider leaving a review on Amazon or Goodreads to help others find and enjoy it.

Extract from The Infinity Pool by Jessica Norrie, available in ebook and paperback from Amazon:

May 2011

Adrian Hartman wasn't expecting to die that day, so he hadn't thought to make a will. Now, as he lay slouched across the pool edge, pink shirt and copious shorts plastered unflatteringly to his spread belly, he realised this would cause difficulties for his numerous children and their mothers. At times, with some glee, he had mentally designed his funeral. A double slot would be booked at the crematorium, and the captive audience of friends and family would have to sit through an hour of his favourite music, without prayers or eulogies. But he had never written down his choices, because they changed and it didn't seem urgent. He hadn't foreseen what would be needed, yet in certain circles he was considered very wise, and the happiness of many people depended on him.

Crawling ants and buzzing flies soon clustered about his wounds. Somehow he retained enough sense to realise that to stay under the burning sun would lead to worse injury, and with much groaning and creaking he managed to heave himself away, only to collapse again in the shade of the nearby pine trees. He had no idea how much time passed.

At some point steps padded along the side of the pool and he heard what he thought might be somebody scrubbing the congealing blood from the tiles where he had struck his head as he fell – the work of seconds, but surely to get rid of blood in the water would be a bigger challenge. It would take nearly two days to empty, clean and refill the pool, and would draw attention at a time of low local water pressure. They might just rely on the natural disguise of blowing debris and dust which disturbed the surface play of moving light and shadow all the time, since the pool was set – fabulously – among wind blown pine trees above a cove. In any case, whoever was doing the cleaning must think the job finished, for the footsteps moved away, down the steep stony path leading to one of the pebbled beaches that punctured the rocky coastline. Adrian, lying supine and exhausted, half remembered seeing the owner of the sweaty seaside restaurant fishing from his makeshift jetty for the evening menu. But it was too far for his weakened voice to carry even if he did shout for help, and in his growing confusion he could think of nothing else to do.

Besides, it was easier and even rather pleasant just to give in to the situation, and lie still under the forest canopy. Adrian had practised meditation almost all his adult life, so he could switch his attention at will, and the blue sky glimmering through the branches high above him, the scent of the pine needles, the occasional flutter of a bird and the warmth of the soft ground were far more restful to contemplate than his thudding head or the peculiar sensation of having lost something important. He lay still, dizzy but calm among the lulling sounds of the island, and time passed.

At first he wasn't missed. He liked to cut himself off from the outside world, and people who knew him respected this, so they would wait for him to contact them and think little of it if he didn't. This year he had deliberately but discreetly arrived in the area earlier than usual, and for a change was staying on the mainland with the intention of spending a few quiet days by himself on a personal project, before he resumed his annual role as director of Serendipity for the next four months.

~~How much des~~

How did you research the different cultural backgrounds of the families in your AMERICC

#B What tips are you give to writing a novel with multiple points of view?

What prompted you to develop a second career as a writer after finishing teaching?

What was it like
writing outside your own
heritage for 4 or the 5
families in the novel.

Which authors who ~~initiate~~
capture multicultural
Britain / do you admire?
~~Which bo~~ in their fiction.

~~suffe~~
prejudices discrimination

~~turaloo~~
pleasure

wider than
3rd generation
- beyond the question
- When does an
immigrant become
British/free?

Shows commonalities
in concerns & whines
about and across
diff backgrounds.

Wh
[illegible] is the
heat of the
[illegible] in MMC
— [crossed out] is that
is that the experience
[illegible] is
across [illegible]?

Printed in Great Britain
by Amazon

57672897R00251